MW00467321

THE SOMALI DECEPTION

THE COMPLETE EDITION

DANIEL ARTHUR SMITH

This book is a work of fiction and any resemblance to persons, living or dead, is purely coincidental. The characters are productions of the author's imagination and used fictitiously.

The Somali Deception The Complete Edition
Copyright © 2010-13 Daniel Arthur Smith
All rights reserved Holt Smith ltd
Second Edition
Cover Design and Formatting by Daniel Arthur Smith
Edited by Crystal Watanabe

Published by Holt Smith Limited
ISBN: 0988649373
ISBN-13: 978-0-9886493-7-8

Also Written by Daniel Arthur Smith

The Cameron Kincaid Adventures
The Cathari Treasure
The Somali Deception

The Literary Fiction Series
The Potter's Daughter
Opening Day: A Short Story

The Horror Series
Agroland

~*~

For Susan, Tristan, & Oliver, as all things are.
&
To all of the others that choose to use crayons to color
their rainbows.

~*~

.

EPISODE I

CHAPTER 1
SEYCHELLES TUESDAY
02:35 HOURS SCT

Christine woke to yells from the decks above. She slid her hand over to the still warm spot where Nikos had been sleeping and then began to raise herself. Wine and darkness pulled her back toward her pillow. She pressed her hand down hard on the mattress to steady the spinning bed and then pushed herself up further.

Softly she spoke to the darkness, "Nikos."

No one answered.

Again she said his name, this time louder, "Nikos."

The yacht was still.

Christine shifted to the side of the bed, dizzy from the subtle movement. The shouts above were scattered, unclear, and the voices strange.

The yelling stopped. The darkness, stillness, and silence enveloped her. The cabin air became thick and the remnants of the wine again pulled at her forehead, down her neck, into her stomach. The blood rushing through her core caused her to gag.

The handle of the cabin hatch came to life suddenly.

The stillness broken, her chest went tight. Breathing ceased, her lungs held hostage by muscles squeezing deep into her neck, chin, jaw. She felt the sensation of falling back and away, the urge to vomit, to escape, and then, a rapid eruption of adrenalin. Christine's body was overcome in a wave of forced compensation as all of her muscles released. Her breathing returned, faster than measure. Clenching the edge of the blanket, she pulled the velour in tight to her lips to stifle the sound of her low feeble sobs. Hard forced clicks from the latch filled the stateroom. Though the cabin was a shroud of black, Christine set her eyes wide in the direction of the imminent intrusion. Futilely, she began to back pedal against the slick silk sheets, sinking deep into the cushioned headboard.

Across the room, metal slapped against metal, repeated two, three times, and then abruptly stopped.

The hatch was locked yet the chemicals flooding her system offered no quarter. The intrusion was imminent. Muffled whimpers continued to betray Christine despite her efforts to shield her mouth, and the hot rapid breaths that coursed through her nose were thunderous in the silence of the cabin. Throughout her chest and throat, her mouth and nose, the sensation of more breath out than in, each gasp a magnitude of terror.

A volley of gunshots interrupted the silence, followed by a barking shout.

She broke down what was happening on the yacht into a series of actions spaced eternally apart. Each silent divide an escalating stretch of anxiety towering over the last.

Nikos had assured her that to anchor on the far side of Curieuse was safe. The beach was in view from the deck, a far swim at most in the warm azure sea, and they were so close to Mahé, a mere forty kilometers to Victoria.

From the edge of the room, she heard the smooth metallic grate of a key being slid into the hatch and then tumblers falling into place.

Christine wanted Nikos to be the one turning the key.

With a final click of the lock, the hatch smoothly fell ajar. A seam of light sliced through the cabin. Christine winced. Her eyes tightened, opened, then tightened again.

She was initially blinded by the glare from the hall, then her eyes adjusted to the form before her.

The open hatch was cut with the backlit silhouette of a towering man, his arms contoured, his head a smooth sphere. Two other men of smaller stature stood behind the first. Christine focused her green eyes onto one of the sconces lining the hall. The two men behind the silhouette were both dark Africans, one in a light soiled t-shirt, the other was shirtless, each with a Kalashnikov strapped over a thin shoulder.

The tall bald man hunched down into the stateroom. She watched the outline of the fingers of one hand spread wide then slip away to the dark inside edge of the doorway. The man's arm snaked up until he found the switch he was seeking. With a click, the sconces fastened above each side of the master bed illuminated the cabin with an amber glow. The man, another African, darker than the others, surveyed the room. His eyes scanned the dressers snug under the side berth and cabin windows. He inspected the closet doors and the opened entrance to the head. Not once did the bald giant's eyes focus on the near naked woman, a model by trade, peering at him from the master bed.

With a wave of his hand, the tall man gestured the two gaunt Kalashnikov bearers into the stateroom. The men reached down between them and from the floor lifted a shirtless Caucasian. The two men effortlessly dragged the unconscious man toward Christine.

As the men moved closer, Christine's feeble whimpers rose to convulsive sobs. Frozen against the cushioned headboard, her eyes began to flood.

The bright green of her eyes glazed over with the well of tears and her head and neck pressed back so tightly against the headboard that with each thudding pulse, the thundering rush of blood pained the base of her skull.

The two men carried the ragdoll of a man over to the bed and then with a dip and a lift, they heaved the lifeless figure next to her. Her eyes shot to the bloody face. The beaten man was Nikos. Her heart swelled, throbbing against her lungs, preventing air from getting in.

Nikos looked dead.

Christine dropped her hand to Nikos' forehead to move his blood-matted hair away from his face. She ran her thumb over his brow, first smearing, and then clearing blood away from the small cut near his eye.

Nikos coughed weakly. He was alive. She was able to take in a deep breath.

She caressed Nikos' cheek, "It's going to be okay, Nikos." She was unsure if more than a soft wisp had escaped her dry throat.

Nikos' eyes were already swelling shut and he was having trouble opening them. His jaw opened and then closed, only a faint breath escaped.

She exerted more effort into her voice, "Shhh, don't try to talk."

The hatch slammed shut, followed by the metal clack of the bolt. Christine raised her head, her eyes frantically darting to the hatch and then searching the rest of the still lit room.

Christine and Nikos were alone.

CHAPTER 2
UPPER WEST SIDE, NEW YORK

Cameron reached deep into the loose right pocket of his slacks for the key to Le Dragon Vert. He usually threw jeans on after taping down in Chelsea, but tonight he didn't bother. He walked alone along West Eighty-first Street. This time of night, the sidewalks of the Upper West Side were near empty. To his right, the massive Hayden Sphere glowed soft indigo in the six-story glass cube Rose Center, a nightlight for the wealthy residents of Central Park West. Cameron sucked in the fragrance of the daffodils carpeting the small Roosevelt Park bordering the museum. Two taxis drove under the traffic light from the Central Park crosstown entrance. Cameron waited for the yellow cabs to pass and then jaywalked across Eighty-first Street to his restaurant.

Cameron slipped his key into the front door of Le Dragon Vert, closed for the evening an hour before. He skipped down the three steps from the vestibule into the amber lit lounge, his attention immediately drawn to the bar. The dark oak bar jutted into the edge of the lounge then ran the length of the tunneled hallway that led to the dining room. Midway down the dimly lit tunnel two men, one thin, one stout, sat on leather seats conversing softly. The wide man, his back to Cameron, concealed all but the shoulder of the second. Without seeing their faces, Cameron recognized them both. His mentor and partner in the restaurant, Claude Rambeaux, owned the thin shoulder, and the girth and thick black hair of the other belonged to his friend Pepe Laroque, visiting New York from Montreal.

Cameron approached his two friends, both former members of the same super elite Legionnaire regiment that he himself had belonged to years before. He placed a hand on each of their shoulders. "I see you found the Ardbeg single malt," he said.

"Claude says you charge seventy dollars for a drink of this," said Pepe.

Cameron curled his lip, "It is thirty years old. Everything okay? I wasn't expecting you."

Since Pepe had been in the French Foreign Legion with Cameron and Claude, he was far more than just a dear old friend. Cameron knew Pepe as a man would know a brother. Pepe was never too far from a glass of wine or brandy. Hard liquor, however, was not his drink of choice. On the bar was a bottle of whiskey and three glasses.

Claude picked up the rock glass he had set aside for Cameron and then poured two fingers of the single malt.

"Have a seat," said Claude. "I expected you back from the studio a few hours ago."

Cameron reached behind Claude for a stool and then pulled the seat to where he stood. "I took my competitor out for a drink. Life on the soundstage isn't what he thought it would be."

Claude handed Cameron the half filled glass. Cameron held it up, and the others followed suit.

"Vive la Légion," said Cameron.

In unison, Pepe and Claude responded, "The Legion is our strength."

"That is good," said Cameron, after sampling the single malt. "So I take it there's no funeral. What are we celebrating?"

"No celebration, I'm afraid," said Pepe. He placed his palm on his forehead and held his hand there, letting his eyes slowly close. After a pause, he wiped his hand across his brow, let his eyes rest open, and looked into his palm. "The whiskey heats you up," he said, and then feigned a smile.

Pepe's smile was that of a cherub, high into his puffed cheeks. Still, Cameron suspected bad news. "What is it, Pepe?"

"Tell him," said Claude, "Go ahead."

"Remember Langdon?" asked Pepe.

"Sergeant Langdon? Yeah, I remember him."

"Well, he's Adjutant-Chef Langdon now."

Adjutant-Chef was the equivalent of Lieutenant in the Legion and essentially a sub-officer. "Huh, the world keeps changing," said Cameron. "What about him?"

"He called me this morning. One of Langdon's men is the IMB liaison."

"The International Marine Bureau," said Claude. Cameron nodded.

Pepe nodded his head and then said, "Langdon gets all the reports from the IMB piracy reporting center in Kuala Lumpur. Five days ago the Kalinihta, a forty-five meter yacht, sailed from the Seychelles at 0300 local time without notifying anyone. Kuala Lumpur is tracking the yacht. Her heading appears to be south of Mogadishu."

"What," said Cameron. "So you're saying the yacht was taken?"

"The reporting center is not sure, they cannot make contact."

"I don't understand," said Claude.

"The owner of the Kalinihta hasn't reported her missing."

"If she's not missing, why are they watching the yacht from Kuala Lumpur?" asked Claude.

"Because of who owns the yacht," said Cameron.

"Somebody important owns the Kalinihta."

"Exactly," said Pepe. "The Kalinihta is owned by Demetrius Stratos, the Greek shipping magnate. The GPS on the Kalinihta links directly to the IMB. They monitor its movements and the Captain checks in regularly. If the yacht moves a meter, they know."

"Sounds like the Somali," said Cameron. "Though I didn't think the pirates went that far out." He sipped from his rock glass. "I'm sure Stratos is keeping it quiet to deal with it himself."

Pepe nodded and made a soft grunting sound in the back of his throat.

"Why did they notify Langdon?" asked Claude. "Is the Kalinihta flying a French flag? I know our boys have zero tolerance for French hostages."

"The flag is Panamanian. Demetrius has a son, Nikos. He was last seen on the yacht the day before with a model he has been dating. She is the French citizen."

"So the IMB called Langdon," said Cameron. "I'm missing something. Why did Langdon call you?"

Pepe's eyes appeared sunken, and from beneath his meaty brow he peered deeply at Cameron. The corners of his mouth went taut into his full cheeks.

"What?" asked Cameron.

"Cameron," said Pepe. "The model is Christine."

"Pepe," said Claude. "Your sister Christine?"

"She was with Nikos on the yacht," said Pepe.

"Are you sure?" asked Cameron. He leaned forward to set his whiskey on the bar. "I mean, she takes off all the time. Are you sure she was on the yacht?"

"I'm sure," said Pepe. "I called her roommate in Paris. She told me Christine had flown to the Seychelles with Nikos and that she has not heard from her since."

Cameron pushed his hands into his knees and tilted his head back to face the ceiling. His mind flooded with youthful images of a smiling, laughing Christine.

"And Langdon," said Claude. "What's he going to do,

take a team to board the yacht?"

Pepe shook his head, "No, until the Kalinihta is reported hijacked there is nothing he can do."

"I see," said Claude.

"Hostages are held on the average of forty-five days before a ransom is paid," said Pepe. "I don't think it would take Stratos that long to come up with the money. If he sends in his own team, who knows."

Cameron brought his head back forward and straightened his neck. He lifted his hand from his knee and firmly gripped Pepe's shoulder. "So when do we leave?"

Pepe grinned. He reached across his chest, patted Cameron's hand, and then from his jacket he brought out a pair of heavy rimmed black glasses and a folded sheet of paper. He slipped on the glasses, opened the sheet, and leaned his head forward, tilting the paper toward the dim light behind the bar.

"We fly out of JFK at 7:50pm for Nairobi," said Pepe. He lowered the paper and peered over the rim of his glasses toward Cameron. "We layover in London for a few hours. In all, it should take about twenty."

"That will give us time to make some calls," said Cameron. "I take it you already contacted Alastair?"

"I have, his people will meet us in Nairobi and take us to meet him at the eco-lodge."

"Eco-lodge, I like that." Cameron's right hand was still on Pepe's shoulder and the other was retrieving his whiskey from the bar. "Claude, I'll need you to—,"

"I know, don't worry," said Claude. "Just get Christine home safely."

Cameron lifted his glass into the air. "To Somalia via Kenya we go."

Pepe lifted his glass to the toast and then the three drank.

CHAPTER 3
ATLANTIC OCEAN

Cameron pulled the light blanket over his chin. This flight contrasted the countless missions he'd flown as a young Legionnaire. In the Legion, there were far more takeoffs than landings and never had a flight been this comfortable. Pepe had arranged sleeper service for the two of them. They were served a full dinner pre-flight at the JFK VIP lounge and then as soon as the Boeing 777 left the runway, the flight attendants started a turn down service. Next to each other in opposing directions, the back and front of their two sleeper seats reclined and lifted to create two-meter berths. A little tall for the mattress, Cameron was still able to relax, though sleep would not come easy. Cameron was well aware that on the other side of the divider, Pepe was reviewing the latest details of the hijacked yacht.

Six days had passed since the Kalinihta had been hijacked. The last GPS coordinates had put the Kalinihta, still not reported missing, near the small port city of Kismayu, 500 kilometers down the African coast from Mogadishu. Pepe had shared with Cameron what he'd learned from Langdon. On board the yacht were Christine,

Nikos Stratos, the captain, cook, three crewmen, and two other women, one a maid and the other a steward. The captain, Warren Lewis, was an older British man, well seasoned with a commercial background. The cook and two women were Greek, the steward the cook's girlfriend. Two of the crewmen were brothers from Genoa, Aberto and Donato Disota, and the third was a Seychellois, local to where the Kalinihta was anchored. Langdon had told Pepe that for a crew that size, the pirates would most likely ask for a million US dollars, expecting to get half.

Cameron had done some homework as well. Before leaving New York, he'd made some calls concerning Demetrius Stratos. As a civilian, a commando, and later as undercover ops, Cameron had come across men like Stratos, powerful men unabashed by their actions, men with egos that forbade them from receiving insult without swift response. Stratos would not turn his back on his son and he was not the kind of man that would easily pay a ransom. For men with the power Stratos possessed, there was an alternative resolve. Cameron and Pepe were undoubtedly not the only former soldiers on their way to Somalia.

The top of the cabin reflected the pale blue glow of Pepe's MacBook Pro. Cameron could visualize the drill. Pepe was checking the coordinates of Kismayu and key points in the vicinity against Google Earth or some other plat map. Christine was Pepe's little sister. Pepe spoke of her as if she were tough, but Cameron thought differently; they'd had something years ago. The tough exterior was an act, Christine was softer than Pepe wanted to admit. Sophisticated and well traveled, to call Christine fragile would be a mistake, yet a week as a hostage would be enough to break most anybody.

Cameron took a breath in through his nose as he again processed the thought of Christine being held hostage. He drew a mental picture of Christine on the yacht. The image of Christine was of her the last time they spoke. That would not be right though; almost ten years had passed since the

11

last time Cameron had seen her in person, and though she was still beautiful, she had matured, lost the girlish features. Cameron thought Christine would more closely resemble the woman she portrayed in the ads, a visage combined from cosmetics and Photoshop.

The beauty was real though.

What Cameron and Christine had together had been real.

Cameron told himself that Christine was the one that got away. He'd let her slip away. They had met in Paris when Christine first began modeling. Pepe had introduced them over lunch and, in fear of insulting or hurting Pepe, the two began seeing each other in secrecy. When Pepe did finally confront them, he was not angry. Pepe gave them his blessing and told them that nothing would please him more than seeing his brother-in-arms marry his sister.

That probably would have happened had Cameron and Christine chosen different careers. They spent too much time apart, each with jobs that took them far around the world, Christine to the fashion meccas of the wealthiest countries and Cameron to the hot spots of the poorest. As Cameron's work began to involve deep cover operations, the time they spent apart grew from weeks to months. The missions Cameron became involved in were dangerous and with each, the risk of fatality increased. Looking back, Cameron could see that Christine would have understood, would have waited for him. At the time, Cameron thought it best to let Christine go on without him.

Cameron had more than once imagined a different life where he and Christine had gone farther together. There were children that looked like them with chestnut hair, his chin, her cheeks, and her green eyes below his brow. Cameron always imagined them all happy.

Yet thinking about a past that had never occurred and a present that did not exist was futile, so when nostalgic thoughts arose, melancholy or pleasant, they were expeditiously warded away. Chased away as other futile thoughts were by simple sage advice that Claude had given Cameron years before. "Men like us," Claude had said, "should not tally regret."

Regardless of a past shared and unshared, Christine was in trouble and her rescue was up to Pepe and Cameron. A rescue from captors that did not know the mistake they were making by boarding the Kalinihta.

CHAPTER 4
LONDON HEATHROW AIRPORT

The flight attendant appeared no older than a teen. She leaned in toward Pepe, her shoulders tight, arms straight, and her hands pressed against her knees. She spoke softly, as though sharing a secret, her British accent both formal and kind, "Mister Laroque, when you and Mister Kincaid disembark, a London crewmember will be waiting outside the Jetway."

"Thank you, Rachelle. I appreciate your extra effort contacting Heathrow," he said.

"Nonsense, Mister Laroque, it is my pleasure. Can I get you anything before we land?"

"No, I'm quite fine."

Rachelle gave Pepe a departing smile and then shifted her focus to Cameron. "Can I get you anything, Mister Kincaid?"

"I'm quite fine as well. Thank you," said Cameron.

"Very well gentlemen, please prepare for landing."

Cameron and Pepe gave Rachelle a friendly nod and then locked eyes with each other.

"Cameron," said Pepe.

"I know," said Cameron.

Cameron peered out the window beyond Pepe. White billows enveloped the large jet airliner as she fell through the clouds.

Rachelle opened a cabinet near the ceiling and pressed the first of five buttons that crossed the face of a black metal console. In the next cabin, a voice as formal and kind as Rachelle's relayed an automated message asking passengers to please check that their tray tops were up, their seatbelts were fastened, and that their seatbacks were in an upright position.

Outside the window, white wisps of moisture revealed first hazily, then concisely, the details of soft green terra firma fields, roofs of row houses, and then lastly, the myriad of utility sheds and parcel depots skirting London Heathrow.

A muffled thump rose from the deck as the Boeing triple seven kissed the Heathrow tarmac coupled with the immediate roar of the engine's reverse thrust. The travelers lurched forward and then eased back, the engines lulled, and applause filled the coach cabin. Rather than take part in the transatlantic landing ritual, Cameron gathered his gear. Time in London was to be short, hurried by the departure of the Kenyan flight. Pepe had gathered his gear together moments before and was now bent slightly forward at the waist, his feet and knees together, eyes open, chin to chest, elbows tight into his sides and his fingers spread wide from his extended hands. Cameron recognized the posture. Pepe held the posture paratroopers assumed before leaving a plane. Pepe was in jump position and prepared to launch himself when the cabin door opened.

Pepe did not have long to wait.

As the jet taxied toward the terminal, Rachelle walked passed Pepe and into the small service area demarcating the sleeper section of the cabin from coach. She pulled the privacy curtain from the side of the fuselage to clear the exit and then waited in front of the hatch. The jet stopped, bumped forward, and then began moving again under the power of a small tow vehicle below.

Cameron could see from his seat the glass Jet Bridge closing in on the side of the Boeing.

The two men stood and approached Rachelle. She was awkwardly hunched forward, peering up through the hatch window, coordinating with the Jet Bridge operator by means of a black telephone receiver jacked into the side of the cabin door. Rachelle turned and smiled widely at Pepe and Cameron, flirtatiously raising her eyebrows as they approached. The men appreciated they were to have remained seated. She merely continued to respond to the operator with monosyllabic statements, "Clear... Clear... Five and... Clear..."

With a subtle jolt, the Jet Bridge fastened to the side of the fuselage. Rachelle seated the receiver and pulled the latch to release the cabin door.

"Welcome to Heathrow, gentlemen," said Rachelle, pulling the door clear for Pepe and Cameron to exit.

"Merci," said Pepe.

A series of faint bells rang through the cabin. Passengers began to lift themselves from their seats and gather their carry on luggage from the overhead compartments.

"Ms. Conroy will be to the right of the Jet Bridge," said Rachelle. Her voice raised an octave, "Thank you for flying."

This time Cameron responded, "Thank you." Then he shot out the hatch to catch up with Pepe, who was already halfway up the glass corridor.

~*~

Ms. Conroy, a petite woman with blonde hair fashioned no hassle pixie style, briskly walked toward Cameron and Pepe from the entrance of the Jet Bridge. She wore a Heathrow blazer and on her arm, a clipboard filled with sheets of itinerary that had been shuffled and flipped through a number of times before her latest wards had arrived. In her other hand, she held a two-way mobile.

"Good morning, Mister Laroque, Mister Kincaid. My name is Ms. Conroy. Welcome to London Heathrow. If you could follow me, please."

Before Pepe or Cameron could respond to Ms. Conroy's greeting, she had spun around back toward the Jet Bridge entrance and in two steps was leaning on a side door that led down to the tarmac. In the same motion, she lifted the two-way and spoke into the device, "I have them with me. Side alpha-2, word of the hour," Ms. Conroy paused and tilted her wrist to see her watch, "Giraffe." The magnetic lock buzzed and Ms. Conroy pushed the large metal and glass door open, giving her small frame the appearance of great might. The moist air surged in thick from the rainy grey world outside of the enclosed terminal. Pepe and Cameron had to pick up their step to keep in stride with Ms. Conroy as she shot down the steps and onto the wet tarmac toward a waiting van directly below the Jet Bridge. She jerked the side door of the van open with the hand holding the two-way and then stepped back.

"Please step aboard, gentlemen," said Ms. Conroy, an expedient machine a moment before, now poised and courteous. Cameron and Pepe climbed into the van, each nodding to the smiling young woman. She threw the door closed once they were clear and then hurled herself into the front passenger seat. Cameron raised a brow to Pepe and both were rocked back into their seats as the van accelerated away from the Jet Bridge out onto the tarmac across a road designated only by two white painted lines. The van shifted to either side, negotiating the course, the large single wiper slicing the gathering water from the windscreen, the onboard radio chirping porter information across the complex. Ms. Conroy was on her two-way as well, a different channel, flipping through her clipboard and marking the lists of flights with notations of names, checkmarks, and times with numerous circles.

Cameron and Pepe had spent years of their lives on tarmacs and found the ride familiar. While thousands of patrons roamed the terminals, the hidden underbelly of the great animal that was London Heathrow functioned as a giant organism. The van a corpuscle surging through with momentum under the wings of jets, around trains of baggage carts, petrol trucks, and dozens of other vehicles that were all part of the Heathrow eco, all moving to a breakneck choreography to accommodate the two hundred thousand people being served each day.

"Mister Laroque," said Ms. Conroy. "As London is not your final destination, arrangements have been made for Mister Kincaid and yourself. This will only take a moment. Please have your passports ready."

The van cleared the back of a petrol truck and then spun a 180-degree turn, pulling up next to a small white concrete block building. Ms. Conroy threw open her door and in a single borderline acrobatic maneuver, swung out and slid the side panel of the van open.

Every time Ms. Conroy spouted an order, her voice would raise to a polite pitch. "This way, please," she said, again marching away before Cameron or Pepe could respond.

The white building was as Spartan on the inside as out, consisting of four walls and a glassed-in customs agent on one end. To the side, a small room divider lead away from the customs desk, masking a table. Cameron and Pepe followed Ms. Conroy through the door and waited for her cue. "Wait here, please," said Ms. Conroy. She approached the agent then said something the two men could not hear that prompted him to nod his head.

"Very good, then," said Ms. Conroy. "Mister Laroque, you first please, and then Mister Kincaid."

Pepe walked the four steps to the glass. The agent held up his open hand and said nothing. Pepe offered his French passport. The agent placed the passport on his desk. He did not scan the passport or even bother to look at the picture. He opened the passport to the middle and then, finding the pages full, flipped until he found a blank. With a thud, he stamped the ID, then handed the passport back. Cameron stepped forward and the process was repeated. Before Cameron had his passport back in his hands, Ms. Conroy was at the door.

Ms. Conroy led Pepe and Cameron to the rear of a black Bentley that had driven up to the door of the discrete Customs building. Seeing his passengers exit, the driver stepped out of the black limo and opened the rear door. Ms. Conroy handed Pepe a packet. "The tickets for your next leg are here. Instructions with the flight time and where to enter the airport are included." Ms. Conroy smirked, "Please be prompt. The driver your friend has arranged also has these instructions, so you should be fine. You will not need to go through Customs again as you have never left the airport. Your friend felt the formality of the stamp beneficial in the event your stay is prolonged. One never knows."

"One never knows, Ms. Conroy. Merci," said Pepe.

"Good day, then," said Ms. Conroy, flashing a broad smile. Then, in her manner, she briskly marched back to the van, already back to chatting into her two-way and flipping through reshuffled itineraries.

CHAPTER 5
LONDON MAYFAIR

Cameron rubbed his temples. He peered up and out the window of the Bentley to the London sky, and then over to Pepe.

"The man we are going to meet here in London is a Somali expat," said Pepe. "I was made aware of him by a contact back in Montreal."

"Did your contact mention how he knows this man?" asked Cameron.

"The man in Montreal said that he and the London man used to be fishermen. I was told we would find him at The May Fair Hotel."

"You sure? A lot of workers move in and out of that place."

"I am sure. I was told he does not work there," Pepe threw an eye to Cameron. "He lives there."

Cameron arched a brow, "He lives at The May Fair?"

Pepe nodded, "He used to be a fisherman. We are not all what we were."

The driver glanced into the rearview mirror, "Excuse me, gentlemen. We will be at The May Fair Hotel shortly."

Pepe gazed far out into the grey day. "This area of the city is nice. What is that large building in the center of the park over there? It is very familiar. Is that a museum?"

"In a manner of speaking, sir," said the driver. "That would be Buckingham Palace, home to her majesty the Queen. The May Fair Hotel is around the next corner."

Pepe tilted his head forward for a better view, "Very nice, eh Cameron?"

"The May Fair Hotel is a five star hotel, one of the finest in the world," said Cameron. "It appears our friend is living rather upscale."

"My contact did mention that the man we are meeting with is a bit of an entrepreneur," said Pepe.

~*~

A porter opened the rear door of the Bentley and Cameron began to exit from the car.

"Sir," said the driver. He was looking in the rearview mirror again, this time directly at Pepe. Cameron elbowed Pepe's upper arm.

"Oh, excusez-moi," said Pepe, putting his hand into his jacket.

"Oh, no sir," said the driver. "That is not necessary." Pepe stopped reaching for a tip and waited. From over the top of the seat, the driver presented Pepe with what appeared to be a small black key fob.

"Please take this," said the driver. He tapped the flat panel screen on his console. "I will know when you are approaching the lobby and are ready to be taken back to the airport. You can tap and hold the button as well."

"Tap and hold?"

"Yes, sir," said the driver. "Tap and hold."

"All right then," said Pepe. "We will only be a short while."

The driver nodded. Pepe nodded back, uncertain what to say next.

"Let's go," said Cameron. He shifted out of the Bentley toward the waiting doorman.

"Right," said Pepe, and then he scooted out behind his friend.

The few short steps from the Bentley to the lobby were a contrast of worlds. Cameron and Pepe entered the lobby below a ruby-laden Baccarat chandelier and surrounding them were eclectic Russian, Thai, and Vietnamese objects d'art, the finest London had to offer. Cameron immediately approached the Clef d'Or concierge, the two crossed golden keys on the man's lapel shimmering in the lobby light.

The concierge clasped his hands together when he saw Cameron. "We are graced by the Dragon Chef. Mister Kincaid, we did not know you were arriving today," said the concierge.

"My visit was not announced," said Cameron.

"We have missed you since your visit with our last Chef. I will call the restaurant at once and let them know you are here. Our new Chef is out, yet I believe she will be back from the market shortly."

Cameron lifted his hands, "I would rather you did not. Though I would love to hold court with the Queen of Eastern European Cuisine, I am actually here on different business."

The concierge let his face go blank. "Discretion is my business."

"Thank you. My friend and I are here to see someone who is living at The May Fair."

"I see. A private audience with the Dragon Chef and..." the concierge lifted his gaze to Pepe.

"My sommelier," said Cameron.

The concierge drew his brows together, "And sommelier. Of course, what is food without wine? And who is it that we are going to see?"

Pepe leaned into the concierge and whispered into his ear. The concierge's eyes grew wide. Cameron took note.

"Discretion," said Cameron softly.

The concierge composed himself. He reached below his counter to prepare a magnetic keycard. "The guest you wish to see is staying in one of our signature suites, the Amber. The suite is on the fourth floor, this key will take you there, and I will ring them of your arrival."

"Thank you," said Cameron. "We are expected under the name of—,"

"D'artagnan," said Pepe.

The concierge swallowed hard, "D'artagnan, yes, of course," he recovered a cordial smile. "Discretion."

Cameron did not directly look back at the concierge, though through his trained attention to peripheral detail, he noticed the concierge's friendly and genteel gaze shift to a leer as the two made their way to the lift.

"Who is this guy we're going to see?" asked Cameron under his breath. "What is his name?"

Pepe also had metered the concierge's response, "I do not know who this guy is. The name I was given was Smith, Ibrahim Smith. The concierge though, he was very disturbed."

Cameron curled his lip, "Of course he would be a Smith."

CHAPTER 6
THE MAY FAIR HOTEL, LONDON
MAYFAIR

Cameron and Pepe entered the lift and then inserted the keycard into the slot next to the button designating the fourth floor. The cabin rapidly ascended to the luxury level. Immediately they saw which door led to the Amber suite. Halfway down the corridor, a massive bodyguard stood sentinel outside of a doorway, his eyes glazed and fixed on the wall to his front. Cameron and Pepe approached the door. The large man, a giant, did not shift his gaze or girth. The door opened without Cameron or Pepe having to announce their presence. Shadowing the inner frame of the door was another titan as large and solid as the sentinel, though this second guard was animate. He gestured the two men into the suite where, by the door, they saw a chair and a table topped with a monitor displaying the hallway. Behind them, they heard the door close and then the clicks of several locks engaging on top and bottom. The titan then strode past them. "This way," he said, and led them into the heart of the beige and brown apartment sized suite.

As the name of the room implied, amber was the

predominant theme. The numerous objects d'art in the room were all made of amber, as were the many lamps. The centerpiece of the room was a large L-shaped sofa upholstered with amber hued crushed velvet. In the center of the sofa, so as to treat the room as his dominion, sat a well-groomed dark African man. The man was not young, though he appeared in fine health. The man's suit was impeccable, and certainly, Savile Row tailored. The man, undoubtedly Mister Smith, was watching a football match on the 42-inch Bang & Olufsen plasma television centered on the wall. Mister Smith was indifferent to Cameron and Pepe entering the room. Pepe and Cameron stood silently and watched the match from the side of the sofa. One of the players kicked a far pass and a raucous noise shot from the stadium crowd through the many surround sound speakers hidden throughout the suite. Mister Smith flashed a glance at the large bodyguard still standing to the side of the two and then wagged a finger at the screen. The bodyguard held up the television remote.

"Just the volume," said Mister Smith, his voice deep and absolute. The volume went down. The man still made no eye contact with Cameron or Pepe. "Please, sit. I apologize. Like most men, sport takes me to my youth."

"I understand," said Pepe. He and Cameron sat on a small matching sofa perpendicular to Mister Smith.

"Our friend in Montreal believes I may be able to help you," said Mister Smith.

Pepe nodded, "I would like that. He said that you know Somalia, that you and he were fishermen."

Mister Smith chuckled. "Yes, that is true. All of us on the coast were fishermen once, when there were fish. Now I am a diplomat."

Pepe scanned the suite, "Our friend also said you were an entrepreneur. I see diplomacy has perks."

"Yes, perks. Can I get you anything?" Mister Smith raised his hand again to the bodyguard.

"No, thank you. We are really on a tight schedule,"

said Cameron. "I am sure you understand."

Mister Smith let his hand suspend for a long few seconds and then reached for a rock glass on the dark wooden table before him. He lifted the glass, relished a sip of the clear liquid inside, and then continued to speak, "Yes, you have a plane to catch. Listen, I am sorry I do not have any news for you."

Pepe dropped his head, "I see."

"I have made inquiries though, and I am sure I will have a name for you shortly. Give your number to my man. I could not hold this position without having a pulse on who is responsible for such actions."

"Thank you for your time," said Pepe, rising with Cameron from the small sofa.

"Do you need a driver or a pilot back to Heathrow?" asked Mister Smith "It is the least I can do. For now."

"No, we have a car waiting," said Cameron.

Mister Smith again wagged his finger toward the screen. The suite filled again with the sound of the football match. The bodyguard raised his arm toward a sidebar behind Cameron and Pepe. On the end, Pepe found May Fair Hotel stationary and pens. He wrote down a number where a message could be left then turned to tell Mister Smith, but Mister Smith was once again indifferent to their presence. The titan held his hand out and Pepe relinquished the number to him.

Cameron waited until the two were in the lift before he spoke. "Did you recognize him?"

"Even after all of these years, his face has not changed," said Pepe.

"I was thinking the same," said Cameron. "He calls himself a diplomat now."

Pepe pulled the key fob from his pocket that the driver had given him and then pressed the button. "He can call himself a diplomat all he wants, the man is still a warlord."

CHAPTER 7
THE MAY FAIR HOTEL, LONDON
MAYFAIR

The lift descended past the lobby down to a sublevel.

"I thought you tapped the button," said Pepe.

"I did," said Cameron. "We probably have to go to the bottom and work our way back up."

Cameron heard a slight grunt from Pepe. The meeting with Mister Smith had not been fruitful. A ping rang from the digital panel and the cabin doors opened to two dark African men, one attired in a brown suit, the other blue, both suits cheap. Though they were in a subterranean level, the man in the blue suit was wearing dark sunglasses.

"Please step out of the lift, gentlemen," said the man in the brown suit, gesturing toward an older model white Bentley parked behind him.

Cameron and Pepe shared a glance and a slight nod.

"I have been to this hotel several times and was unaware there was underground parking. I believe I will have to speak to the concierge," said Cameron.

"Apparently this level is invite only," said Pepe.

The brown suited man's eyebrows lifted, "If you

27

please."

"Why would we want to do that?" asked Cameron.

The man in the brown suit smiled widely then took a step back from the doorway. The man in the blue suit stepped back as well, then lifted the corner of his jacket to reveal a revolver.

"Please," said the man in the brown suit. "Our employer only asks for a moment of your time."

Cameron lifted his hands to the height of his chest and Pepe did the same. "Okay," said Cameron, "Since you said please."

"Invite only," said Pepe.

Cameron and Pepe eased from the lift toward the white Bentley, keeping their hands raised high. Leery of any sudden action, the two men in suits shadowed them from a wary distance on either side, careful not to step too close.

Now out in the open, Cameron could see down the row of parked cars in the garage. At the far end of the aisle, easing slowly into position, was the newer Bentley they had arrived in. Between Pepe's thumb and index finger, Cameron could see the key fob their driver had given them. Pepe was subtly holding the button down and though they were in a lower level, a level previously unknown to Cameron, the signal was strong enough to reach the driver, a man obviously of privileged information.

Cameron and Pepe stopped short of the vintage white Bentley.

"You know we are not getting into that car," said Cameron.

The men in the suits said nothing, and stopped as well, one at the rear of the Bentley, one at the front. The front door then opened and out stepped the Bentley's driver. The driver was also an African man and rather than acknowledge the two men standing with their hands raised, he disregarded them altogether, instead reaching for the handle of the rear door.

The white suit that exited the rear of the Bentley was

neither cheap nor small. Though an odd choice of color, the suit was another tailored on Savile Row, and as impeccable as the one Cameron and Pepe had seen upstairs moments ago. The bald giant towered high over Cameron and Pepe.

"Relax, gentleman," said the bald giant.

Cameron and Pepe eased their arms down. "I suppose you don't want to call attention to the cameras," said Cameron.

The tall man lifted his hand and twirled his finger in a circle, "The cameras went away when the elevator missed the lobby."

"I see," said Cameron. "So what do you want?"

"Me," said the tall man, his face not gathering expression, "I want nothing."

"Then why the detour?"

"The man I work for, now he wants something."

"Okay, now we are getting somewhere. What is it?"

"The two of you came here to visit a man, to ask questions. Is that so?"

"So what if it is?" asked Pepe.

The tall man fixed his eyes on Pepe, "My employer wishes for you to stop. What is the expression? You are sticking your nose where it does not belong. Into the business of others."

"And if we do not stop?" asked Pepe.

"First, we will harm your sister, Mister Laroque, then we will come for you."

Pepe spoke cool and slow, "It's a shame those cameras are not on."

"And why is that?" said the tall man, for the first time showing a sense of inquisitive interest. He tilted his head and focused a threatening leer toward Pepe.

In a fluid motion, rotund Pepe propelled himself up and threw his forehead toward the tall man while Cameron simultaneously pulled the chrome Magnum from inside the white belt of the tall man's suit. As Pepe fell back toward the ground, Cameron put a bullet through the forehead of the brown suit, then spun and put two scarlet holes into the head of the blue suited man. The blue suited man had drawn his revolver free from his waist, yet had not raised his weapon in time. Upon hearing the shots fired, the new Bentley squealed down the aisle toward them. When Cameron spun back around, Pepe already had the tall bald man pinned on the ground with his knee pressed against his chest. The tall man's African driver was standing beside the Bentley shaking, easing his hand toward his waist.

"Don't do it," said Cameron.

The driver then made a darting motion toward the grip of his gun only to find himself sliding back against the Bentley on a slick of his own blood. His fingers had not even made a firm grasp.

Pepe leaned in close to the tall man, "It's a shame those cameras are not on," said Pepe once again. "Because I have to let you live to deliver this message to your boss. Tell him, I am coming."

CHAPTER 8
JOMO KENYATTA INTERNATIONAL
AIRPORT, NAIROBI

The fierce Nairobi heat blanketed the tarmac,
penetrating the fuselage and enveloping Cameron and Pepe
inside. The pilot had cut the air conditioner early, stifling
the cabin. Cameron and Pepe took their duffels from the
overhead and waited for the steward to open the hatch. The
pungent evening air flooded the fuselage when the hatch
swung open.

The jet had traversed from Heathrow, midway to the
polar cap, down to this equatorial heat and was now parked
away from the terminal. Cameron and Pepe followed the
queue out of the hatch and onto the mobile Airstair that was
raised to the door from the back of a small truck.

The balmy darkness hung snug over the tarmac.
Porters in brown canvas vests pulled handcarts stacked with
luggage and parcels to smaller single and double engine prop
planes on either side of the passenger jet Cameron and Pepe
were now exiting.

Between two tattered red velvet ropes leading out of
the Jomo Kenyatta international terminal stood a small

crowd, above them a large number two marked the entry to the customs desk. As passengers disembarked, the crowd began to thin. Drivers quickly came forward to take whatever luggage their employer or assigned businessmen held in their hands. Family members embraced those returning home and those visiting from as far away as Cambodia and Australia. Halfway down the Airstair, Cameron saw Alastair Main standing at the back of the group with a well-groomed dark haired man.

Alastair may as well have walked off the cover of National Geographic. Alastair's hands were at his hips, his elbows wide akimbo, his chin high, and his yellow mane glowed bright against the backlit tarmac. Alastair threw a nod to Cameron and Pepe and then raised his hands out high into the air as he began to saunter toward them.

Alastair was a Brit, more so a colonial, though he despised the term, as he was born and raised in Kenya. He had served with Cameron and Pepe in the Legion and to them he was a brother.

When Alastair reached Pepe, he threw his arms around him and pulled him tight. Pepe kissed each of Alastair's cheeks.

Alastair threw a firm grip onto each of Pepe's shoulders. Gruffly, he said, "Will get this beat old man, don't you worry."

Then Alastair released Pepe and threw his arms around Cameron. "The great Dragon Chef of New York."

Cameron met the Brit solidly, eye to eye, "Al, good to see you, I didn't expect you to meet us in Nairobi." Cameron flashed a glance at Pepe, then back to Alastair, "I'm sorry it's under these circumstances."

"Me too," said Alastair. "That's why I came myself. I don't want you to have to waste time." He grabbed the shoulder of the dark haired man to his side. "This gentleman is Ari. The best bush pilot I know, and Ari, this is Kincaid and Pepe. My brothers."

Pepe and Cameron in turn each shook Ari's hand.

"Ari will be taking us out to Lanta. First we will need to get you checked in," said Alastair. He spun around to search back toward the terminal, scanning the tarmac until he found what they needed. Near the hatch of a small plane, two Kenyans in customs uniforms were reviewing a clipboard. Alastair raised his hand to signal. One of the uniformed men responded with a nod.

"Do you have any other bags?" asked Alastair.

"This is it," said Cameron, referring to the duffels he and Pepe each held on their shoulders.

"Good," said Alastair. "That way we don't need to go inside."

The uniformed man approached the four men.

"Get your papers ready," said Alastair. "I assume you're travelling French."

"Whenever I can help it," said Pepe.

"Ha, that's funny. I'll take them please."

Alastair lifted his arm in the direction of Cameron and Pepe as the customs agent approached. "These are the two men I told you about." With his other arm, Alastair presented their passports. The man's face held little expression. The agent slowed as he neared, a self-righteous scowl crawled across his face, and then he stepped closely in front of Alastair to receive the passports. Alastair may have paid this man, yet the sudden drop of his brow and quick pierce of his eyes removed any ambiguity, he was charged a fee for service, not for employ. The agent flashed a quick glance at the other three men beside Alastair to ensure all eyes were on him, for what good is power without witness. Without opening either passport, the agent unsnapped a leather pouch on his belt, dug his fingers around inside, and then took out an automatic rubber stamp. He flipped open the first passport to the last page with no interest in seeing the photo. The uniformed man placed the automated stamp on the page and then peered up at the four men under the rim of his hat, his eyes scanning in a threat of authority.

"No other bags?"

33

Alastair answered quickly, "No."

The customs agent pushed down on the stamp, flipped the other passport open, and brought the stamp down again in one smooth action. He handed the passports back, then slipped the stamp back into his pouch.

The customs man pulled slightly at the front of his hat, "Good evening, gentlemen." The men nodded in return as the uniformed man headed back toward his colleague.

"That was efficient," said Cameron.

Alastair sighed, "Cheap as well. Pretentious lot, these airport trolls."

"My helicopter is over here," said Ari.

"Let's get to it before somebody we don't know starts asking questions," said Alastair.

They walked toward the small planes near the domestic end of the terminal. That end of the terminal was dark; there were not that many flights that came through Nairobi at night. The area of tarmac past the planes was also without light. With the terminal and runway lights to their backs, they could only see a short way in front of them, after that, only darkness.

The night enveloped them and then the stars revealed themselves.

Cameron could not resist looking into the early evening equatorial sky. Few, if any, stars could be seen from Manhattan. Above and around him was the Milky Way, seemingly close enough to touch. He sought out the distant horizon and then let his eyes circle above, around, and back to the terminal, an oasis behind them, a luminous dome that had shielded the stars from them moments before, now silhouetted with a million points of light.

In front of them, the dark form of the helicopter further materialized with each step.

Ari opened the side and then front doors. "Al, you'll want to get your mates set," said Ari, and then he climbed up into the cockpit.

Pepe leaned over to Alastair, "Do you usually fly at

night?"

"Heh, heh, no worries," said Alastair softly, "Most don't. Ari can, by instruments or blindfolded." He clutched the bridge of his nose between his thumb and middle finger, pressing his index finger into his forehead. "Like a pigeon."

A light flipped on inside the cabin. Alastair grabbed an interior handle to pull himself up. Pepe grabbed his arm, stopping him.

"I don't want him to fly blindfolded," said Pepe.

"He won't have to," said Alastair. "Ari learned to fly in the Israeli military, he can comb the bush and desert better than most anyone." Alastair turned his head to Cameron, then back to Pepe, "Then there is the intelligence training."

"Ari is Mossad?" asked Cameron.

"Was, is, does it matter?"

"Not at all," said Pepe. He let loose Alastair's arm.

Alastair flashed his eyes at Cameron.

"It's never mattered to me," said Cameron.

Alastair grinned and then pulled himself up. Alastair opened a panel and then Cameron and Pepe in turn tossed him their duffels to stow. After he secured the panel, he climbed back out of the chopper, circled around to the other side of the cockpit, and then jumped up front. Ari was finishing his preflight checklist. Pepe and Cameron boarded the cabin and fastened their seat belts. Panels separated Alastair and Ari from the rear cabin. Between the panels was an opening. Alastair leaned into the opening and handed back two aviator headsets.

"I brought the good ones, you can jack them up above," said Alastair.

Cameron took the headsets and handed a one to Pepe. Across the side of the large clunky headphones was the word Bose. The headsets were heavily cushioned on the top and around the large earpieces. Cameron slipped the velvet pillow equivalent over his head. When he jacked them, the air sucked away from his inner ears. Cameron pressed a hand up on each earpiece, opened his mouth wide, and moved his jaw around to see if his ears would pop. To his side Cameron could see that Pepe was doing the same. While his jaw was twitching side to side, he glanced up toward the front of the cabin to see Alastair smiling back. Alastair tapped a small switch on his headset and then tapped his earpiece.

"These A20's have noise cancelation," said Alastair.

Cameron could hear him through the headset crystal clear.

"Christ, these are great," Alastair continued, a sudden serious look across his face. "These would have been so nice when we were lads coming up."

Pepe said something that sounded muffled. Alastair placed his finger near the switch on his headphones and Pepe found his. Pepe spoke again, this time Cameron could hear him clearly as well.

"These are nice," said Pepe. "I need a pair of these."

"No problem, mate. I'll put a pair in the post for Christmas."

"This is style," said Pepe.

"The best of the best," said Ari through the headsets. "This is a Eurocopter AS 350 B3plus Squirrel, also known as the Dark Star. This little baby can go anywhere from the bush to the top of Everest."

Pepe pushed his lower lip high, "You mean somebody landed one of these on top of Everest?"

"Heh," said Ari. "I mean I landed one of these on top of Everest."

Cameron and Pepe watched Ari flip a switch above the windscreen and then heard his voice again.

"Dark Star 1 requests engine start, Mount Kenya, Flight Level 320, two passengers, two crew, eleven and a half hours of fuel."

A voice from the tower came over the headsets, "Clearance to Mount Kenya, Dark Star 1."

CHAPTER 9
LAIKIPIA PLATEAU

Pepe was finally able to sleep. Countless ops in years past spent in the backs of planes, trucks, and boats made the copter, gliding softly through the hot Kenyan night, as comfortable as a waterbed. The light ache of fatigue in Cameron's thighs and feet reminded him how they had spent the last twenty hours. Cameron had slept as they crossed the Atlantic. Pepe had never closed his eyes.

The dense blanket of lights that had been Nairobi had funneled out into streams of wide lit super highways that in turn diminished to single lane roads, and then eventually stray beacons in the landscape. The course of the copter was a direct flight path. The silhouette of the far off mountains remained constant against the African sky and Ari maintained a bead toward the highest point in the horizon.

"Take a look to your left," said Alastair.

Cameron leaned forward and peered down at the ground. Below them, among a field of black, was a large thick glowing white crescent.

"Beautiful," said Cameron. "Is that a hydroelectric dam?"

"No, not yet anyway," said Alastair. "They call that the Fourteen Falls. The eight lane highway out of Nairobi may reach here soon."

"Really," said Cameron.

"Bloody shame," said Alastair. "We're on a bit further on. Relax if you can."

Soothed by the subtle vibrations, Cameron rested his head against the wall of the copter and closed his eyes.

~*~

Christine shifted her weight to her side and threw a hand onto each of Cameron's shoulders, pinning him on the picnic blanket. The loose strands of her mussed chestnut hair glowed from the sunlight above, creating a halo around her smiling face.

"Hey," said Cameron.

"Why can't you just tell me when you are going back to the island," said Christine.

"Why so many questions?" asked Cameron. Before Christine could say another word, he reached up and pulled her next to him on the blanket, so that they faced each other side by side. Christine lifted her brow, sighed, and rolled onto her back.

"So that is it. You are the man of mystery," said Christine.

Cameron remained on his side facing Christine. He softly drew his finger down the bridge of Christine's nose, then onto her lips. She lightly kissed his finger, then staring up through the branches of the oak, took his hand into hers.

"I like that you're man of mystery," said Cameron.

"Does it please you to taunt me?"

"Taunt you? How so?"

"You tease me by not telling me when you and Pepe have to return to base. You make me anxious," said Christine.

Cameron rolled from his side onto his back so that

they were both now gazing up into the branches of the oak tree.

"I thought there would be less pressure if you did not have to count down the minutes until I left again. I thought that if we could enjoy all of our time together, our time would not diminish."

"Men," said Christine.

"What does that mean?"

"You think of yourself always. You know when you are going to leave. By doing this you do not spare me anxiety. You make me anxious."

"I make you anxious?"

"You upset me because I do not foolishly think we have all of time. I feel you could leave at any time. I feel you are always going to leave."

~*~

Cameron awoke to the jarring of the copter touching down. Ari switched off the rotors and began to power down the engine. Beyond the windscreen, the shrub filled flat landscape to the east rolled far out to a predawn eastern horizon, lit with hues of fuchsia and vanilla. Through the side window, night still held. Through the thin tree line, Cameron could make out a structure in the dim light, not far from the copter.

"Here we are," said Alastair. "Lanta Resort in the heart of the Laikipia wild country."

"Wild country?" asked Pepe.

"Well, Lanta is a bit of an oasis as are a few other resorts about the area. We are, however, in the central highlands of Kenya. Laikipia covers almost two million acres from the Rift Valley in the west to Mount Kenya in the East. The main lodge is over the ridge. You will be bunking with us in the cottage."

Alastair glanced to the back of the cabin to inspect Cameron and Pepe and then pulled the jack of his headset out of the console to stow. Cameron and Pepe did the same and the three exited the copter leaving Ari to finish his post flight duties.

Alastair led Cameron and Pepe to a slate path that slightly inclined toward the cottage, a fairly modern building, new perhaps forty years prior, built on a small ridge. The light was coming on fast, and though they could not see far into the surrounding morning, the ground and grass at their feet and the trees nearest them were detailed and clear. At the top of the path were wooden steps that led up to a deck. Pepe and Cameron trudged behind Alastair across the deck and then waited for him to unlock the glass door.

"Pepe, will you look at that," said Cameron, looking back at the copter. Their climb had been short and gradual. The deck was above the tops of the small acacia trees, elevated enough to exaggerate their vista of the horizon.

"Hmm," said Pepe.

Having unlocked the door, Alastair now joined them. "She's a beauty. The sunrise is close to breaking. Wait 'til then."

Pepe turned toward the door, placed his hand on Alastair's shoulder, and then walked past. "I'd rather not wait."

Cameron and Alastair peered at each other. Ari stepped onto the deck. "Is he okay?"

"Not yet," said Cameron. "He will be, when his sister is safe."

CHAPTER 10
LAIKIPIA PLATEAU

Behind the billiards table, a large map of Kenya and the Northeast African Coast filled the wall. Crackled decoupage and hues of patina gave the map, no more than a few years old, an antiqued quality that dominated the decor of the game room. Tribal knick-knacks carved as tourist souvenirs were scattered across shelves along with a myriad of classic novels.

"While you were sleeping, I checked the service Pepe set up," said Alastair. "Your friend in London not only left a name for us, he also told us the location of the Kalinihta."

"My sister," said Pepe.

"Yes, your sister, and the crew."

Alastair put his finger in the center of the area of the map marked Kenya. "We are here, and he said," he dragged his finger across the wall to the southern Somali coastline, "the Kalinihta was brought to port here. A bit south of where we would expect. We knew the GPS coordinates from Langdon, of course. Now we have specifics."

"I am guessing that intel came quickly," said Cameron.

"You most likely had not even left the Heathrow tarmac. How did you know?" asked Alastair.

"The man in London was General Ibrahim Dada," said Pepe. "We recognized him straight away."

"Ibrahim Dada?" asked Ari. "He goes by Admiral Dada now. If there were a pirate king, he would be the man. What is he doing in London?"

"Admiral, eh?" said Cameron. "Well, he told us he was a diplomat. I don't think he realized we knew who he was."

"I have heard this before," said Ari, "high-level pirates working with the Somali Government to cut out the low-level competition. How did you recognize him?"

"A past life," said Alastair. "The boys and I met up with Dada's lot outside Mogadishu when we were active. He was a warlord calling himself General Dada then. He became Fleet Admiral when he took over the Somali Marines."

"The Somali Marines?" asked Cameron.

"Marines as in fishermen," said Alastair. "At least that is how they started out. While Dada and his cronies were battling it out inland, Russian and Chinese trawlers moved into Somali waters. You know the story. At first, the fishermen just banded together to defend their fishing waters, cutting off the trawlers with their speedboats. Soon they were organized into four main groups," Alastair pointed to different areas of the coast, "the National Volunteer Coast Guard here in the south, the Merca Group above them, here below Mogadishu, the Somali Marines based out of Haradera ran the coast north of Mogadishu, all along here, and the Puntland Group close to the horn here. The big fisheries caught on to pay to fish, and wasn't too long before the fishermen had a new lucrative business."

"Why sell your fish at market when you can sell them at sea," said Cameron.

"Exactly," said Ari. "That is when Dada took notice."

Alastair continued, "Dada took over the Somali Marines and expanded business. Under his leadership, they evolved to be the most powerful and sophisticated of the pirate groups with a military structure, an admiral, vice-admiral, a head of financial operations, and of course, Dada appointed himself as fleet admiral. Hell, he has a bloody navy to go with his army."

"Yesterday's warlord is today's pirate," said Cameron.

"Today's diplomat," Pepe corrected.

"I suppose," said Cameron. "And the people of Somali?"

Alastair frowned, "Those that have not been recruited by Al Shabaab are at the mercy of the warlords, as always. Starving, desperate, a lot of the crimes that actually go reported are the desperate poor or rogue soldiers not following orders."

"Or street thugs," said Ari.

"Well, once they take up the sword," said Alastair, "they're all thugs in the end."

"I don't know about that," said Cameron. "Anyway, Alastair, you said the Kalinihta was a bit south of where you would expect. We had the coordinates, why would you say that?"

"I meant for a hijacking. These pirates essentially operate as cartels with established territories. The Kalinihta first headed toward Mogadishu, then south. I thought the port a bit of an odd choice. Well, that was before I knew that the message came from Dada. Now it makes perfect sense. As Ari said, high-level pirates like Dada have been working with the Somali Government to cut out the low-level competition. So far the Merca Group has been pretty much forced out and Dada's people have moved in," Alastair drew his finger down the coast, "Dada's message said Abbo Mohammed of the National Volunteer Coast Guard took the Kalinihta." His finger stopped on a port town south of the location of the Kalinihta. "Their territory is pretty specific to Kismayu," he then dragged his finger back up to the reported coordinates. "The yacht came to port in a territory that belonged to the Merca Group and is now predominately run by the Somali Marines."

"That explains how Dada knew so quickly. The Coast

Guard are expanding their operations northward into his new territory," said Cameron.

"And he does not like it," said Alastair.

"That also explains why the men in the garage wanted us to stay away," said Pepe. "I am sure Dada was more than happy to pass along this information."

"Hell, we're doing him a favor," said Ari. "That's absolutely beautiful."

"Strange bedfellows, surely gentlemen, regardless of where they are spreading out landside, the attack in the Seychelles is consistent with the International Maritime Organization records," said Alastair. "The Coast Guard have been seen out that way recently so this is only more reason to believe that we will find the Kalinihta there." Alastair saw Pepe's brow drop and added, "and that is where we will save Christine."

"Great," said Cameron. "Let's get to it."

"Right," said Alastair. "Listen, I have a confession. I didn't want to mention this until the two of you had rested."

"Mention what?" asked Cameron.

An array of framed photographs covered the sidewall of the game room. Portraits and vistas featuring Alastair posing with resort guests, many recognizable celebrities, at various locations around Laikipia. "You see that photo, second from the left," said Alastair. "The one with the elephant cub."

Pepe pointed toward one of the photos, "Here?"

"No," Alastair approached the wall. "This one," he gestured at a photo of himself and another man kneeling on either side of an elephant cub.

"Yes, so?" said Pepe.

"That is a picture of my friend, Nikos Stratos," said Alastair.

"You know Nikos?" asked Pepe.

"Well enough. He has stayed at the resort more than once."

"So you know him," said Pepe.

"I know him, and his father Demetrius."

"And you called his father?" said Cameron.

"And I called his father."

"And?" asked Pepe. "Has the Kalinihta been reported missing?"

"No. The yacht still has not been reported missing, though Demetrius did not seem surprised to hear she was. He has given us substantial funding. Nikos' father would like to see everyone safe. As he puts it, he is greatly disturbed by the circumstances, yet finds relief in that we are able to assist."

"Sounds a bit cold," said Cameron.

"He is Greek, I assure you he is not cold. Cunning yes, not cold."

"The Kalinihta still has not been reported missing," said Pepe. "Langdon's people would have contacted him as well."

"You do not get to where Demetrius Stratos is without holding a few cards. To report the Kalinihta would be to tell the world that he, a shipping magnate, could not even be trusted to care for his own personal craft. I am sure he already had a team assembled before I called. We are a convenience."

"True enough," said Cameron. "Do we have a place to put this funding to use?"

Pepe smiled, "I already know the answer to this."

"You mind sharing?"

"Some ballistics boys," said Pepe.

"A couple of Ari's mates," said Alastair. "You'll like these guys. He leaned his shoulder against the wall and glanced down at the floor, lowering his voice, "They're blooming crazy."

Cameron winked at Alastair. "Great, and when do we head out to see these fellas?"

"We are to meet with them tonight, after dark," said Alastair. "So I had cook prepare a meal. I think we grab a bite now, put our heads down for a kip until dusk, then head to their bunker. They already know the target and have started the logistics." Alastair then peered at Pepe. "Brother, we'll have your sister safe at sun up."

Pepe raised his brow and conjured a smile.

"Did you say bunker?" asked Cameron.

"Heh, yes," said Ari. "That is why we leave at dusk. They don't take well to daytime visitors."

CHAPTER 11
LAIKIPIA PLATEAU

An array of dishes had been prepared in the main house and then brought to the large table on the cottage veranda. Bowls of fresh fruits and platters of vegetables orbited a large centerpiece tray that held a mixed grill of lamb, beef, and chicken smothered in long green beans.

Though there were only four men eating, there was enough food for eight.

Alastair grinned at Cameron and then said, "I think you will find the cuisine sufficient."

"This spread is a feast," said Cameron.

"Well, cook does a fine job regardless. Yet when he heard he was preparing for the Dragon Chef, he may have gone a bit overboard."

"You told him the Dragon Chef was coming?" asked Cameron.

Alastair stared deeply into Cameron's eyes and held his face straight until Pepe, for the first time since arriving from New York, became his usual jovial self with a blurt of laughter.

"Are you daft?" asked Alastair. "If I told him such a thing the entire staff would be running for the hills."

Ari took a seat at the table, "They would have been expecting a giant Komodo lizard man, I would imagine."

Cameron slightly frowned and let his cheeks pucker as he sat, "What is this in these little glass jars?"

Beside each plate was a small jar filled with a mix of what appeared to be diced apples and vegetables.

"That is a house specialty, spiced courgette chutney," said Alastair.

"Really? Courgettes?" asked Cameron.

"Courgettes, tomatoes, onions, garlic, and ginger with a mix of brown sugar and spices. I figured this would get your attention."

"This is good," said Pepe, already sampling a jar.

Ari offered to pour the wine. "I think you will find the wine to your liking as well," he said. He filled the glasses in front of the four, all now seated. "The vines grow not far from here. Though you probably do not want too much for now."

Pepe raised his brow, "Well, we do not want too little."

"I'll drink to that," said Alastair. "Cheers."

"Cheers," the other three echoed as they touched their glasses together.

The toast was more than a mere token. Though Cameron had just met Ari, he knew he was kin to him. They were all kin, the four men at the table. They were brothers-in-arms, veterans of the hidden and silent shadow wars that were the true commerce of government.

Ari had his training in the Israeli forces, then later Mossad. The other three men were at one time Legionnaire super commandos, and later served clandestine as well. Cameron was not alone in Corsica, home of the Second Foreign Parachute Regiment. Alastair and Pepe were members of the special elite unit as well, the elite of the elite. The training that almost killed Cameron, had exacted the same toll on the other two, and the three were among the few to land a Dragon badge, the badge of a commando. The Green Dragons at this table were part of the same team; they had gone from being the tip of the fighting spear on the battlefield to global undercover operations, from the cites of the new fallen eastern bloc to the newly democratized Mongolia.

A little wine was good.

Regardless of their native born nationalities, being in the French Foreign Legion meant they could easily pass the hours with drink. For a brief time, Pepe was smiling, eating, and drinking, and as the tangerine bush of Laikipia, extending from the veranda out to the horizon, began to give way to darker hues of rust, and the cotton white clouds creamed to vanilla, then gold, Cameron could almost forget why they had traveled to Kenya. They could be in Laikipia merely to see their old brother-in-arms once again. Yet as the evening waned, Cameron could see that if a pause lagged too long between a story or a joke, the corners of Pepe's face would begin to drop. They would not be going in anytime soon to earn the rest they needed for the mission to come, rather they would fortify their friend. Each time there was a gap, Cameron was alert to fill the space. That is, if Alastair, also sensitive to the pain behind Pepe's veil, did not fill the void first.

Alastair was the one to finally lure them from the table, before a fall of silence could imminently take hold. Terry, a tall Maasai in the shirtless garb of the local Laikipiak people, came onto the veranda to clear the last of the platters. Only Alastair took note of Terry's soft glance away from the table.

"What is it, Terry?" asked Alastair.

In a nonchalant manner, Terry answered, "She's back."

Alastair stood from his chair and then peered hard out past the acacia trees at the far end of the cottage.

"Oh, you fellas will love this," said Alastair. From inside the French doors he grabbed a pair of binoculars from the side table, and then headed to the edge of the deck. The other three remained in their seats.

"Well, c'mon then," said Alastair to the other three,

already scanning the acacias with his binoculars.

Cameron and Pepe joined Alastair by his side. Ari stayed behind them. Alastair fixed the binoculars on a point past the last tree, then handed the glasses to Pepe.

"What do ya think?" asked Alastair.

"She's beautiful," said Pepe, and then shared the binoculars with Cameron.

Lurking slowly through the brush beneath the tree was a leopard.

"What is she doing out this early?" asked Cameron.

"She is moving closer to where she will want to hunt tonight. Now she will rest," said Alastair.

"We should do the same," said Pepe. "In a short time we must go."

CHAPTER 12
LAIKIPIA PLATEAU

Alastair leaned forward to scan the inky darkness.

"We're close now," said Alastair.

"And there it is," said Ari.

To the southwest of their position, Cameron saw the spent phosphorus cartridge of a flare-gun arc up and then burst high in the air. Ari piloted the helicopter toward where the flare had ignited. As they approached, first one, two, then three bright green fluorescent dots appeared below, forming a triangle. Ari landed the helicopter in the middle of the makeshift landing zone.

"I'm going to power down to save fuel," said Ari, flipping a series of switches that cut power to the rotors.

"Most pilots like hot action," said Cameron. "To keep the equipment running for efficiency."

"I told you," said Ari, "This is an AS 350. This little squirrel will start cold every time."

The last few interior lights flicked off and the cabin flooded with the green glow of the fluorescent signal sticks that surrounded the helicopter. Cameron unplugged the headset from the jack above and slipped the Bose from his head. He opened his mouth and worked his jaw side to side to ease the pressure on his ears.

"Let's hit it," said Alastair, disappearing from his seat into the night. Abruptly, he stuck his head back into the copter. "Oh, careful of the wait-a-bit trees."

"Wait-a-bit trees?" asked Pepe.

"Acacia with thorns like cats claws. They grab you then you have to wait-a-bit to get free."

"Ah."

Alastair pulled his head back into the night.

The other three men exited the copter, the darkness surrounding the makeshift-landing zone chirping to an incessant beat.

"All alone in the wild," said Pepe.

"I assure you, we're far from alone," said Alastair. "If you had your infrared specs on you would see we're standing in the middle of a crowd."

On cue, a hyena cackled in the night. Then, in front of the copter, at the edge of the landing zone, a flashlight switched on. Alastair held his hand up over his eyes.

"Christ, mate, watch it with the torch."

The beam lowered.

"Sorry about that," a deep voice said from behind the light. "This way." The accent was Dutch. The man was Afrikaner.

"Just a minute, boys," said Alastair. He and Ari each switched on their own flashlights. "Here's a torch for each of you," said Alastair. Under his beam, he held two mini Maglites.

Cameron and Pepe took the Maglites, twisted them on, then all four men walked toward the deep voiced man.

Cameron had initially thought the man was holding his light at his shoulder. Then Cameron stepped behind the giant and briefly shined his beam the length of the man. In the dark, Cameron could not gauge the true height of the man.

Pepe whispered into Cameron's ear, "Two meters, and maybe five centimeters."

"Close," said the deep voice. "Two meters, ten centimeters."

"That's Dakarai," said Alastair. "We call him Charlie."

"Pleased to meet you," said Dakarai, without turning back.

"And you," said Pepe.

Away from the green fluorescence, their eyes adjusted quickly. The beam of Dakarai's light ahead, cut with his tree high silhouette, rendered their beams unnecessary. The chatter of the wild heightened and lowered as they made their way through the black. A bright celestial blanket, pulled taut to the horizons, surrounded them. The distant mountains tore into the stars and every few steps, branches of the wait-a-bits rose from the brush, cutting into the night sky.

Ten minutes from where Ari had landed the helicopter, the group entered a flattened circle of gravel that somewhat glowed against the night. Even in the darkness, the area appeared to be a landscaped oasis in the middle of the bush, clear with the exception of two small dark structures on opposing sides of the clearing, silent sentinels, not quite the size of proper toolsheds, each barely larger than a phone booth. Dakarai led them to the dark pillar to their right. The terrain of the gravel crunched differently than the sandy red soil they had been hiking through. Not until Dakarai cracked the door did Cameron first hear the tinny resonation of electric guitar riffs. The sound came from a bowel too deep for so small of a structure. The weathered wooden door opened to a small room that revealed the lemon lit outline of a second door. Cameron thought of the TARDIS, a machine that carried Doctor Who, the television time lord, through time and space, a machine that looked like a small phone booth on the outside yet was paradoxically larger within.

Cameron realized where they were going and it was confirmed when Dakarai opened the second door to reveal a shielded room no larger than a broom closet. Illuminating the space was a clear glass bulb dangling from the top of the closet at the end of a rugged insulated wire. The dim filament burned lemon yellow. The wire was staple tacked to the back wall, leading down to another bulb, and then another below the floor where they stood, deep into the ground.

Dakarai took hold of the rungs of a metal ladder fastened to the left sidewall of the closet, then swung inside. "Close the doors on the way down," he said as he glanced down at his feet and then dropped out of sight.

"Really?" said Pepe.

"You are going to love this," said Alastair. "Go ahead."

"You're going to love this," said Pepe, his face scrunched. "You use that phrase too often, I think." Then in a lower voice, "Qui est telle connerie."

Pepe took hold of the rung and leaned over the shaft. He saw Dakarai still sliding several meters below. Pepe lifted his head, "Oh."

"Do it," urged Alastair.

Cameron slapped Pepe on the back, "You weigh enough, you'll drop fast."

"So funny, you two. See you in a moment," said Pepe, and then he too swung himself onto the ladder rung and let himself disappear into the depths below.

Cameron and the others followed Pepe down the shaft that led to a large music-filled tunnel space meters below the surface. More of the insulated wire was strung in a wide mesh across the naked rock ceiling and walls of the tunnel. Rows of tables, workstations setup at many of them, filled the center of the cave. On the far side of the space, next to a freight lift that led up to the other structure in the clearing above, were uniformly stacked pallets of crates.

The music was coming from a console system to their right, set up in a small makeshift entertainment enclave that included leather chairs, a sofa, and a large flat panel that was silently screening a zombie movie. Funnily enough, the images on the screen were aligned with the rough electric guitar blaring out of the oddly out of place tall pyramid speakers. To their left was a kitchenette with a microwave, mini-fridge, portable range, and espresso machine. The back of the tunnel narrowed to a passage that led further into the earth.

At one of the tables, a man with thick magnifier goggles was hunched under an engineer desk lamp, the variety with several joints and springs for precise managed maneuverability. The goggled man was working meticulously on a clamped electronic device. Another man in a safari vest was hovering closely above the first, inspecting the work. Dakarai was at the kitchenette pouring water from a bottle fountain. An air bubble traveled up through the bottle producing a loud glug. The hovering man raised his head toward Dakarai, still almost cheek to cheek with the man working beside him.

"Oh, good. You're back," the man in the safari vest barked, a breath from the ear of the other.

"Really," exclaimed the goggled man, and he jabbed his elbows up to his sides.

"Sorry," scowled Safari as he eased back from the table. He then turned his attention to the group at the entrance, "You made it from the States. You must be exhausted. How about a little pick up, eh? Arabica, grown local." Safari gestured to the espresso machine then began to move toward the kitchenette.

"Cameron, Pepe," said Alastair, "this is Isaac and at the table is Ezekiel."

"Pleasure," said Isaac, "and he likes to be called 'Eazy'. Being so relaxed and all."

Eazy again raised his hands from his work, this time to acknowledge the group. Without removing his magnified goggles he spoke, "Hello, sorry. The pleasure is mine Pepe and... uh."

"Cameron," said Cameron, "a pleasure,"

"I'm sure," said Eazy, already back to his work.

"Excuse him. He went ahead and armed that thing and now the timer is not functioning the way he wants," said Isaac.

"That device is armed?" asked Pepe. He craned his neck to see if he could identify what Eazy was working on.

"I told him the thing was not ready and he still went ahead and armed it."

"I unarmed it," said Eazy, intently focused on the small screwdriver and pliers in his hand.

Isaac raised his voice, "I was standing right next to you. You did not unarm it."

"There, the timer is fixed, and I did too unarm it. See right here," said Eazy, and then he paused and leaned in, "You are right. The thing is armed."

"I told you. I was standing next to you."

"Yes, here we go. I forgot I had to rearm the device in order to disengage and then reengage the timer. All better now."

Cameron and Pepe shared an intent glance with Alastair and then shifted their concerned gaze to Isaac. Isaac looked back blankly.

"You know we are messing with you," said Isaac. He, Eazy, Alastair, and Dakarai all began to laugh, Ari merely grinned.

Cameron and Pepe collectively sighed.

Cameron glanced at Alastair. "They do this often?"

"Any chance they get," said Alastair. "Isaac and Easy are also former Mossad. Their expertise is demolition."

"I get that," said Pepe. "They have what we need?"

"We will hook you up," said Eazy.

"We are more than happy to do so," said Isaac.

"I would love to have some of that coffee you offered," said Cameron.

"Me as well," said Pepe. "Though now I am feeling quite awake."

CHAPTER 13
LAIKIPIA PLATEAU

The group had moved into a large canvas tent in another section of the tunnel. The tent created a sense that they could be anywhere other than below the earth in the abandoned mine turned bunker. They sat along one side of a table that held current weather charts and a paper model of a seaside compound. Before them, a large physical map of the Somali and Kenyan coast hung on the wall, draped with a plastic overlay. The southern Somali coast was heavily marked with coordinates, circles, and crosses in red and black colored pen. The Indian Ocean portion of the map along the right side was plated with several satellite images of the target area terrain and close-ups of the buildings from the compound modeled on the table. On the left side of the map were photographs of the Kalinihta, her crew, Nikos, and Christine.

Cameron recognized the photo of Christine. The image was from a magazine advertisement she had appeared in a few years before for Estée Lauder. Her face had been cropped and enlarged to fill the photo. There were eight pairs of eyes on the wall next to Christine's yet Cameron was drawn to her's alone.

"They call this the Tactical Center," said Alastair.

"I can see why," said Cameron.

Isaac raised himself from the table and approached the map. "I have to tell you that when Alastair rang us, we were happy to jump on board even before we knew the meat of the situation. We want to see those pirates—and this is, of course, whom we are talking about—gone in general." Isaac placed his hands on his hips and peered directly at the map of the Somali coast, studying something that the others in the room could not see. "There have been far too many rumors that Israel is funding the pirates, rumors that say Israel is attempting to secure a presence in the Gulf of Aden." Isaac's voice softened, "Ridiculous, the CIA knows a lot of the ransom money has changed hands in Lebanon."

"We're not here for the politics," said Cameron, his voice elevated.

"Fair enough," said Isaac, and he spun back toward the table. "Let us tell you how we can help you. As I was saying, we were happy to jump on board right away. As you are aware, the Kalinihta," Isaac gestured to the photograph of the yacht, "is owned by billionaire Demetrius Stratos and as Alastair told you, he has already secured substantial funding for our operation."

"Is that how we were able to get the satellite imagery so fast?" asked Cameron.

Eazy spoke up, "There are many international satellites directed at the Middle East region and I have a direct feed into several of them."

Cameron glanced at Alastair and raised his brow. Alastair raised one brow in return. They had utilized satellite imagery like the photographs on the wall on nearly every mission while in the Legion and after, and Cameron was aware that to gain access to the level of detail displayed in these pictures was near impossible. Anyone could pay to task a satellite down to one meter and big money could easily get half of that. These super sharp pictures were down to a quarter of a meter easy.

Eazy anticipated Cameron's next question. "The hacks are old and unnoticeable," he shrugged his shoulders, "maybe tolerated. You know they seldom risk upgrading the firmware. If the upgrade knocks out a satellite, well..." he raised his hands in the air.

"I am glad we have them," said Pepe. "How recent are they?"

"All from within the last twelve hours," said Isaac, "most an hour before sunset, and the infrareds after. We pulled from the birds right after we heard from Alistair. As you can see, the Kalinihta is anchored here as reported." Isaac referenced an aerial picture of the small harbor at the edge of the building compound. The photograph displayed the buildings closest to the water, a small beach, a dock, and man-made break walls hugging around them. At the mouth of the tiny port was a yacht flanked by buoyed skiffs. The detail of the image was pristine. The chaise lounge pillows on the deck of the Kalinihta were clear, as were the side tables.

"The Kalinihta does not take much water. Why not use the dock?" asked Ari.

"Same reason the skiffs don't," said Cameron.

"You're right," said Eazy. "Good eyes."

"We have done this before," said Alastair.

Isaac ran his finger through the center of the picture, "The road is guarded by a tower and from movement we think that building number four, adjacent to the main building number one here on the courtyard, is a barracks. The clearest point of entry is directly through the harbor, up the beach, and right up the steps to the compound." He gestured to an image of the entire complex, "You see here, and by the model on the table. The walls are three meters high surrounding the compound."

"Ah," said Ari, "There is something in the water."

"Mines would be my guess," said Cameron.

"And you would be right. We also have intelligence that the beach is mined," said Isaac. He gestured toward another two photographs, "We have images of individuals crossing so there must be a safe line... Still."

Eazy continued Isaac's thought, "We believe the safe line would be monitored electronically, or at least as guarded. You can see the guards there." He shot the bead of a laser pointer onto three shadows near the water's edge of the compound, two at the ends of the wide steps, and one obvious sentry on the dock.

"Electronically? That's far more high tech than I imagined for these fellas," said Cameron.

"Well, that is the meat of it," said Isaac.

"How's that?" asked Cameron.

"One of the reasons our friend Dada was so glad to help," said Alastair. "This is not only a stronghold of the National Volunteer Coast Guard. According to Dada this is the home of their leader Abbo Mohammed."

"Their leader?" asked Ari.

"And all that implies," said Isaac. "A lot of men, a lot of guns, and I expect an RPG or two."

"The man that wanted us out of the way," said Cameron.

"The bald man in London Alastair was telling us about?" asked Isaac.

Cameron nodded his head, "I think this is pretty straight forward then, we do a helodrop a kilometer out, then take the yacht from the water."

"I thought you would see it that way. Our helicopter is a modified Sikorsky Black Hawk. She's already fueled and loaded in the launch bay."

"In the launch bay? This place is full of surprises," said Cameron.

Isaac nodded at Cameron. "I think you will find we have all of the gear you require in the armory," said Isaac. "We leave in three hours."

"And if they are not all on the boat?" asked Ari.

"Need be, I can clear the way to the compound," said Eazy. "There will be a lot of noise, which means the team going ashore will have to be fast and surgical."

"If anyone has been taken to the main house it will have been my sister," said Pepe. "Cameron and I will go."

"Not without me," said Alastair. He placed a hand upon Pepe's shoulder, "Vive la Légion." Pepe's eyes matched Alastair's, "The Legion is our strength."

CHAPTER 14
SOMALI COAST NORTH OF KISMAYU

Cameron slipped another clip into a pocket of his wetsuit, then for a third time, in the dim light of the cabin, inspected the MP-5 submachine gun he had selected from Isaac and Eazy's armory. The bewildering variety of weapons amassed in their munitions store amused Cameron. A matter of tactical operation protocol was that all of the munitions were interchangeable. Perhaps confidence in experience was high or maybe the years between field and undercover ops had forgiven rigor and set them in their ways, because each armed by personal preference.

In the cockpit were Isaac and Dakarai, the towering Afrikaner. Isaac and Dakarai were to stay on the helo after the drop. Across the cabin of the Black Hawk, Eazy was inspecting his CTAR-21, an Israeli commando submachine gun. Alastair sat next to Eazy with his hands on his lap, his back arrow straight. Pepe was sitting in the back leaning against the corner, inspecting the MP-5 he had selected. Cameron watched Pepe maneuver the safety toggle from single fire to rapid then back to single. Pepe's gaze was not on his weapon. He stared vacuously into the interior of the cabin, sliding the toggle to different hot actions. Cameron recognized that Pepe was running a combat simulation.

Though the small team was well equipped, no one else wanted to see battle this morning. The plan was a direct action infiltration exfiltration, a commando specialization. The four of them were to shadow the yacht with the zodiacs and then rescue the crew. If anyone was missing, Eazy was to evacuate with whatever hostages were on board while the other three went ashore, and they were only going ashore if necessary. Their team was too small to take any great risks. Somewhere outside of the Black Hawk was Ari in the Dark Star. Ari had not hesitated in his role of the mission. If everything went well on the yacht, they would not see Ari again until the mission was complete. If they had to get to the main house on the beach, what they referred to as building number one, then Ari was going to come in like the cavalry, strafing with the guns newly fitted at the bunker, and lift them out, or at least provide cover for the Black Hawk if all of the hostages had been moved to shore.

That was a major kink in the plan.

The team was counting on the hostages being left on the yacht and even with the satellite images that Eazy was able to retrieve, there was no way of knowing if that was the case. The team had debated as to whether the zodiacs should be brought to shore or the Black Hawk brought in. In the end, Pepe made the call. If the compound was still too hot to evacuate with the Black Hack, there was no way the three of them were going the get all of the hostages onto the beach and out. "If we fail, we fail big," said Pepe. So that was Plan A, the yacht, Plan B, the compound with Ari, Plan C, the compound with the Black Hawk, and if Plan C went awry, their last resort Plan D would be the zodiacs on the beach with strafing fire from Ari. No one wanted Plan D. They all agreed the Kalinihta was to be utilized if the yacht had fuel and the captain was in shape to pilot the ship, yet they had no time to discover if the hull was rigged with explosives and they certainly could not outrun the skiffs that would have GPS locks on the yacht.

If the uncertainty bothered any of them, none of them blinked. Cameron, Pepe, and Alastair had been on missions less certain, missions deemed impossible, missions deemed suicide. Cameron did not know the history of his new ex-Mossad and Afrikaner comrades, yet he knew brothers-in-arms. Certainly every soldier regardless of status prefers black and white, but the reality is that every mission is colored with hues of grey. Besides, there was never a time this mission was going to be a no-go. Pepe's sister was being held hostage. Regardless of the financial incentive sent down by Stratos, the three Legionnaires had been destined to make this trip from the moment the Kalinihta was boarded.

Cameron checked if the knives he had strapped on were secure. He unsheathed the knife on his ankle and began to sharpen the blade against a small accompanying stone.

"Look at you," said Pepe.

Cameron lifted his gaze to Pepe, "What?"

"What was that show you were taping? Steel Chef?"

"Uh, ya, something like that," said Cameron.

"Ha, ha, if they could see you now."

"You would probably win more with that steel," said Alastair, his eyes now open. Pepe began to boisterously laugh.

"You could really," said Pepe, having a hard time getting the words out, "put an 'edge' on that show."

Alastair and Eazy now joined in the laughter.

"Might help you 'cut out' the competition," said Alastair, causing the three to laugh even harder.

"Oh, you're funny," said Cameron. "The both of you, clowns." Cameron pointed the end of the blade at Eazy, "What are you laughing for? You even know what they're talking about?"

"I don't need to," said Eazy. "Everyone appreciates the Dragon Chef's 'sharp wit.'"

This caused all three to bellow with laughter.

Cameron raised his brow and shook his head, "Open the door so I can jump out of this bird."

Over their headsets they heard Isaac's voice, "You'll have your wish soon, Dragon. Three minutes to drop. Prep the zodiacs."

The laughter stopped. "Clear," each said into their headsets.

The four men secured their kits and prepped for the door.

Eazy dropped to his knees and pulled two large duffels to the center of the cabin. "We will need one of these in each of the zodiacs."

"Explosives?" asked Pepe.

"More than just that. The contents will get you across the two mine fields if the three of you have to get up to the compound," said Eazy.

Dakarai entered the cabin from the cockpit to open the hatch.

"On target, H2 check in," said Isaac.

"H2 at your eleven," said Ari.

"H2 affirmed," said Isaac. "Open hatch."

Dakarai opened the hatch, "Hatch open," said Dakarai. "Get ready for bump one." Dakarai released the first zodiac and the helo lifted slightly.

Ari's voice came on the headsets, "Zodiac one in the water."

"Get ready for bump two," said Dakarai. He released the second zodiac and the helo lifted again and tilted before straightening out. "She's caught."

Ari's voice came on the radio again, "Zodiac two is dangling."

Dakarai pulled a ten-inch blade from his belt and slipped the edge into his cuff, "Back in two, H1."

"Affirmative," said Isaac. "Don't damage the boat, we only brought two."

Dakarai slipped over the side.

The team did not need to wait long. In less than a

minute, the helo lifted slightly.

"H1, Zodiac two is in the water," said Ari.

Dakarai put an arm up onto the hatch and then Eazy and Pepe pulled him in.

Dakarai composed himself quickly and swung around into position, "You should be able to stay dry. The water is glass, the boats are below."

"Great. Let's drop the ropes," said Pepe.

As soon as the ropes were uncoiled, Pepe and Eazy stepped into their positions to fast rope.

"Team ready, H1," said Dakarai.

"Then team clear," said Isaac.

Eazy and Pepe slid down the ropes into a zodiac below. As soon as they were clear of the ropes, they secured the zodiacs together while on the helo Alastair and Cameron clipped the first duffel onto the ropes.

"Package ready," said Dakarai.

"Ready for package," said Eazy.

Cameron and Alastair let the duffel drop. Eazy and Pepe secured it and then moved the duffel to the second zodiac.

"Package ready."

"Ready for package."

The second duffel dropped from the helo onto the zodiac, followed by Alastair and then Cameron.

"Team clear," said Dakarai.

"Team is in the water," said Ari.

"See you soon, boys," said Isaac.

The two helicopters moved off and within minutes the zodiacs were separated and motoring toward shore.

CHAPTER 15
ABBO'S COMPOUND

The equatorial sky densely glittered above while below the two zodiacs glided across the mirrored surface of the early morning ocean. The water was so still and silent that the two-man crews had pulled the rotors up and were now bent over the sides rowing in rapid uniform pace. Before the small inflatable crafts, the profile of the Kalinihta glowed white bow to stern, hugged between the two hilly shadows of the breakwalls that extended out into the water beside her. On shore, the compound was dark, no lights in the windows, or the exterior, and the western sky beyond the large structure, darkest before the dawn.

Careful to not nudge the hull too harshly, the team gently steered the zodiacs to the stern of the Kalinihta. Pepe eased a small mirror around the corner of the swim platform. He flashed a hand gesture to Cameron and Alastair to signal the deck was clear. The crews used their hands to slide the crafts along the hull and then when the first zodiac was in position, Pepe rolled from the inflatable up onto the platform, keeping out of view of the aft deck and salon steps above. Pepe extended his mirror, then pointed two fingers at his eyes. This meant the salon was dark and that they would need the night vision gear. Eazy quietly handed each of the three men a headset that included a monocular lens and a battery pack. Alastair and Cameron fit their gear into place; Pepe passed, preferring to trust the darkness.

In three quick movements, Cameron allowed himself to be boosted by Alastair up onto the deck and into a gun ready point position. To his left, the Jacuzzi sat flat, reflecting iridescent green to his night glass; on his right, the chaise lounges were unspoiled. Cameron scanned the dark void of the aft salon through the open glass doors. The ceiling mirror and heavy metal trim brought a lot of light into his scope. He took three hunched steps forward, ready to dodge if needed. The luxury of the fine wood paneled lounge was in no less a state than earlier in the week. Original artwork still adorned the walls and the fabrics of the cushions, though tinted green by the night glass, were untainted. The neat and unwrinkled placement of the pillows on the furniture did not appear to be in any way abnormal. The Kalinihta was in stasis, immune to the circumstance of her crew.

Alastair sidled Cameron's left and then Pepe his right.

The three men shared a glance and a nod. They had reviewed blueprints of the Kalinihta at the bunker. There were two decks above, the sky deck and top deck, and below were the cabins and engine room. Alastair was to work his way skyward, Cameron to the bow, and Pepe was going to the compartments below where most likely the hostages—and his sister—were being held. A standard sweep the three had performed countless times before. Eazy was to stay with the zodiacs unless requested.

The three strode forward in unison, a rhythmic machine, Alastair and Cameron with MP-5s ready and Pepe wielding a blade. At the back of the salon, a decorative spiral staircase shot up to the sky deck while to the side a second stairwell slipped to the stateroom and guest cabins below. At the point of the stairwells, Pepe and Alastair split off to their own appropriate preplanned routes. Cameron pressed forward toward the bow of the yacht.

Cameron entered the dining salon next. The large dining table and small side bar were in order, as was the rest of the lounge, preserved as the aft salon had been. Even the compliment of liquor lining the corner-mirrored shelves above the bar was untouched. Then again, the men who took the yacht did not think of themselves as pirates, rather as an Islamic coastguard, and as such were Muslims bound to a Sharia law prohibiting alcohol. The team's overall boarding plan took advantage of the fact that these captors were likely devout. In moments, dawn would begin and the morning call to prayer would come. As worshipers of Islam, the devout believe God's most favored prayer of the day is the Fajr dawn prayer. Muslims believe all others sleep while the devout pray. The plan hinged on infiltrating the yacht, and then, if necessary, the compound, just before the prayer, and then evacuating while surrounding reinforcements were still praying.

A large mural of a silver olive tree covered the wall at the back of the dining salon. Cameron knew from the blueprints that a television was behind a retractable panel and that behind that was the galley. On either side of the wall was a door, the one to the left would lead up to the pilot house, the one to the right would lead down to the crew's mess. Cameron placed his back near the edge of the left side entryway, then eased the door open. The hallway was dimly lit from the forward pilothouse. He disengaged his night glass so as not to be blinded by a flood of light. From a pocket, Cameron pulled a thin scope and then began to ease the glass to the corner to catch the reflection. When he noticed how reflective the dim light was on the gold trim of the hallway sconce, he stopped. The scope could betray him, yet the fixture could be his ally. Cameron slipped the scope back into his sleeve pocket and then nuzzled close to the corner to use the sconce fixture as a mirror. Within the golden shine was a pocket of clarity, a slight window of reflection onto the helm. In the image, Cameron saw a man hunched forward.

Cameron pivoted the edge of the door and swung into the galley with a sense of immediacy.

The galley was empty.

Cameron took in a breath and then burst around the corner of the hallway onto the four-step stairwell leading up to the pilothouse. The MP-5 leading, he steadily marched up the short steps, and when in contact squeezed the trigger twice. The only sound was the rapid clack of the bolt and the clink of the two metal casings hitting the floor, rapidly followed by two more. The second man in the pilothouse, the man that had not been in Cameron's view, did not even have time to turn to see what had caused the sound of the first two clinks. Cameron had not had to think. The decision to shoot the second man was neither rational nor irrational, not a decision at all, not instinct, merely a simple motor response, even after all the years away from active duty. Vive la Légion.

Cameron placed a finger to his headset, "Helm clear."

"Top clear," said Alastair. Cameron crossed the pilothouse to ensure the other entrance was clear, then entered the sky deck. Alastair was already crossing the lounge.

"Any resistance?" asked Cameron.

"Nothing up top except the yacht's tender," said Alastair, "tarped and tethered aft of the communications tower."

The two quickly crossed back through the pilothouse and then slipped back down the steps in the event anyone at the compound or on the breakwall could see into the dimly lit room.

Cameron led Alastair into the cleared galley. They each clipped their night scopes back on. Traversing the galley, Cameron spun quickly toward the crew's mess. There was no light emitting from the stairwell below, yet that did not mean the cabin was empty. Cameron floated down the four steps into the mess, squeezing two rounds into the heads of the men sleeping face down on the table. These devout would not be waking for prayer.

As Cameron made his way back up the short stairwell, Pepe's voice tinned into his ear, "Below deck clear."

Cameron nodded to Alastair standing at the door of the dining room.

"Main and top all clear," said Alastair. "Do you have the targets?"

Cameron and Alastair waited a moment for Pepe's reply, then headed for the stairwell when no reply came. Pepe was rapidly climbing the steps.

"Pepe," said Cameron. "The targets?"

"What's going on in there?" asked Eazy.

Pepe stopped at the top of the stairs, "In the stateroom. All but two."

Pepe began to step past Cameron and Alastair.

"Hey, where are you going?" asked Alastair.

"The compound," said Pepe.

CHAPTER 16
ABBO'S COMPOUND

Cameron did not need the light to see the darkness buried deep in Pepe's eyes.

"Just hold on a minute," said Cameron.

Pepe stopped.

Cameron continued, "Let's get those people out of here and storm the compound properly." He placed his hand on Pepe's shoulder, "Together, as planned."

Alastair placed his hand on Pepe's other shoulder, "Vive la Légion."

Pepe inhaled deeply, "Vive la Légion."

"Sounds like you're going in," said Eazy over the headset. "I need one of you to come out here and give me a hand with this gear. I think you'll like what I brought."

"Sure thing," said Pepe.

"The captain was down below?" asked Cameron.

"Yeah, everyone except... and they look pretty good," said Pepe.

"Great, let me go see if he wants to pilot this boat out of here," said Cameron.

Cameron squeezed Pepe's shoulder tightly, then raised his hand and slapped back down. Then Cameron slid around Pepe down into the stairwell. At the bottom of the stairs, the green tint of the scope was far dimmer by comparison to the light-touched upper decks. The lower landing opened to a hallway that led aft to the main stateroom. Immediately adjacent from the landing was a double pane glass door shielding a large collection of wine. Hatches to small cabins lined one side of the hallway, while on the other side there was only the door to the engine room. Cameron knew that Pepe would have swept the engine room first for signs of sabotage, not that they expected any from these captors, only because training is training.

On the floor at the end of the hall, a throat slit body was curled and gnarled with eyes wide and unaware. The door to the stateroom was open and a dim light flowed out. Cameron removed his scope and peeked in. The cook and the two women were seated on the large bed along with the Seychellois. On the sidewall berth sat the captain and the two Genovese.

"You know you are liberated," said Cameron.

The captain, aged by the days and the dark purple contusion along the side of his face, nodded slowly, "Yes. Thank you."

"Are you Lewis?"

"Yes."

"Can you pilot out of here?"

"Yes." The captain's own answer struck him and his eyes lit, "Oh, yes."

"Good. Come with me," said Cameron. "The rest of you, I'm sorry. Unless the captain needs you, you should probably stay out of sight."

Those on the bed nodded their heads while the two Genovese on the berth turned to their captain. The captain met eyes with his crewmen yet directed his question to Cameron. His authority returned to his tone. "Is the yacht clear?"

"Yes."

"Aberto and Donato, you two make ready the engine room," said the captain.

" Sì," said Aberto, echoed by his brother.

"The rest of you stay here as this man said."

"Okay," said Cameron. "Follow my light. Watch your step here by the door."

Cameron made his way back toward the stairwell. The captain was a step behind him. Cameron noticed the captain did not flinch at the body on the floor, nor did the Italians. Cameron stopped at the engine room hatch so that the brothers could see to enter. Once inside, they switched on the interior cabin light and then Cameron and the captain were on their way.

"Thank you," said the captain. "I'm at a disadvantage, you know my name."

"I'm Kincaid. Don't thank me yet. There's a compound full of enemy combatants fifty meters from your hull."

"I see."

"What shape is she in?" asked Cameron.

"She'll motor fine. That's how we got here," said the Captain.

"And fuel?"

"There's enough fuel to get clear. You're thinking south to Lamu?"

"I am."

"We can get there."

At the top of the stairwell, Alastair was waiting in the dark.

"This is Alastair," said Cameron.

"Captain Lewis," said Alastair, nodding. "Cameron, we good to go?"

"Yeah. One more thing, captain, how fast can you push her?"

"We can hold twenty-five knots easy in this clear water. The diesel will burn though," said the captain.

"Twenty-five should be good," said Cameron. "We

only need to clear here."

"Won't they be sending anything after us?" asked the captain.

"I wouldn't worry about them getting too far from shore," said Pepe as he entered the cabin. "Our man has some truly special toys."

"Good to hear," said Cameron. "All right, Captain, we'll leave you to it. Wait for our signal, then haul out of here."

Cameron and Alastair joined Pepe. Alastair gestured to what Pepe was holding in his hands, "What the hell is that?"

"Eazy calls it a lobster," said Pepe.

"A robot lobster," said Eazy over Pepe's shoulder. Eazy held up two more, one in each hand.

The machines were indeed robots and looked remarkably similar to lobsters. The core bodies were large rectangular blocks lined with coils and servos along the sides where eight long insect like legs shot out. From the front of the block were two very long copper antennae and on the tail end a mechanical lobster tail, fin and all. In place of the claws were two large black oval discs, obviously sensor plates of some type.

"What are you going to do with these?" asked Alastair. "Are they mines?"

"The opposite," said Eazy. "We detected mines in the water and on the beach from the satellite shots. These little fellas are going to seek out the underwater mines between us and the compound and..." Eazy lifted his arms in a makeshift explosion, "Boom."

"Heh heh," chuckled Pepe.

"Are you sure this will work?" asked Cameron.

"Yes, of course," said Eazy. "It's biomimetic, a machine designed to function like a biological system. Works perfectly, like a lobster, swims through the water straight to the mine."

"You've done this before?" asked Cameron.

"I've tested blowing things up. I use them mostly for

75

underwater surveillance."

"He has a lot of them," said Pepe. "If they move through the water the way they're supposed to, they're bound to hit something."

"Hmm," said Alastair.

"With what Stratos is paying I figure I can get some upgrades," said Eazy.

Cameron took an electronic cephalopod from Eazy to observe the metal monstrosity more closely. "These will clear the beach too?"

"No, I have something a bit more conventional for that," said Eazy. He reached into his pocket and pulled out a .50 caliber dart.

"Is that an antipersonnel venom dart?" asked Cameron.

Eazy nodded. "This one is empty," said Eazy. He twirled the long blunt nosed dart between his fingers, "good thing too, because DETA is deadly. I have some modified mortars. These little babies cut through surf and sand like butter. Whatever does not go boom is then neutralized by the DETA. DETA is a caustic chemical."

"Caustic?" said Pepe.

"I would watch my step," said Eazy.

"Sounds good to me. When can these things go into the water?" asked Cameron.

"Whenever the captain is ready."

CHAPTER 17
ABBO'S COMPOUND

The first mine blew halfway between the shore and the Kalinihta. The undersea lobsters were doing their job. The sea erupted into a high pillar, followed immediately by a cascade of others across the small harbor. Eazy and Alastair did not hesitate to launch the first package containing the venom darts. The blunt missile shot up out of the mortar with a loud thunk, arcing above the beach, and then soundlessly separated to release an uncountable number of shadowless spikes high above the surf. A wall of quick shimmer washed in front of the compound as the darts accelerated down. On the metal daggers' point of impact, a rapid succession of detonations blanketed the beach and surf, lifting sand and water high from the shore. Additional liquid columns sprouted up in the harbor as the deep-water mines began to clear, some in reaction to the darts, others to the robot lobsters.

Eazy and Alastair fired another package to clear the remainder of the beach. Before the second package had even arced, Alastair was in the zodiac with Cameron and Pepe. He dropped a knee forward at the bow beside Cameron as Pepe eased the throttle. The inflatable gently lifted above the dark water's surface and floated forward.

On the bridge of the Kalinihta, Captain Lewis eased the throttle forward and began the journey starboard out to sea.

So far, there was no movement from the compound.

If the scene were to be transcended from the zodiac's strongan duotex, the carbon, the steel, and the flesh of the men, to one large piece of marble, no pose would need to change. In the spray of the surf, the faces of these men were statuesque. These men, stoic in their deed, were operating textbook. Pepe was a master with the throttle. The zodiac pressed on with varying momentum to negotiate the bomb made swells. Cameron and Alastair each were prone against the inflated sides of the assault craft's bow, their weapons set to discharge on impulse. Though all three men still had vision gear, none chose to cover. A medley mist of water and harbor bottom coated brows and cheeks with heavy muddy droplets that ran down, and then spouted from, each chin. Their faces were a contrast to the dripping white foam and shadows from the night's last low indigo hues.

The first light of dawn shot from the eastern sky, illuminating the five-story face of the now docile compound and cratered beach. Two boat lengths from shore, a final water column erupted to the starboard of the zodiac, the last of the mines. Four seconds later, Pepe cut the throttle as the craft slid into the bright effervescent spume at the shoreline. In a fluid motion, Alastair launched from the bow, towline in hand, and as he did, two shirtless men with Kalashnikovs ran from a near door. The two men immediately fell, the second falling into the first before either hit the ground. Cameron, positioned to fire again, waited for Pepe to clear the inflatable so they could complete their three-man beachhead.

Cameron, Alastair, and Pepe went directly to the door the two shirtless men had exited from. This shore side structure was main building number one and the most likely to hold hostages. Cameron and Alastair climbed the short porch first. The stucco wall of the compound was caked with muddy sand, as were the steps up the porch to the door. From the side of the building, four men came running out onto the large break wall, oblivious to the three commandos on the beach below them. The four men were yelling and waved behind them to someone unseen and then frantically pointed to the Kalinihta. Cameron raised his MP-5 submachine gun toward the four men and then, before discharging, yielded to Pepe's gesture. Pepe, below the small porch on the beach, could see something Cameron could not and had tilted his MP-5 up on a slight angle. Alastair shifted his attention from the open doorway he and Cameron stood in front of to the side of the compound.

Cameron and Pepe were focused on the four on the breakwall and their unseen friend.

From the edge of the building another man came running to join the first four. On his shoulder, bobbing back and forth as he clumsily jogged, was an RPG-7 already loaded with a single stage warhead. Trailing behind was a younger man, maybe an older boy, half carrying, half dragging three more warheads. The four men on the breakwall were ecstatic, still waving and pointing to the Kalinihta. When the grenadier got into position, Pepe flipped thumbs up to Cameron and in six easy headshots the frantic breakwall mob became a pile of corpses.

The Kalinihta slipped safely south out of view of the small harbor.

Through the outer doorway, a second door, solid iron and locked from the inside, blocked their entrance into the building. Alastair secured a small cake of C4 to each of the two hinges, then signaled Cameron down to the side of the outer doorway. Alastair then slid himself around to the other side of the outer door. Pepe positioned himself on the second step of the porch, hunched clear. With a nod to Cameron and Pepe, Alastair thumb punched the detonator to the explosives. From inside the vestibule came a thud and a mist of dust.

A door opening out was a bad design for security, yet an advantage for the three.

Pepe was the first up and into the vestibule. He immediately assessed the space that once held the upper hinge and from one of his long pockets produced a thick, wide shiv. He jammed the shard into the newly formed crevice. Pepe's portliness gave him easy leverage to jar the heavy metal door to the side.

Alastair and Cameron's MP-5s filled the new-formed void; they found the room empty.

As they had with countless other incursions, Cameron, Pepe and Alastair began to clear the first building of the compound, room by empty room. The rooms were large and interiors out of place for this region and time. The furnishings were fine and intact, paintings, murals, lamps with detailed trim, and the amount of fine woods impeccable. This was truly the refuge of a rich man, and in southern Somalia in these times that meant a warlord.

That each room was coming up empty in the first building did not surprise Cameron. The assault during the Fajr dawn prayer was meant to minimize confrontation.

Still, someone had locked that metal security door behind the first two shirtless men, and somewhere in this building or the next, someone was holding Christine.

CHAPTER 18
ABBO'S COMPOUND

At the beach level, the sheer walls of the compound were windowless in defense of monsoon force or tsunamis that could clear the small harbor breakwalls. The top two stories of the ocean facing building were walled in industrial glass, allowing the dull, blue hued low morning light to wash through. Easily confused with a penthouse suite from any metropolitan city, the upper two floors of the five-story compound were adorned with an array of modern art, luxurious sofas, panel televisions, and flowing white panel curtains that punctuated the ocean vista.

Cameron and Pepe entered the top floor, an open loft space, from a spiral staircase in the center of the room. From where they stood, the room was clear, their only blind spot a short wall behind the stair. The two each chose a different side and circled the divider.

On the other side of the division wall was a lounge. A wooden bar was at the far end and occupying the space between them was an Olympic size billiards table. Seated on the floor at the end of the billiards table was Nikos, his back against the division wall. Nikos was clean, well dressed, and although very shaken and bruised, he appeared otherwise unharmed. Also sitting on the floor, at the end of the billiards table, was a thin man of dark Somali complexion. This second man was also clean and well dressed, yet holding a large golden handgun. He held the gun tightly with both hands wavering to either side of Nikos' head. He held the gun too tightly, as the weapon quivered in his hand.

The gunman did not move his watery glazed eyes away from Nikos. He waved the cannon side to side, his breathing getting noticeably heavier.

Though muffled by the glass and the five floor distance to the courtyard below, yelling could be heard as men rallied to discover what had caused the beach cacophony a few moments before.

Pepe waited and watched the heavy gun, a gold-plated .50 caliber Israeli Desert Eagle, hover in front of Nikos' face. He eyed the man holding the expensive weapon, dressed in a silk shirt, linen slacks, and Prada shoes. Pepe was certain this man had never fired the fancy trophy that he was now waving dangerously in the air. Pepe also knew that the action on the .50 caliber was sensitive and that if this man became any further stressed, there was going to be a hole through Nikos, on through the wall, and into the next building.

Pepe paced the rhythm of the nervous man's breathing with the sway of the .50 caliber, and when the small cannon was pointed at the wall beside Nikos' head, he acted. A shell from the MP-5 made a small clink against the floor and blood from the man's head sprayed Nikos.

"Bloody hell!" said Nikos, his eyes wide, his feet shuffling him into the wall in a failed attempt to put space between himself and the recently departed.

A fleeting moment passed and Nikos sucked in a deep breath, tossing his head back against the wall.

"Êtes-vous d'accord!" said Pepe. "Everything is okay."

Nikos ran his fingers across his face then, seeing blood on the ends, flexed them in an odd attempt to rid them of the stain, "You just blew a hole through Feizel's bloody head."

"Are you okay?" asked Pepe.

"Yes," said Nikos. He began to stand, "I'm fine."

"Where's Christine?" asked Pepe.

"She's gone. They took her," said Nikos. He went to the bar across the billiards table. "By helicopter, two, three days ago."

"Who took her?" asked Cameron. "Did Abbo take her with him?"

"No. Not Abbo. He was never here." Nikos surveyed the bar, then found a bottle of seltzer. "It was the man who boarded the yacht," he doused his hands with the seltzer, "A Somali. A really tall bald fellow."

Cameron flashed his eyes at Pepe, "I think we've met."

The sound of rapid fire and single shots rose up from the courtyard.

"We have multiple shooters out here," said Alastair into the headset. When the shooting had begun, he had gone down to secure the door leading out of the building into the courtyard.

Cameron put his finger to his headset, "Are you engaged?"

"No," said Alastair. "They're shooting at shadows and each other. We better get out of here though. I have a feeling it's going to get pretty hot. You have the packages?"

"We have one package and we are on are way," said Cameron.

Nikos paced to the side of the room, both of his hands clasped behind his head. He spun back to Cameron and Pepe, "This is shit. We're dead. Do you know who you just killed?" Nikos waited for a response that was not coming. Cameron and Pepe watched him with still faces. "Well, do you?" asked Nikos again. "You just blew a hole through the head of Abbo Mohammed's son. We are so dead."

Cameron glanced down at the corpse sprawled below the billiards table, "Is that who that was? Pepe did you know who that was?"

Pepe did not take his eyes away from Nikos, "No."

"Pepe did not know who that was," said Cameron. "I'll tell you this though. If we don't get out of here, you are dead. Your friend Alastair is downstairs if that makes you feel any better."

The presence of someone familiar appeared to calm Nikos, "Alastair is here?"

"For the moment," said Pepe. "Shall we?"

Nikos lowered his hands slowly at first, then dropped them to his sides. "Yes, let's go." Though Nikos was clean, fed, and dressed, his face was horribly bruised. There was no mistake that Nikos had taken a beating.

The three began to walk around the divider. "Wait," said Nikos. He bent over and relieved dead Feizel's still warm hands of the .50 caliber Desert Eagle.

"You sure?" asked Cameron.

Nikos lifted the .50 caliber and pulled the slide back from the barrel, allowing a round to flow into the chamber, "Unlike Feizel, I know how to use this weapon."

CHAPTER 19
ABBO'S COMPOUND

Alastair nodded toward the door that led to the harbor. "We head out onto that beach there is no way to guarantee that inflatable stays inflated." He shifted his gaze to Nikos. Beads of sweat poured from the young Greek. Alastair pursed his lip. "The zodiac is out of the question."

Nikos' tone was rushed, "So that was your plan?"

From the courtyard came a booming concussion, then a barrage of rapid machine gun fire followed by the ever closer rhythmic chopping of rotors.

Alastair stretched the back of his neck, extending his height. "No, that's our plan," Alastair arched a brow, "You remember Ari?"

Nikos bobbed his head, "Of course, right."

Cameron peeked past the edge of the window. The courtyard was full of silhouettes backlit by the stucco of the compound's other buildings, and from above by the indigo glow of the brightening predawn sky. Some shadows were frozen in position while others were frantically trying to evade the sheets of strafing fire from the copter.

"What do we have, Al?" asked Cameron.

"They're consolidated in building four as we

suspected," said Alastair. "The three you see scurrying are positioning from there. From the sounds of it Ari has compromised tower one."

"You left the gifts Eazy packed?"

"I found a beautiful place to stash the satchel."

Cameron nodded and then touched his headset, "H2, check in."

"This is H2," said Ari over the headset. "Are you ready to come home?"

"Affirmative, H2. Four to pick up, repeat, four to pick up. Ready when you are," said Cameron.

"Now is good," said Ari. "Landing zone one, repeat, landing zone one."

The rhythmic chop of the Dark Star rotors grew louder as Ari maneuvered the copter to the clearing they'd designated as landing zone one across the courtyard. The commandos instinctively did a periphery check of their gear, a rapid weapon inspection, and an up down of each other, the type of actions trained into their core.

Cameron placed his hand on the handle of the door. "Nikos, you're going out with Alastair first, then Pepe, you'll go. I'll cover from the back. Straight to the chopper, got it?"

Nikos nodded his head and then Cameron pulled the handle of the door.

Cameron peeked out, his nose filling with the pungent fumes of the burning tower hidden from his view by the barracks. He then threw the door open wide, "Go, go, go!"

Outside warmth flooded into the doorway with the thunderous rotor of the Dark Star copter touching down directly across the courtyard. Nikos and Alastair broke from the building in a dead run. The courtyard was far brighter outside than when Cameron had peered through the window. The silhouettes and shadows now had detail, though nothing showed true color, rather varying hues of blue with the exception of the stucco and stone wall which appeared in odd scales of grey. In a few quick heart pounding seconds, Nikos and Alastair were in the copter.

"Go!" said Cameron.

Pepe launched from the doorway toward the copter.

When Cameron heard the Kalashnikov, he instinctively turned. The rotors muffled the rapid burst, yet the compound walls surrounding the courtyard created a loud echo trail back to the barracks. Fortunately, the shooter had been leading his target too far, so Pepe had seen bullets pummel the top of the stone well at the center of the courtyard in time to dive safely below the line of fire.

Cameron fired at the barrel of the Kalashnikov protruding from the doorway of the barracks. The shooter still had a clear bead on the well and when Pepe tried to ease out of cover, he was chased back with a rapid succession of rounds.

Pepe was pinned down at the well by the shooter.

Cameron expected the inside of the barracks to be wide open and without walls, so he targeted the windows. The barrel in the doorway still did not waver. He decided to go in close and broke into a run toward the side of the barracks. The gunman in the doorway paid no attention to Cameron running along the side of the courtyard. When Cameron reached safety behind the corner, he pulled a grenade from his pocket.

Across the courtyard, Cameron saw another fighter running up behind Pepe's position.

Pepe launched himself from behind the well toward the assailant. One hand to a shoulder and the other to the waist, he hurled the man onto the ground out into the open, away from the well. Like a cat to his feet, the man was back at Pepe fist-to-fist, hand-to-hand. Cameron raised his MP-5. The two men were moving too quickly for Cameron to target and fire.

Alastair's voice shot over the headset, "We have an RPG."

"Where?" asked Cameron.

"The other side of the barracks. Can you get to him,

Kincaid?"

Cameron engaged the grenade he still held and then lobbed the small bomb blindly around the front into the direction of the RPG.

A second later there was an explosion.

Debris shot past the corner where Cameron stood, and a bloody flesh-filled boot landed near his feet. "Did I get him?" asked Cameron.

"No," yelled Alastair over the mic. "The shooter ran out and got in the way. I have a shot. Ari can you lift us up?"

Ari did not hesitate at Alastair's request. The Dark Star lifted to hover above the ground and gently spun to the side. Alastair immediately shot toward the grenadier Cameron could not see. Alastair fired too late or missed, from the far side of the barracks, a rocket flew.

The ghastly slow white smoke trail of the rocket cut across the courtyard, not to the copter as intended, but toward the center of the courtyard. The stone well blew to pieces. Cameron threw one leg in front of the other, almost falling. He could no longer see Pepe or the other man. Cameron put his other leg forward, strong yet slushy. The next moment across the courtyard felt like an eternity. When Cameron reached what was left of the stone well, he found Pepe, struck down by the rocket.

~*~

"Let's go!" screamed Alastair over the headset. Cameron suddenly realized Alastair had been screaming for a while. He lifted his head toward the copter and saw Alastair waving his arms. Nikos, his face contorted, was beside Alastair, shooting a submachine gun out into the courtyard. Across the courtyard, soldiers were running and falling. Cameron dropped his head down again to Pepe. Pepe was bloodied and half buried by heavy stone and limbs. Cameron hovered above him in an elongated moment stretching in time and pain, then dropped to his knees to shift the weight of the stones.

The intense roar of the rotors and gunfire around him faded. Smoke billowed throughout the rubble, pushed down to the ground by the rotating blades of the Dark Star, close, yet far away. Cameron realized that Alastair was kneeling down in front of Pepe.

Alastair was trying to lift Pepe. Alastair screamed at Pepe again, still all muffled, this time without the headset. Then Alastair struck Pepe. Pepe's eyes sharpened and cut into Alastair's. Pepe shook his head violently side to side. Wherever he had gone, he had now returned. He let Alastair lift him by his shoulders. Alastair pulled Pepe up from the rubble and the mutilated remnants of the Somali fighter, and then sent the large man running past Cameron.

Cameron still did not move. Real time did not return until Alastair shoved his shoulder. Sound returned to normal. He heard Alastair yell, "Let's go, let's go!" With that, Cameron turned behind Alastair and followed him to the waiting chopper.

Cameron climbed in with a liquid motion. In position, he pointed his weapon pointed out the door. As Ari began to lift the Dark Star, Cameron saw a fighter run into the courtyard from the far side of the barracks. Cameron dropped the man thoughtlessly without wasting a second round.

"Eazy, check in, this is H2," said Ari. "We have cleared the compound."

"H2, this is Eazy, do you have the package?" asked Eazy.

Ari peered over to Alastair, "We have the package."

"Bombs away," said Eazy.

Ari glanced at Alastair again. Alastair reached into his pocket and pulled out a small detonator, radio linked to the satchel of explosives Eazy had given him to leave on the first floor of the main building. With his thumb, he flipped back the safety cover then crushed the igniter. Back in the main building of the compound below, large explosions began that dwarfed all of the early detonations, and as they flew south over the beach berm the sky filled higher and higher with the aftermath of the incendiary devices.

Cameron did not watch the fireworks above the exploding compound. He found solace deep in the eyes of his brother-in-arms. Pepe, his face blackened and bloodied, held his head high, his gaze fixed on the ocean abyss, and though Cameron had no words, he felt no need to search for them. Cameron and Pepe were committed to a shared resolve. Finding Christine.

EPISODE II

CHAPTER 20
SHELA VILLAGE, LAMU

Nikos' frantic blubbering had driven Cameron out of the suite. He stood alone on the veranda watching the Lamu dhows glide by, the tall full single sails lifting the crafts forward. The ageless sailboats brought him a soldier's zen. Then the commotion to his back subtly dulled. Cameron sensed someone was physically blocking the chatter. He decided to acknowledge the friend at his back. "Graceful, isn't she?" he said. "The way the captain maneuvers that giant lateen sail as effortlessly as a jib."

"Like a photo," said Alastair from behind.

Alastair might have stood in the doorway the whole of the afternoon, hesitant to disturb Cameron. With his friends acknowledgement he sauntered to the edge of the veranda.

The two brown glass bottles Alastair held by the necks were perspiring. The hotel suite interior was far cooler then the veranda by contrast, yet nowhere near as comforting as the quieter adjacent space. Cameron had not said much to Alastair, or anyone else, since they arrived in Lamu. Eazy and Isaac had handled the logistics of docking the Kalinihta and securing transportation to the Peponi Hotel. Cameron did not need to say much as everything had gone according to plan. Well, almost everything. The primary goal of the mission was to liberate Christine, yet she had not even been at Abbo's compound. Christine had been moved by the warlord days prior.

As if to himself, Cameron said, "They look a lot like the jolly-boats up in the gulf."

"Lamu dhows are jihazi, similar to the jalibut," said Alastair.

"Jihazi? Doesn't that mean..."

"It's a Persian word for ship, I think."

Cameron allowed himself some levity and let out a slight grunt. Alastair offered him one of the brown bottles, "Here, Charlie dropped a few of these by before he went to check on the crew. They're cold." He shrugged, "Well, sort of."

Cameron held the beer up. On the label was a black stencil of an elephant head. "Finest Quality Lager, eh?"

"Try it, Tusker is pretty good. Best you'll get here in Lamu, anyway."

"What does this mean on the label? Bia yangu, Nchi yangu."

"Swahili," said Alastair, "it means, 'my beer, my country.'"

Cameron drank from the brown bottle and let the cold fizz down his throat, letting out a satisfying sigh.

"I told you it wasn't bad," said Alastair.

"Hmm. Thanks," said Cameron. "I was meaning to tell ya, for being out of service, that was a quite maneuver you and Ari pulled on the chopper, despite the rocket."

"Oh, the rocket man. Well, we tag rhino that way," Alastair wobbled his head to the side and back and then sipped his lager, "and the odd poacher."

"The odd poacher?"

Alastair raised his Tusker, "Conservation. I noted you still handle yourself quite well."

Cameron raised his Tusker in return, "Vive la Légion."

Exiting the suite behind them, Pepe added, "The Legion is our strength."

Cameron and Alastair allowed themselves to smile for a moment. Pepe and Isaac joined them on the veranda. Pepe's mere presence reminded Cameron all too quickly of the dread of the day.

"Nikos is talking," said Pepe. His eyes were dark and drawn in.

"What is he saying?" asked Alastair.

Isaac spoke for Pepe, "He is saying the Volunteer National Coast Guard kidnapped him and Christine to leverage his father."

Cameron arched one brow, dropped the other, then twisted his head slowly away from the Lamu dhows, toward Isaac and Pepe, "He said what?"

Isaac continued, "Abbo Mohammed was attempting to leverage Demetrius into increased protection of his shipping fleet."

"So this wasn't merely a ransom. He told you two this?" asked Cameron.

"No, no," said Pepe. "Nikos finally reached his father directly and was quite loud when he spoke to him. We could not help to overhear his yammering." Pepe shook his head.

"Tell me about it," said Cameron.

"Anyway," Pepe locked eyes with Cameron, "Demetrius is apparently paying the Coast Guard to allow passage, and whatever that amount is, Abbo decided it should be more."

Isaac walked to the edge of the veranda next to Alastair, "That explains why the Kalinihta was never officially reported missing. This was a business maneuver from the beginning."

Pepe's gaze was still locked, "A mistake that Abbo will not live long to regret."

"You told me you took out Abbo's son," said Isaac. "That is no small thing."

"That is nothing at all," said Pepe.

"Not with these people," said Isaac. "I know he has your sister, but I'm telling you that for men like Abbo Mohammed, the death of a son by another's hand is a catalyst for a Godob, a Somali blood feud. And let me further tell you that all of these clans were established and perpetuated by blood vendettas going back hundreds of years. They live and breathe this. Abbo may be looking for us already."

"Let him come," said Pepe. "He should have thought of such consequences before he took the Kalinihta."

"I'm sure he did and this was nowhere on his radar," said Alastair. "If what Nikos is saying is true, Abbo never meant to harm him. He was flexing old school tribal muscle. I don't think he ever meant to harm anybody. I mean, bloody hell, we found Nikos with his son in a luxury apartment."

"From Abbo's perspective," said Isaac, "his son was killed by a hit squad."

"Isaac's right," said Alastair, "he'll be seeking some bloody twisted flavor of Somali vengeance."

"Then we need to hit first," said Cameron. "Alastair, do you think we can get Stratos on board for more financing?"

"I don't see why not. He's a pretty honorable fellow, perhaps he can get Abbo to simply hand her over," said Alastair.

"I doubt that is going to happen now that Abbo is less one son," said Cameron. "If Isaac is right, then Abbo may be under the impression Stratos himself offed the kid. Pepe, can your contact back in Montreal put us back in touch with Dada?"

"I don't know. I will make the call," said Pepe.

"Why would you want to contact Dada?" asked Isaac.

"We may need some additional connections and intel to hit Abbo and if we're doing Dada a favor, he can do us one."

"That's a dangerous game," said Isaac.

"I game we're already playing, Isaac," said Cameron, "and it's too late for Pepe and I to quit. Pepe, do you suppose your contact would know where to find Abbo?"

"Perhaps, but I doubt they are that informed," said Pepe.

"If not, I have another friend close by," said Cameron.

"Here in Kenya?" asked Alastair.

"Here in Lamu."

CHAPTER 21
SHELA VILLAGE, LAMU

Maggie Soze began life as a socialite and then, after finding her way through the world, found herself in West Africa married to a lodge owner she affectionately nicknamed Tarzan. When the marriage ended, she parlayed her experience and connections into a career in freelance journalism. Cameron had become acquainted with Maggie in New York. When stateside, she was a frequent guest of Cameron's restaurant Le Dragon Vert. Maggie had moxie, something Cameron appreciated. She was as likely to order a rock glass of scotch as a glass of wine.

"It's like we're on a boat," said Maggie, "floating right through the channel along with the dhows."

"Yeah," said Cameron. "The suite I'm in is recessed behind the beach and lawn, no air flow. I think there is actually a breeze here."

Maggie eased her eyes shut, tilted her head back, and inhaled deeply through her nose. "I do believe there is."

Maggie slowly brought her head forward and opened her pool blue eyes into a fixed lock on Cameron's. "You know I love the Peponi. You picked a great hotel. The food here is outstanding. Is that what brought the Dragon

Chef?"

Cameron laughed. "No, though I am a bit hungry. What do you suggest?"

Maggie relaxed her gaze. She slid her turtle shell glasses over the bridge of her nose and reached for the one sheet menu. "Well, let's see what's on special today." She peeked over the rim of her glasses. "The Peponi is not Le Dragon Vert but still pretty good." She veered her attention back toward the menu, "Oh yes, you'll love the prawns."

"Right, I read about them in the New York Times."

"Is that how you heard about this place? I have to say I was surprised when Claude called me."

"Yes, I did read about the Peponi in the New York Times but no, that is not why I am here. Actually, a friend made the arrangements for us."

"Us?" The corner of Maggie's mouth curled up mischievously.

"Us as in a group of friends," said Cameron. "Men. We were in Laikipia and..."

"Oh, and you wanted to get to the coast. I get it. I can't be land locked too long either. There's nothing like a seafront stroll through Shela. Did you know this is a world heritage site? UNESCO." Maggie arched her eyebrows and then removed her glasses, holding them away from her in the air for a moment to inspect, and then, finding no flaw, she set them on the table.

"I was not aware of that," said Cameron.

"That's why there are no cars. Have you been on the seafront when the fishermen bring in the afternoon catch?"

"No, why?"

"Quite a spectacle, cats by the herds show up."

"You don't say."

Maggie sat back in her chair and straightened her back. "Spit it out. What's up?"

Cameron sighed, then furrowed his brow. "Remember that article you wrote a while back on the kidnappings near here?"

"Hmm, the Manda island abductions across the channel. How could I forget? After I wrote that article I had to watch my back, as did every other journalist. Various mzungu and wazungu around Lamu—"

"Mzungu and wazungu?"

"Foreigners and whites, Swahili, dear," Maggie arched her brows again and nonchalantly looked to either side of the table for eavesdroppers. "I was threatened more than once by foreigners and whites with business interests in the tourist sector, and in one case I was physically assaulted because I wrote that magazine article."

"You were physically assaulted?"

"Well, I wasn't beat up. I was doused with a bucket of ice water. Kind of refreshing in a hot place like this, actually. The intent was there, though. Hey, I just wrote the article and the Associated Press picked it up. No fault of mine if there is no security over on Manda. Tourist cancellations started coming in way before I wrote a story about the pirate-slash-tourist kidnappings in Kenya. I mean they have three police patrol boats that never leave the dock because the money that's earmarked for hotelier security ends up in some politician's pocket."

"Really?"

"Oh yeah, this place is paradise but there is a reason they call the government serekali."

"Swahili again, and why is that?" asked Cameron.

"As I understand, the Swahili words siri and kali mean secret and fierce."

Cameron nodded his head. "And the pirates?"

"Probably no different than the rest of them, taking payoffs. Those abductions were just some strays, off the reservation, if you will. As were the other abductions you have heard about. The female journalist that was held and raped a few years ago, and the aid workers. Thugs took those poor people, the equivalent of teenage street gangs. Those gangs are not the real power up there. There is a lot more going on."

"Like Abbo Mohammed?"

Maggie's eyes lit up, "Wow, now we cut to the quick. You picked a hell of a name to drop."

Cameron let his smile go subtly coy, "So is he a local player or what?"

Maggie sat silent for a moment, smiling at Cameron.

"You're sizing me up," said Cameron.

"You're a chef," said Maggie.

"Among other things," said Cameron. "So off the record, what can you tell me about Abbo?"

"Off the record?"

"All off the record. I like to keep private."

"Okay, I'll play. So, Abbo Mohammed is 'the' local player. If you did not know, he runs a little group not far north from here called the Volunteer National Coast Guard, and that little group, like some other groups up the coast, has a nasty reputation as a band of pirates. But they're not."

"They're not?" asked Cameron.

"No, they are not. Well, they are and they aren't. Semantics."

"What are you saying?"

"Their designation as pirates is a bit of a misnomer. A better word might be..."

Maggie pursed her lips pondering a word choice.

"Warlord, militia," said Cameron.

"Cartel," said Maggie. "Their reputation as pirates has actually helped them in the past, creates this picture of a rag tag group of unwashed men in rags tearing around in little wooden skiffs. Detracts from what they actually are."

"And what is that?"

"The strong arm of the northern horn of Africa. They control shipping in the Indian and western Pacific oceans, parts of Indonesia and South America now too, and they run grift across all of these waters."

"Grift?"

"That's their big money. All of those yachts, ships, and freighters that are picked up bearing precarious flags, a good

101

portion of them are prearranged insurance scams or illegal cargo transfers under the guise of a siege. There's protection money for the giant fisheries, and Lord knows what they're dumping in the waters out there."

"That sounds like a lot," said Cameron.

"It is. As pirates, they're documented around 120 million US dollars a year. I hear the real numbers are more like three billion."

"Whoa."

"Yeah," said Maggie, "probably still a lowball. It's never where you see it."

"I guess not. No wonder they have such a strong foothold."

"They're allowed a foothold because they're suppressing Al Qaeda in the Arabian Peninsula. The cartels are clan driven and even though Al Shabaab is predominantly intertwined, the cartels are the decision makers. As long as they're funded, they are in charge," said Maggie.

"Al Shabaab means the youth," said Cameron.

"And the clans are run by the elders."

"And Abbo is an elder."

"Technically a sheikh maybe, I don't know. He is the cartel elder."

"Where can I find him?" asked Cameron.

"You want to find Abbo Mohammed?"

"Do you know where he is?"

"Sure I know. He's not that hard to find. He holds up where all the shady billion dollar deals take place. You'll find Abbo Mohammed in Dubai. What do you plan to do, march in and cook him something?"

"You'd be surprised," said Cameron. "Actually, we have a friend to help us make contact, Ibrahim—"

"Ibrahim Dada!"

"You know the name?"

"Don't be fresh. You should be real careful of the friends you are making lately."

"I can use the help, so right now I am going with the old saying 'the enemy of my enemy is my friend,'" said Cameron.

Maggie leaned back and peered into Cameron's eyes, "I hope you know what you're doing. The old saying you should be concerned with is 'with friends like that, who needs enemies?'"

CHAPTER 22
PARIS, FIFTEEN YEARS BEFORE

Christine entered the small galley kitchen and agilely slipped her naked body behind Cameron as he buttered golden chunks of the egg-fried bread he had prepared from the remnants of last evening's loaf. She wrapped her arms tightly around him, rested her cheek on his upper back, and made a warm purring sound. Cameron felt her nakedness through his thin cotton shirt. Her warmth prompted his chest to flex as she squeezed.

"Bonjour, l'amour," said Cameron, his voice soft and sing song.

"I cannot believe you were up so early," said Christine, her eyes still closed, heavy with sleep. "What time is it?" she nuzzled further into Cameron's shoulder muscles.

"I did not want to wake you until breakfast was ready," said Cameron.

"Did you make coffee?"

"Yes, and it's not that early."

"No? I do not believe you." Christine softly nudged her head deeper into Cameron's shoulder. "We should go back to bed."

Cameron smiled contently and began to place the

bread onto a plate, "What happened to going out today? Remember? A walk by the river, a gallery, maybe a trip to the country."

"Yes, yes," said Christine. "I want to do those things today." She lifted her head and tugged Cameron's shirt, turning him toward her. "That would be so nice. To have you for myself today." She lifted her arms up over his shoulders and pulled herself close to him. He met her with a kiss. First a long one and then two fast smooches. Her lids sprung open, her green eyes lively and jubilant, awaken by his touch.

"Whoa," said Cameron. "Where did that come from?"

"You remind me, I love you." Christine grabbed a piece of the bread from the plate and the jar of jam from the counter, "First you must feed me. I am so hungry." Her eyes and mouth both went wide as she tore off a chunk of the bread. Mouth full, cheeks puffed, she smiled at Cameron, and then slipped past him toward the table.

Cameron set the plate of egg battered bread on the table along with some goat cheese, honey, and the coffee. When he sat, Christine was already voraciously under way with breakfast. Cameron laughed and Christine returned a full smile. Cameron bit into a piece of bread and then chuckled. He placed his hand over his mouth.

"What?" asked Christine.

Cameron pointed at the corner of his mouth as if he were Christine's mirror. She put a finger near her lip, "Oh," she said, and wiped away a splotch of honey. Cameron's smile did not fade. Christine lifted her brows in question. "And um," Cameron tapped his chest. She looked down, "Oh," she said. She gave him a toothy bread-filled grin. Then with her pinky she dabbed at the drops of honey that had drizzled upon her breasts, rubbing them into her flesh.

"I guess they were hungry," said Cameron.

"I cannot help myself, this food is so good. I did not know I had spices on my shelves."

"Only cinnamon and sugar."

Her eyes went wide again, her head wobbled side to side, "Only cinnamon and sugar? I would not know the first thing to do. You, my love, are in the wrong line of work."

Cameron took in a slow breath. The flat was shielded from the morning light by shadow and curtains of lace, yet Christine's green eyes shone bright. To him, she embodied beauty. Her physical beauty was undeniable, her long chestnut hair wildly flowing over her bare shoulders. No man could resist the charms of perfectly formed pert breasts slathered in shining droplets of honey. Certainly, they shared lust. To Cameron though, Christine also held the beauty of innocence, happily rocking side to side as she ate, now humming a song, most likely one of her own creation. Most of all Cameron believed—wanted to believe—that Christine did not know the work he did when he was away from her. When Cameron was by her side, that man was someone else.

"Cameron," said Christine.

"*Oui, l'amour*," said Cameron.

Christine tilted her head to the side and gazed into Cameron's eyes. He could become lost in those eyes and never go back to Corsica, to the regiment. Maybe one day.

"Today," said Christine. "I want to look at puppies."

"You want to look at puppies?"

"Yes, puppies. One of the girls has this beautiful new labrador. She says he is a chocolate Lab. He is very cute and keeps her company when…"

Christine shifted her eyes down to the table and bit off a small piece of bread. She chewed the piece more slowly than needed. Cameron waited for her to finish her sentence and when she did not he prompted her, "When…?"

Christine sighed and then sat upright in her chair, still peering at the table. "I do not want to think bad thoughts today. I need you to go with me to find a puppy to keep me company for when you are not here." She slid her eyes up from the table to meet Cameron's again, at the same time grasping his fingers into hers. Playfully pleading, she said, "Would you do that, Cameron? Would you go with me to find a chocolate Lab puppy?"

Cameron leaned forward and responded in the guise of a playful lover, "Oui, of course I will go with you to find a chocolate Lab puppy."

Christine lurched forward and planted a kiss on Cameron, wrapping her hand around his head so that he could not escape. When she sat back into her chair, the toothy smile returned to her face. "Fabulous," she placed her hands flatly together, "I know just the place in the country, and then we can have a picnic."

Seeing Christine so satisfied and joyful, Cameron could not help feeling the same. To simply make her happy made him happy. Cameron again imagined a world where he could easily stay here in Paris.

Again Christine's face became serious, "Cameron."

"Oui, l'amour."

"Thank you for being here with me."

"Where else would I be?" Cameron placed his arm across the table and Christine rested her hand in his.

Christine smiled. Then a brief moment later, "Cameron."

"Oui, l'amour."

"Thank you for making this lovely breakfast." Christine offered her cup to Cameron, and then sheepishly asked, "May I have more coffee?"

CHAPTER 23
AL MARMOOM CAMEL RACETRACK, DUBAI

From his seat in the grandstand, the stringy twelve year old flung his naked arm down toward the starting gate pit. From the sea of owners, trainers, and entourages packed tightly behind the twenty-three painted camels, the boy singled out one man. "That's him in the full body thobe and ghutra."

"Very funny, little one," said Pepe. "They all are wearing thobes and ghutras."

"We're wearing thobes and ghutras," said Cameron. "Can you be more specific?"

In his tattered desert tanned t-shirt and matching light denim pants, the boy, Rehan, was the only person on the grandstand not wearing a thobe and ghutra. The boy shrugged the shoulder of protruding arm, "You said you wanted the younger man from the Kingdom."

"Yes," said Pepe.

"He is there in the white thobe and red checkered ghutras." The boy pressed his arm out farther, wagging his hand toward the man. "There behind the red painted camel with the green robot. The one with the number nine on the side, talking to the tall bald man."

"Yeah," said Pepe. "I see." He fixed his eyes on the man the boy had described, the only one of the small Arab horde to wear a red-checkered ghutra, was close to his trainer, passionately gesturing toward the length of the track. "Yes, that's him." Pepe tilted his head close to Cameron, "And look who is with him, our friend from the London garage."

"That's the man from London, all right," said Cameron. "Looks like he is stepping away. Good."

Cameron slipped his hand into his thobe and retrieved a bright pink folded note revealing a picture of a hawk and the number one hundred. He held the paper toward the boy.

Rehan's eyes widened. He snapped for the money.

"Hold on," said Cameron, lifting the bill above the boy's reach. "This dirham is yours as well as the others we promised." He handed Rehan the bill.

"And the rest?" asked Rehan.

"First I need you to go down there and tell the Saudi that two Frenchmen are here to see him."

"But you speak English."

"And so do you," said Pepe, "so what?"

Rehan nodded and scurried down the grandstand toward the camel pit, his dusted shirt and trousers blending into the tan sand and shadow below the grandstand. He wove his way through the crowded staging area, disappeared, reappeared, and then popped up in front of the man. The Saudi, elegant in his pristine white thobe, froze mid-gesture of explanation to his trainer of how he saw the race that was to be run, and then tilted his head down to the urchin pauper boy before him. Rehan held his clasped hands up to the man and then swung back around toward the grandstands and pointed with the same overextended arm and waggling hand he had used a moment before. The Saudi fixed his gaze near Cameron and Pepe, his eyes searching.

"Smile and wave," said Cameron as he subtly raised his hand. Pepe did the same.

Having seen their signal, the Saudi smiled, slightly bowed his head, and waved back. He held up his hand with the palm upwards and all of the fingers together and made a small movement with his wrist to signify he was almost finished and then he turned back to his trainer.

"Watch this," said Cameron.

"He will not leave until he has a reward," said Pepe referring to the boy, still standing in the Saudi's shadow. The Saudi appeared surprised to realize the boy was still there. He said something to Rehan, and then attempted to return to the trainer.

"Not that easy," said Cameron, and he was correct, as the Saudi next gave Rehan something out of the leather pouch. Only then did the boy disappear again into the crowd.

"I don't know about this guy," said Cameron.

"Considering he is friends with Abbo, that should tell you enough. Then again, he is willing to betray him to us, so..."

"Even that makes me queasy. I mean, we're here for the morning races. Only sheikhs race in the morning and this fella owns a camel."

"A lipstick wearing camel."

"I think they are all wearing lipstick. Anyway, if this guy is a Royal Saud why is he willing to talk to us? What's the deal between him and Abbo anyway?" asked Cameron.

"He owes Abbo money," said Pepe. "A lot of it."

"This fella appears to be loaded."

"All appearances. My contact tells me this man is way down on the Saudi food chain, barely on the radar. He is in hock over his head. That is why he will talk to us. We erase Abbo and—"

"His debt is erased," finished Cameron.

"Voila."

"Must be quite a debt."

The boy shot up from the bottom the grandstands. "He is coming. He says he has to be fast as the race is to begin."

"I'm sure he has a lot riding on that little robot," said Cameron.

"Excuse me, sir?" asked Rehan.

"Wagered, I am sure he has a lot wagered."

"Oh, no. I am sure he does not."

"Why is that?"

"Gambling is strictly forbidden."

"Then why is he so pumped up?"

"Oh, the prizes are great. A luxury SUV, a luxury car, and yesterday someone won twelve luxury cars. And in the morning race, if you win, or place in the top three, another sheikh will surely purchase your camel for great riches."

"Bingo," sad Pepe. "He wants the prize money. A passive way to stay liquid."

"Okay, here he comes," said Cameron.

"Run along for now, little one," said Pepe, a fifty-dirham bill already extended. The boy grabbed the bill, then rolled his eyes at Pepe. Pepe began to stand, "Go on, and come back when the race begins."

Rehan scurried back down the grandstand steps the way he had come, circumventing the Saudi along the way. The Saudi raised his arms, scowling as the boy passed around him.

Cameron and Pepe began to rise as the Saudi reached their seats. He waved his hand to gesture they remain seated. The Saudi faced the track, smoothed the length of his thobe, and then without shifting his focus away from his camel, took a seat next to Pepe.

"Ahlan wasahlan," Pepe greeted the Saudi, being sure to mirror the man's mannerism of keeping his attention toward the track and not obligating him to make eye contact.

"Ahlan feek," said the Saudi.

Now that the man was up close, Cameron and Pepe were able to see that the Saudi, as described, was a younger man, perhaps late twenties, with the handsome look of an aristocrat. His face was smooth and his eyes jeweled. Having met this type before, they were able to discern this man was arrogant and spoiled, most likely the flaws that were key to his undoing.

"A fine morning for a camel race," said Pepe in his most congenial manner.

The Saudi's voice betrayed his disdain and disgust for the two men beside him. His eyes remained fixed on his camel down below, "So you are the Frenchmen from Montreal?"

"Oui," said Pepe.

"Have you ever been to a camel race before?"

"No. I cannot say that I have."

"Well, let me tell you. There has not been a good morning for camel racing in years, not since they started wrapping these electronic devices in Arabian cloth and weaving them into the saddlebags. Age old tradition tossed aside for public relations."

"I see. The human jockeys were better?"

"Much better," said the Saudi, and for the first time, he allowed himself to inspect Pepe and Cameron. Then he returned his focus to the red painted camel, "Anyway, I understand you are looking for a mutual friend."

Pepe and Cameron, of course, were not unnerved at this joke of a man and continued to feign interest in the pit below, even in the brief moment the Saudi had turned to them. "Yes," said Pepe, "I was told you would be able tell us where to find this…friend, in Dubai, and more importantly, assist us in getting us close to him."

"You understand correctly."

"So will you do this?" asked Pepe.

"Yes. I will help you, though there are some conditions."

"Conditions? What do you mean?"

"It was made clear to me that your intentions are to kill our friend."

"That may happen," said Pepe.

Cameron slipped his hand into his thobe, wanting to be near his weapon if needed.

"I am good with this. And though your business is not my own, I did have to ask myself why you would want to do such a thing."

"I assure you, our action will serve us both," said Pepe.

The Saudi turned his head and faced Pepe, "Well, I did some digging, and it is like this, Mister Laroque." Pepe took measure of the Saudi's expression. The Saudi continued, "I need to think of my best interest. Were you not to succeed, how do I benefit?"

Pepe, his face calm and voice kind, matched eyes with the Saudi, "We are here to do business. What do you want?"

The Saudi patted Pepe on the leg, "I am glad you understand. I need a small fee. Insurance, if you will."

Pepe's voice drew cold, "How much?"

The Saudi again put his attention on the camel pit, obviously annoyed, "What is he doing now?" The Saudi fruitlessly raised his hand toward his trainer.

Pepe repeated his question again, his voice deeper, "How much?"

The Saudi faced Pepe and this time placed his hand on his shoulder, "The fee will be one million US dollars, Mister Laroque." He then smiled and began to stand.

"That is no small amount," said Pepe.

"No," said the Saudi, "that is the amount, however, that Abbo is offering for information concerning his son. Listen, I have to get down to the track. When I have finished I will return for your answer." The Saudi began to start toward the camel pit then stopped himself. "Oh, there is one more thing."

"Yes," said Pepe.

"Something to help you decide."

"On with it."

"A new woman has been brought into Abbo's harem," said the Saudi. "A woman with chestnut hair and green eyes."

CHAPTER 24
AL MARMOOM CAMEL RACETRACK, DUBAI

Scattered shouts rose to howls and then a collective roar as people began to rise in the grandstands. On every tiered level, those nearest the front massed forward, tightly pressing against each other, folding those at the edge over the railings.

"Would you look at that," said Cameron.

Still a kilometer away, an elongated cloud of dust rapidly rounded the outside turn of the Al Marmoom Camel Racetrack, a rolling haze that covered all except the front-runners of the consolidated pack of painted camels and the pace keeping armada of white four-by-four Land Cruisers. Sporadic bursts of sunlight gleamed off the windscreens of the Land Cruisers that briefly slipped the grasp of the looming dust to shuffle for position. Striding forward at remarkable speed, the camels appeared to hover above the hot desert track—a Fata Morgana, a mirage—the trailing racers obscurely fading in and out of view.

"They are making good time," said Rehan.

"They seem to be running themselves," said Cameron.

From the grandstands, the tiny electronic robot jockeys appeared to be mere colored cloth atop the lean camels' backs.

"They are not," said Rehan.

Cameron flashed a glance to size up the boy, unsure of the response. He decided to go along, "The remotes are in the four-by-fours?"

"Yes, and some of the cameras are on the bonnets."

"The bonnets?"

Rehan gestured, "On the top."

"Right, the people riding rigs on the tops of the Land Cruisers. There are so many."

"I once saw a race with forty SUVs, they will not allow more."

"Too many camels?"

Rehan laughed at Cameron's comment, "No, of course not. The Bedouin will race a hundred camels. The sheikhs race with the SUV. More than forty is too many Land Cruisers."

"Ah," said Cameron.

Pepe leaned into Cameron's ear, "Are you ready?"

Cameron nodded.

"We need to go now, little one," said Pepe. "Take us to where the man's car is parked."

"Can we see the end of the race?" asked Rehan.

Cameron patted the boy's shoulder, "We will watch from the monitors. Let's go while we can."

"This way then," said Rehan, already in motion.

Rehan had a sense of the crowd. He moved through the openings behind and around the large gathered groups, instinctively avoiding the bottlenecks at the stairwell landings and the congested entrance to the interior concession area, where those that had been lining the corridor in wait for the bathrooms were now pushing out toward the track. Cameron and Pepe stayed close behind, choosing to mimic the boy's snakelike maneuvers rather than lose pace and have to awkwardly chase after him. Still,

Cameron and Pepe were grown men and though agile, young boys they were not. Fortunately, the Al Marmoom guests were focused on the last minutes of the race, intoxicated by the elixir of the finish line.

The concession area in the belly of the grandstand was predominantly empty, with the exception of a few men scurrying from the kitchens. Each carried a brass pot of cardamom-infused coffee, fresh brewed for the regal passengers of the four-by-fours about to finish the race. The monitors covering the walls featured the high definition live action of the camels up close, their tongues loosely draping their ears and pasty saliva spewing from their mouths. The small bulk of the robot jockeys on the camels' backs were clearly visible and the attached whips, engaged for the final stretch, could be seen rhythmically striking the rear quarters of the lumbering beasts.

Above the three, the excitement of the crowd began to build.

"It is almost finished," said Rehan.

The roar and movement from above amplified to a thunderous roar in the concrete cavern of the concession space.

Cameron raised his voice, "And then what?"

"As soon as each race finishes, the sheikhs and royals step out of their cars to greet spectators and the people rush to them, eager to congratulate the winners."

"Everyone rushes down?"

"They may all win a prize," said Rehan. "Sometimes the sheikhs are very generous. Like the great Oprah."

A new image dominated all of the monitors, across which flashed first a purple, then an orange, and then a blue-blanketed camel; none of the three belonging to the Saudi. The hollers and applause that had been gradually building now peaked in a raucous crescendo, a final outburst of excitement that expired to a murmur and the unmistakable sound of an exodus from the seating area above.

"This way," said Rehan, leading Cameron and Pepe to

the back of the concession space. Once free from the cavernous echo of the interior, the day drew new calm. Eyes widened and jaws slacked, Cameron and Pepe attempted to refresh their hearing. The space not enclosed by the concession area was used for private parking, which extended to the farther portion of the grandstands and wrapped around to access the racetrack. The palatial back of the grandstands opened out into an oasis of precious green lawn and palm trees, the centerpiece of which was a large, round pool fountain and an aesthetic bridge to the outside parking area beyond.

"I don't think I have ever seen so many Maybachs and Mercedes at once," said Cameron. "This place looks like a dealership."

"Billboard included," said Pepe, referring to the oversized digital monitor mounted above the parked cars.

Rehan was not fazed, "The camel minders wait for their camel to cross the finish line so they can escort him off the track. The trainer will be with the four-by-four, leaving your man to come through here. Everyone else will be trackside with the winners for some time."

"You're sure of that?" asked Cameron.

"His highness Sheikh Mohammed bin Rashid Al Maktoum was a winner today, so he will be greeting admirers. Everyone will be lining up to congratulate him. His highness is very generous."

Pepe smirked, "The number one guy himself. You know, I truly and honestly respect and admire him. From what I hear, on many accounts across sources, he really is a nice person, cares for his people, and for the reputation of his country."

Cameron rolled his eyes, "I'll take note of that."

Rehan reached into his pocket and retrieved a black key fob, "I parked your Mercedes there. That Maybach over there belongs to the man from the Kingdom."

"The white Maybach there?" asked Pepe.

"No," said Rehan. "The black one."

"Okay," said Pepe. He held his hand out for the key fob and the boy pulled his arm away.

"Don't worry," said Cameron. He held two hundred dirham bills up and the boy slapped the key fob into his hand in exchange. Cameron grinned at Pepe. Pepe scowled and then peered up at the monitor.

"What are they smearing all over those camels?" asked Pepe.

"The heads and necks of the three top placers from the race are smeared with saffron paste before being paraded in front of the spectators," said Rehan.

"Saffron?" Pepe glanced back at Cameron, "Saffron is expensive, oui?"

"I believe the winning camels are ceremoniously doused in turmeric," said Cameron, "essentially low quality saffron."

Pepe grunted then shifted his eyes past Cameron's shoulder. The Saudi and his driver, a giant of a man, were walking along the far edge of the parking structure toward the black Maybach. The Saudi was speaking on his mobile phone and had not yet noticed Cameron and Pepe near the concessions entrance. "There he is," said Pepe, "right on time. Good job little one. Get along now."

"Call my mobile if you need anything else," said Rehan, then he slipped past the two men back through the entranceway.

"Call his mobile," muttered Cameron.

"Don't worry, I have his number. Things are different here you know."

Cameron pursed his lip, "I guess, you ready?"

Pepe nodded, "Yeah, let's go."

CHAPTER 25
AL MARMOOM CAMEL RACETRACK, DUBAI

Cameron and Pepe sauntered across the aisle of the parking area to the black Maybach that Rehan had told them belonged to the Saudi. As there were at least three other black Maybachs in this small section of the structure alone, there was a chance that the boy may have been mistaken.

The Saudi and his driver were steps away before they realized that Cameron and Pepe were waiting beside the Maybach to greet them. The Saudi said something into his mobile that they could not hear and then slipped the phone into his bag. He then gazed at Pepe with a closed smile, a smile of contentment and satisfaction.

"Ahlan wasahlan," said the Saudi.

"Ahlan feek," said Pepe.

"I honestly did not think I would see the two of you again so quickly."

"You mentioned you needed an answer after the race," said Pepe.

The Saudi clasped his hands together in front of his chest, "So I did."

Cameron took one half step forward, "How was the race, by the way?"

The corners of the Saudi's mouth dropped. He slowly faced Cameron.

Cameron continued, "I mean, you didn't even place did you?"

The Saudi let both of his eyes briefly rest shut and then reopen, "No, I did not. My robot did not respond accordingly."

"Yeah, funny things, electronics," said Cameron. He reached into his thobe and removed a small object, which he then tossed to the Saudi.

The Saudi opened his clasped hands enough to catch the object, "What is this?"

"Just a piece of electronics."

"I don't understand."

"You see, I know why you are running out of here so quick. I mean, ahead of everyone else." Cameron raised his hand and extended his finger, an insult alone, and then he began to wave his finger, a further insult. "You made a wager, didn't you? And you lost that wager."

"How do you know?" asked the Saudi.

"Oh, I know." Cameron nodded at Pepe. "Tell him."

"He knows," said Pepe.

"You made a huge bet that you cannot cover," said Cameron.

"You do not know what you are talking about. Gambling is forbidden here," said the Saudi.

"Maybe so, maybe so."

"No maybe. Forbidden, I am no fool."

"I have a feeling that you are in a position to make a deal and give us Abbo," said Cameron, "and that little piece of electronics tells me so."

"What are you saying? What is this?" The Saudi held the small piece up, a black plastic cube with small pins protruding from one side.

"That there is the device, or like the device that tells

me you are in trouble. Or maybe that is the device or like the device that tells your camel he is in trouble."

The Saudi's eyes now pierced Cameron. "Did you tamper with my robot?"

"Doesn't matter, you lost and you owe and we are the only friends you have," said Cameron.

Pepe smiled at the Saudi, "What do you say we take a moment. Things have changed from half an hour ago. Our mutual friend will not be happy with you. Maybe you see things our way now."

The Saudi closed his eyes briefly again, "Perhaps you're right. Meet me tonight." From his bag, he retrieved a card. "Here, call this number this evening and I will tell you where I can meet you."

"That's not necessary," said Cameron. "All we need to know is how to get to Abbo and your problems and our problems are solved."

The Saudi composed himself and for the first time signaled his driver to step forward.

"Call me," said the Saudi. "We will eat, start over."

Cameron took another step forward, "I would rather—"

The Saudi threw up his hand in a gesture for Cameron to stop and the driver slipped his hand into his thobe and revealed the top half of a submachine gun.

Cameron threw his hands up and stepped back, "Okay, okay. Dinner then."

"Dinner then," said the Saudi.

Cameron and Pepe stepped from behind the Maybach to allow the Saudi into his car without further discussion. The luxury car backed out of the parking space.

"What was that electronic thing you gave him?" asked Pepe.

The car slowly moved past the two men. Cameron and Pepe smiled, offered a gentle wave, and then bowed their heads at the dark tinted windows of the Maybach.

"Part of the electric eye sensor from the concession

entrance. I figured that would throw him."

"Clever. I believe you succeeded."

"Thank you, I think so too," said Cameron, he lifted the key fob Rehan had given him and tapped a button. The taillights of the Mercedes flashed.

"You know," said Pepe. "He is going to try to make a deal with Abbo to trade us for his debt."

"Well, he thinks he is," said Cameron. "We are about to talk him out of doing such a foolish thing."

CHAPTER 26
AL MARMOOM CAMEL RACETRACK, DUBAI

Cameron let the Mercedes idle in the shaded entrance of the parking structure as he and Pepe watched the Saudi's Maybach follow the service road out of the Al Marmoom Camel Racetrack. When the Maybach reached the first grandstand near the complex edge, Cameron accelerated into the sunlight.

Pepe leaned over the front seat, "How far do you want to follow him?"

"Not far," said Cameron. "Clear of the racetrack, before the Dubai Highway."

"How about that stadium over there, behind us? The entrance is on the left, right before the Highway 77 ramp."

Cameron glanced into the rearview mirror. "You want to get him into that large stadium back there?"

"That's the Sevens rugby stadium. The place was empty when we came in."

"Sounds good," said Cameron. "Hold tight." They turned toward the Alain-Dubai road. "This will only take a minute." The engine revved as Cameron punched the pedals, shifting to a higher gear.

To reach Dubai Highway, Highway 77, vehicles turned right out of the racetrack complex onto the Al Marmoom service road, traveled the opposite direction of the highway a few hundred meters, and then turned to cross the parallel two-lane Alain-Dubai road, properly Highway 66, to reverse back.

The Maybach would be turning onto Highway 66 in seconds and driving directly back toward the Mercedes. If Cameron's timing was correct, he would be turning right onto the service road at the precise time the Maybach exited, giving him the opportunity to catch up before his quarry turned back. Cameron's timing was almost always correct. He evaded out of habit rather than necessity. Providing an evasive pursuit out on this stretch of road really did not matter. The black Mercedes Cameron was driving could have been any one of the many from the parking structure or on the highway. The only vehicles more numerous than the luxury sedans this far from the city were the myriad of high-end four-by-fours.

In less than a minute, the Mercedes was on Highway 66 behind the Maybach and closing fast.

"Are we clear?" asked Pepe.

"Not another car on the road," said Cameron.

"This will be like the Algarve job then?"

"Right, I will pinch the quarter and you—"

"Close the deal."

"Vive la Légion," said Cameron.

Pepe responded, "The Legion is our strength."

The driver of the Maybach would not know what was happening until it was too late, if he ever realized at all. Cameron's years of training and experience made the deadly task effortless in execution, and essentially that is what the maneuver was, an execution. In a country notorious for reckless speeding, the driver of the Maybach most likely took no notice of the black Mercedes rapidly approaching from behind to pass on his right. He probably could have responded better than to jerk the steering wheel to the left when the black car cut him off by too quickly moving into his lane, had his head not been removed from his body by two gun blasts from the other vehicle's rear window. Odds are he never saw Pepe or the muzzle flash, both appearing in the brief instance that the corner of the Maybach's windscreen aligned with the back seat of the Mercedes.

Cameron was surprised as well. The maneuver anticipated bulletproof glass and was meant to jar the driver into a wheelhouse jerk of the steering wheel. Despite the overkill, the Maybach went exactly where Cameron and Pepe had wanted, a billiard ball to Pepe's bullet cue, right into the stadium side pocket. One thing that Cameron and Pepe had not anticipated was that there was no exit to the Sevens rugby stadium from their far lane. This portion of the Alain-Dubai road was a proper multi-directional highway split by a median. Fortunately, there were no dividers of any kind, so coupled with luck, the Maybach made the journey across the median, over the other lane, and onto the Sevens Stadium service road.

Cameron spun the Mercedes around and crossed the median to follow their target. The Maybach traveled a few hundred meters toward the stadium, eventually slowed, and then finally came to a full stop.

"He's going to run," said Pepe, again leaning over the front seat, his handgun dangling in his clutch.

"They always run," said Cameron. "That was an amazing shot."

A light grunt was the only sound Pepe made.

Mere meters away the rear door of the Maybach flung open and the Saudi awkwardly poured himself out of the car.

"There he is," said Cameron. Cameron tapped the accelerator to shorten the tedious task of apprehending the Saudi.

"Oui," said Pepe, "please make this quick. He is tripping over his thobe. Very pitiful."

The Mercedes swerved up next to the Saudi. Pepe swung open the rear door in front of the man. The Saudi, his pristine white thobe now sprayed bright crimson, threw up both of his arms and stumbled backward, then dropped to his knees.

"Calm down," said Pepe.

The Saudi veered up at Pepe and then projected thick vomit onto the asphalt.

"Oh, that is disgusting," said Pepe. "Listen, I promise you I will not shoot. See? I give the gun to my friend."

Cameron reached up behind his head to take the handgun from Pepe.

"Are you sure?" asked the Saudi, his face also speckled with bright red spatter.

"Very sure, now get in before I change my mind."

The Saudi moved toward the Mercedes, slowly at first, and then scampered into the backseat with Pepe, perchance for safety.

"Excuse me," said Pepe, as he reached over the man to close the door, trying not to rest his own thobe against the blood on the Saudi's.

"We all in?" asked Cameron.

"Oui," said Pepe. "Uh, take us around the back of the stadium where we can talk in private." He furrowed his brow to the Saudi, "Relax, we are only going up here a bit. Maybe we should buckle you in."

CHAPTER 27
SEVENS RUGBY STADIUM, DUBAI

Cameron glanced into the Mercedes' rearview mirror. The Saudi had undergone a metamorphosis. Caustic and threatening at the track, he had become something altogether different.

The Saudi rested with his eyes closed, letting his face and jaw go completely lax. He appeared ill, his facial pallor accentuated by brilliant crimson spatter. He drew in a deep breath through his nose that did not give rise to his chest, his body rejecting the cooler air of the Mercedes. His full upper body quivered.

"He's going to wretch again," said Cameron.

"No," said Pepe in a soft voice. "No, he is calming. Go ahead and breathe."

The Saudi began to rapidly mouth some words, a mantra, a prayer, again and again, silently at first, then at a whisper. From the front seat, Cameron could make out the mantra clearly, "A-ozu billahi mena shaitaan Arrajeem, A-ozu billahi mena shaitaan Arrajeem." Cameron understood Arabic; it was a Muslim phrase, mainly used when one was feeling unsafe or when scared by something. Roughly translated, the phrase meant, 'I seek refuge in Allah from the cursed Satan.' Pepe also understood the meaning of this phrase. The overall meaning was that the Saudi was right where they wanted him.

In a still soothing tone, Pepe spoke again, "You pray for Allah to be with you." Pepe nodded his head, "The great Allah is with you. My friend and I, we are not the cursed Satan. Do not feel unsafe, do not feel scared, try to relax."

The Saudi opened his eyes, large and round, wanting to escape Pepe. "Relax?" he said. "You could have killed me. You killed Faheem! You could have killed me!"

"Whoa, whoa, 'could have' is not the same as did," said Pepe. "I did not wish to kill Faheem."

"Then why did you shoot him in the head?"

"My goal was to scare him off the road. You did not have bulletproof glass. Who does not have bulletproof glass? I cannot believe you did not have bulletproof glass." Pepe lifted his hands in frustration, sighed, clasped his hands, and then continued, "Very unnecessary, you know, *we* have bulletproof glass. This is only a rental."

The Saudi sank into his seat, now appearing more a boy and less a man. The blood sprayed upon him was already beginning to dry in the cool air of the Mercedes.

Cameron found a loading dock behind the stadium and pulled the Mercedes down the concrete ramp. The Mercedes lowered from the surrounding view. He stepped out of the car, closed the door, and inspected the bay. With the loading bay doors closed, they were essentially parked in a concrete box. Above, Cameron spied two cameras. Someone could be watching. They would need to be prudent. He walked to the rear door of the Mercedes and pulled the handle.

The Saudi did not move.

"Go on," said Pepe from inside the car. "Out of the car."

The Saudi sat stolid, staring at the headrest in front of him per chance Cameron and the open door would disappear.

Pepe's voice softened further, his always-calming deep accent possessed an additional quality of assurance and he placed his hand onto the Saudi's, "It is okay, Taufiq."

In a meek voice, Taufiq replied, "You are going to shoot me now."

"No, my friend," said Pepe soothingly, "I promised I will not shoot you."

"Then your friend will," Taufiq closed his eyes again. "A-ozu billahi mena shaitaan Arrajeem, A-ozu billahi mena—"

"Now, now. Do not be silly," said Pepe. "Neither of us will shoot you. We need your help. We only want to talk to you."

"Really?"

"Really. Now, let's go."

"Okay," said Taufiq. He placed his arms by his sides to upright his torso and then swung his feet out of the Mercedes, standing as tall and elegantly as he could to regain stature, to save face. He spread his fingers wide and smoothed the front of his no longer pristine thobe and then, without looking down, indifferently tried to brush away any of the dried rust colored blood that may have gotten onto his hands. Cameron stood tall as well, respectfully holding the door for the Saudi as he exited the Mercedes and performed his little ritual. Pepe opened his own door on the other side of the Mercedes and then slowly joined the two, giving the Saudi a further chance to compose himself.

His back to Cameron, Taufiq peered forward as if he could see through or over the top of the ramp to the vast parking area and immensely vaster desert beyond.

"So," said Pepe, approaching Taufiq from the rear of the Mercedes. "Can we now speak?"

"Abbo will kill me for telling you his location."

"You are telling us Abbo's location so that we can kill him. Abbo will not be a threat to you."

"And," said Cameron. Startled by a voice from behind,

Taufiq spun on his heel to face them both. Cameron was still standing behind the open rear door, leaning forward on one arm. Cameron continued, "Your debts will be clear. Abbo will not have sold them. Your slate will be clean."

Taufiq backed away from between the two. He moved toward the sidewall of the loading bay, and then spun on his heel again. He placed a hand flat against the concrete and then faced them, "How do I know you can pull this off?"

Cameron dropped and shook his head chuckling, then gazed up at Taufiq, "Well, you had a back seat view of what we did out there moments ago and let me tell you, we were not really trying."

Taufiq drooped his head, "Oh, yes." He raised his eyes to Pepe, "Not even trying?"

Pepe, sauntering toward Taufiq, shook his head, "Not really."

"Okay, okay. Yes, I guess that is right." Suddenly pensive, the Saudi stared at the ground, placed his thumb to his mouth, and bit. Cameron and Pepe let him spin his wheels and a brief moment later, Taufiq lifted his head. His eyes shifted between the two mock Arabs in front of him. "Who are you two? Why do you want Abbo so bad?"

Pepe stepped closer to Taufiq, "Let's say Abbo took something that does not belong to him."

"And it doesn't really matter if I want to tell you, does it?"

"Not really," said Cameron.

CHAPTER 28
SEVENS RUGBY STADIUM, DUBAI

Taufiq's forehead had gained an oily sheen. His attempt to maintain a confident air was compromised by his feeble and distant words. "You're not going to shoot me?"

"We are not going to shoot you," said Pepe. "Though you can make this easy or hard on yourself."

"Yes, I understand clearly. I will tell you, but it will make no difference. You will never be able to get to him."

"Try us," said Cameron."

"He is at the Burj Khalifa," said Taufiq. "You know this place, the world's tallest building."

"Of course we do," said Pepe. "Can you be more specific?"

"He has a luxury residence in the Armani Hotel, a huge villa suite there. Like a palace really, up in the air, he is safe like a bird in the sky."

"You are sure that is where he is?" asked Pepe. "That does not sound very secure. The Armani is on the lower levels."

"And relatively public," said Cameron. "Like our friend in London."

"But you see," said Taufiq, "he is not in the Armani

residences that everyone knows of. He is high like a falcon on the 105th floor. The residences between floor 77 and 110 are very secure. You must be friend or family to access those levels."

"Or have a key," said Cameron.

The Saudi peered at Cameron.

"Do you have a key?" asked Pepe.

"He has a key," said Cameron. "He has a very special key. Don't you?"

"Taufiq," said Pepe. "Let me see your key."

"It will not help you," said Taufiq.

"Probably not. Let me see anyway."

The Saudi reached his hand into his thobe, removed a golden keycard, and then handed the card to Pepe.

"Hmm," said Pepe. "There is an electronic chip in here, and the card is engraved. Do you mind if my friend takes a look?" Pepe held the card out for Cameron to inspect. Taufiq stared at the ground.

"Well I'll be, that is nice," said Cameron. He held the card up in the air, "A little holographic paint, a chip, engraving. Let's see what this says." He pulled the card closer, "It says here...wow, you live there. That must be nice."

The Saudi, his head still drooping and eyes beginning to well, spoke quietly in almost a murmur, "It is a family residence."

"I bet you have to use a code with this too," said Cameron. "A pin number, maybe?" Cameron peered over the card to Taufiq.

Taufiq began to weep.

"Is that true, Taufiq?" asked Pepe. "Do we need a code?"

Taufiq subtly nodded his head.

"What is the code, Taufiq? Tell us the code. We need your help."

The Saudi spoke in a whisper.

"I am sorry," said Pepe. "I did not hear you."

"823," said the Saudi. "The code is 823. The card works for the elevator and the residence door on the 102nd floor."

"That's what the card says," said Cameron, "102nd floor."

"You see," said Pepe. "That was not so bad. Now we can be close to Abbo. The task is almost complete."

The Saudi nodded again, tears streaming from his eyes.

"And the new woman?" asked Pepe. "The one with chestnut hair and green eyes that has been brought into the harem."

"Also at the Armani Hotel. He keeps his harem there."

"On the same floor?"

"No, one floor below." The Saudi lifted his head, "That key will get you to those floors as well. Except..."

"Except what, Taufiq?" asked Pepe. "Except what?"

"I will need to be with you. Sometimes, not always, sometimes the elevator requests more security."

"Another code?" asked Pepe.

"Or something biometric?" asked Cameron. "Like a voice imprint, a handprint, maybe even a retinal scan."

The Saudi hesitated, then said, "A retinal scan," he paused to gauge Pepe's reaction and then began to speak quickly. "Particularly if you are visiting floors other than your own, it is all very random, hardly ever actually, that's why I didn't think of it, but I will help you, I swear."

"I see," said Pepe.

The Saudi watched Cameron press a thumb to his forehead and make a deep frown.

"I will help you," said the Saudi. "To get Abbo, I will help. Tonight, now. We will go right now."

"That will not be necessary," said Pepe. "You have helped enough. We are finished here."

"Are you sure? There must be more I can do."

"No, you have done enough."

"I have?"

"Now, Taufiq, you must understand we need to be

confident that you will stay silent. If you were to go to Abbo, or run into Abbo, or if Abbo were to come looking for you, there is too great a chance you may say something."

Again the orbs of Taufiq's eyes, plump and pushing from his skull, fought to escape him, "I swear I will say nothing. By Allah I swear, by Allah I swear. Wallah, Wallah."

Pepe placed his hand on the Saudi's shoulder, "I believe, you believe that."

"You promised not to shoot me!" said Taufiq, his face was wet and dripped with tears.

"Shhh," said Pepe. He leaned in close and placed his cheek near Taufiq's. "Shhh."

Taufiq felt a poke in his neck and then great warmth. Pepe pressed on Taufiq's shoulder, easing him slowly down the wall to his knees. Taufiq placed his hand on his neck where he felt the warmth. His fingers immediately became hot and wet and when he massaged them into his neck, sticky. He pulled them away to see his own bright crimson leakage and attempted to cry out, but no sounds came.

"Shhh," said Pepe again. Pepe's face was warm and kind, "Allah waits for you. Close your eyes and go to him."

CHAPTER 29
OLD TOWN DUBAI

Alastair sat at a table near the edge of the promenade overlooking the Burj Khalifa Lake, the building of the shared name towering above them from across the water.

"You didn't bring him with you," said Alastair.

"In a sense, we did," said Cameron. He pulled a chair away from the table and then sat down. "Pepe has his eyes."

"Bloody hell. So it came to that." Alastair's lips pulled tight and the entirety of his face shifted to the side, a scowl that Cameron recognized and always took as a judgment, and a faux disgust. Cameron had adopted many cues from Alastair over the years. Alastair had an upscale upbringing and recognized when to behave in a fashion.

"It always comes to that," said Cameron. "That's why I got the hell out of the game."

A waiter approached Cameron and bowed his head, "Coffee, Sayyed?"

"Yes, coffee please, with lemon and sweet. Do you have artificial?"

"Certainly," said the waiter.

"That will be all then, thank you."

The waiter bowed his head again and backed away from the table before changing direction for the bar.

Alastair picked up where they were a moment before. "You got out of the game for the same reason as the rest of us. You were getting too old and too poor to be doing what we were doing."

"I was tired of killing innocents."

"Collateral happens and you know that. Besides, I would hardly consider Taufiq Sawar an innocent. The man may have lost his money gambling but he made it as a human trafficker, a slave trader. He will not be missed."

Cameron grunted, "Vive la Légion."

"Need I remind you that in combat you act without passion or hatred," said Alastair.

"You are not the only one that can quote the code of honor," said Cameron. "Respect vanquished enemies, I remember that part, too."

"I do as well," said Alastair. "Collateral, we'll have a drink for the bastard later. Does that suit you?"

Cameron flashed a glance and a twisted half smile smirk across the table to Alastair for bringing him back to reality.

"So everything was as we thought?" asked Alastair.

Cameron lifted his hands above the table, "Once again our friend in London had the information right to the tee. The secret Armani residence on the 105th floor of the Burj Khalifa, the golden keycard security, the elevator retinal scanner, and he was even right, unfortunately, that Taufiq would try to double cross us."

"And Christine?"

Cameron sucked in a deep breath, "Right, Christine. He said he saw her, or rather, a new girl with chestnut hair and green eyes that had recently been brought into the harem."

"Harem?"

"Yeah."

The waiter returned to the table and set Cameron's

coffee before him. To the side he set a plate of assorted sugar cubes and sachets of artificial sweeteners. "Shukran," said Cameron.

The waiter bowed his head said, "Afwan," in response and then again backed away from the table.

Alastair watched the waiter from the corner of his eye until he felt he was clear, "Please tell me this harem is on the same floor."

"Close, a floor below," said Cameron. He picked up three yellow sachets from the plate, tore the ends at once together, and spilled the contents into his coffee. He shifted his eyes up toward the tower across the lake, "You come up with any new ideas as to how to get in and out of there while we were gone, or did you spend the whole of the morning with the blonde you disappeared with last night?"

"No and yes, no new ideas and yes I spent a good part of the morning with the blonde. She could not get enough of me."

"I cannot believe you are still using that same line," scoffed Cameron. "'I'm from Kenya.'"

"Well, I am, and the ladies love it."

Cameron twisted and tossed the sliver of lemon rind from the side of his saucer into his cup and then gave a quick stir with the demitasse spoon.

Alastair watched Cameron's ritual and when he was finished, he asked, "Why the artificial sweet?"

"Are you serious?"

"Well, yeah. That raw sugar is good sugar, besides, you're a chef."

"I'm a chef. I eat too much sugar. I am trying to watch my intake."

"Hmm," said Alastair.

"What? I'm getting older. You should watch your diet as well."

"My bloody diet is fine, thank you." Alastair gazed out across the lake. At that moment, the Dubai Fountain, the massive choreographed water system that spread across the manmade Burj Khalifa Lake, erupted and projected water into the air at different heights along the intricate path of the piping.

"Would you look at that," said Cameron.

"Beautiful," said Alastair. The high-pressure water jets and shooters of the fountain pushed streams of water to and fro across each other while the water robots made other streams spin and twirl in such a way that they appeared to dance. "You know that fountain can spray 83,000 liters of water in the air at any moment."

"You don't say," said Cameron, and then sipped from his coffee. He was well aware of where this was about to go.

"I read they installed more than 6,600 lights and twenty-five color projectors."

"Uh huh."

"They even had fire shooting out one year."

"Did they?"

"Can you imagine if that was your job, to be the fountain man?"

"Here we go."

"I mean, what a responsibility to be the man that runs the fountain. What a specialized job. All of that pristine knowledge for only a handful of fountains."

"I've told you before," said Cameron. "These fountains are run by firms, teams, computers."

"But there is one man, Kincaid. One man for each fountain that knows that fountain, that keeps the whole thing running like clockwork. A handful of master fountain men around the world. Sure, the Dubai Fountain is the largest, but think, there is another guy that runs the Bellagio Fountains—"

"Yeah, that reminds me, I read an article in the Times that the same people that built the Bellagio Fountains built the Dubai Fountain, they build all of these fountains."

"That's what I'm saying," said Alastair, "the Fountain of Wealth in Singapore, the Magic Fountain of Montjuic.

Kincaid, the Big Wild Goose Pagoda Fountains were built in 652."

"652, I know, you've told us a hundred times, your fountain fetish is well known and noted, and what I meant was that a firm built these things to be run by firms. I don't think there is just one fountain guy."

"Sure there is."

"I thought we were out here to check out the tower. I should have known."

"Well, I said I have no new ideas, I do have an old one. Watch this," said Alastair. On cue, five super shooters projected streams far above the rest of the water dance. "Whoa, now that is pretty high, at least seventy-five meters."

Cameron followed the jets of water up above the lake. As the water crested, a series of loud booms echoed through Old Town.

"What was that?" asked Cameron.

"The water shooters have to use a lot of pressure to push the water that high. They are very loud. They have extreme shooters they never use that push the water up over a hundred fifty meters. Bloody shame." Alastair winked at Cameron. "They would make your ears rattle."

Cameron slapped his hand down on the table. "Alastair, you are brilliant."

"True," said Alastair. "I have been waiting for chance to be the Fountain Man, at least for a night."

CHAPTER 30
AT.MOSPHERE RESTAURANT, BURJ KHALIFA LEVEL 122, DUBAI

The doors of the express elevator opened on the level 123 sky lobby, 450 meters above the promenade of the Dubai mall, where Cameron and Alastair shared coffee earlier in the day.

"Now this is class," said Cameron, the movement of his lips imperceptible as he spoke. No longer dressed in the incognito local garb of the thobe and ghutra, he nonchalantly adjusted the cuffs of his collar shirt and the Armani dinner jacket he'd purchased from the boutique, "Can you fellas hear me all right?"

From a small device hidden on the inside of Cameron's ear, Pepe responded, "You are coming in clear."

"Crystal," said Alastair. "Can you hear us?"

"Perfectly," said Cameron. From the express elevator, Cameron entered onto the top of a two-story art installation of dynamic light and ambient music. "You wouldn't believe this place."

"I am sure," said Pepe, "though I do not think just anyone can land a same-day reservation for the At.mosphere restaurant, Monsieur Dragon Chef."

"Very true, that's not what I meant, though," said Cameron

"I thought that girl at reception was going to faint," said Alastair.

"Very funny, you two should put on a show. Listen, out of the elevator there is an amazing mahogany cantilevered staircase that is lit up as elaborately as that fountain show down in the lake. Which, by the way, I can see clearly out of the floor to ceiling window 123 floors below, along with everything else in Dubai."

"Cantilevered staircase. You mean suspended in mid-air?" asked Alastair.

"Exactly, I'm telling you, this is surreal. Remember those computer flight simulations we used to sit through? Well oddly, they were more realistic than this. I swear there is a toy city to my left."

"You're high enough up for a low flight plan," said Alastair. "What is to your right?"

"And to my right, below me, is the entrance to the restaurant, mahogany walls, the floors are café au lait limestone and hand tufted carpets, and I am pretty sure the furnishings are Adam Tihany."

"Adam who?" asked Alastair.

"Adam Tihany," said Pepe. "He designs all of the restaurants and hotels. Kincaid goes on about him sometimes."

"Adam Tihany is widely regarded as the preeminent hospitality designer in the world today," said Cameron.

"See," said Pepe.

"Gotcha," said Alastair. "I don't suppose you see the target."

"No, not yet. Give me a moment, here comes Peter, the maître d'. I usually try not to be too obvious."
Cameron lifted his arms and raised his voice, "Peter, good to see you."

Peter, a tall thin Brit, glided toward the landing of the

stairs, his hands clasped and raised to Cameron, still a few steps up. "Cameron Kincaid, welcome, welcome, so great to see you. I could not have been more pleased when you called." Peter placed both of his hands around Cameron's and Cameron in turn lifted his arm to Peter's shoulder. The two walked together side by side.

"What brings you to Dubai?" asked Peter. "Opening a little competition, perhaps?"

"Not on this trip, though I could hardly compete with what you have here. You said if I were ever in the neighborhood to stop by, so..."

"Certainly we are so glad to have you, and thank you so much for the compliment, I so enjoyed Le Dragon Vert. Your restaurant is a true jewel in New York. We have worked hard with what we have. You have to see what the chef has done with the Josper oven."

"I intend to," said Cameron, "literally cooking without gas."

The two entered the lounge area. The dramatic ambience of the suspended stairwell was accentuated with heavy hues of amethyst and a complex blending of ornate velvets. Cameron realized now that the esoteric music he had heard since coming off the express elevator originated from the harpist playing near the end of the bar. Peter led Cameron toward a small table. Cameron veered to the high bar, the sheer white backlit glass reminiscent of the milk bars of the last century.

"I'm fine at the bar, Peter," said Cameron. He rattled his fingertips across the edge of the bar and spun back toward Peter. "Even from here the view is incredible."

Peter shifted his view to the same direction. "Yes, we have a spectacular view of World and Palm Islands from here and of course, Atlantis at the end. And over there..."

"The Burj al Arab. Yes, I see."

Peter smiled and nodded.

Pepe and Alastair had been anticipating Cameron's statement, 'Even from here the view is incredible,' as that meant he had sighted their target, Abbo Mohammed. Now would Abbo see Cameron? The plan was simple. They knew Abbo regularly dined in the At.mosphere Lounge and they knew that Abbo was by nature a connoisseur of cuisine, celebrity, and of all things deemed great and fine. Cameron had dropped his cover to secure a reservation at the At.mosphere, anticipating an encounter with Abbo. Cameron's plan was to have the maître d' place him at the bar near Abbo and let natural events play out. The team had calculated that Abbo, once noticing Cameron, would be excited at an opportunity to meet the celebrity Dragon Chef, and would insist Cameron join him at his table. Abbo, of course, would have no idea that Cameron Kincaid, the famous New York celebrity chef, was one of the numbers involved in his son's disappearance.

"Would you mind indulging me for a closer look?" asked Cameron.

"Certainly," said Peter. He nodded to the bartender, "Edward can you prepare a —" he glanced at Cameron.

"A lemon seltzer would be fine," said Cameron.

Peter again nodded with a closed smile and then led Cameron toward the seaward window, a path that ran directly next to Abbo's table. Abbo sat at the small table's head between two elegantly dressed chestnut haired women. Cameron crossed directly in front of Abbo. He did not make eye contact, yet he revealed as much of his face as he could to be sure Abbo had a good look, at one point pausing to glance across the room. Abbo was not an unhandsome man. Dressed debonair, his dark Somali complexion seemed almost regal in the complimentary interior of the At.mosphere Lounge. The contours of his strong cheeks and jaw were reminiscent of his son Feizel. The women beside Abbo almost caused Cameron to stall in his stride, each a visage of Christine.

Resolute, Cameron pressed forward to the window, "Breathtaking, Peter, absolutely breathtaking. What can't you see?" Another code for Pepe and Alastair, meaning

Christine was not with Abbo.

"We are very fortunate." Peter leaned in to Cameron, "Though this is not New York."

"Beautiful all the same," said Cameron.

The two sauntered back toward the bar. Abbo was speaking rapidly to the woman to his left and she in turn was relating what he said to her mirror on his other side. All three were flashing glances in Cameron's direction as he drew closer. When Cameron and Peter were about to reach the end of Abbo's table, he spoke, his voice deep, booming, "Excuse me, Sayyed, a thousand pardons. My lady friend insists that you are the television chef Cameron Kincaid."

Abbo had taken the bait.

Cameron stopped at the end of the table and smiled a wide, toothy unassuming smile, the smile he reserved for television and fans.

"Yes, sir, I am," said Cameron.

Peter placed his hand on Cameron's shoulder, "Mister Cameron Kincaid, may I introduce Mister Abbo Mohammed."

CHAPTER 31
AT.MOSPHERE RESTAURANT, BURJ KHALIFA LEVEL 122, DUBAI

Many aspects of Abbo Mohammed were fitting for such a man of his physical stature while others were magnified by pure narcissism. Every gesture was flamboyant, surreal, and larger than life. To hear Abbo speak was peculiar; though he had not mastered the English language, his voice was deep, clear, and each word was enunciated at the peril of being missed. His posture was unnaturally erect. His eyes cast a sidelong leer to Cameron across the table, "Mister Kincaid, thank you so much for joining us." Cameron gauged Abbo was a man that sought to peer deeply into the minds of others, to decipher them. "How fortunate for us that you happened by. Can I offer you some champagne?" In a broad flowing display, he extended his arm to present the bottle of Ruinart Rose chilling in a tableside ice bucket.

"I'm afraid I am limited to seltzer and lemon this evening," said Cameron, his voice apologetic, that of the fool to match the toothy grin he still wore. He placed his hand above his stomach, "All of the travelling."

Abbo widely smiled in return, tilted his head slightly to the side, and then nodded. "I understand quite well. My last trip to New York threw me for many days. All of the long flying, I believe."

Through Cameron's hidden microphone, Pepe and Alastair were able to hear Abbo's deep voice stumbling through English with defiant clarity. As according to plan, Abbo had recognized Cameron and invited him to his table. All Cameron's team needed to do was wait for the next phase.

"I am sorry, I have been rude," said Abbo. "May I introduce Mary and Antoinette?" The beautiful dark haired women, one on each arm, wore silk camisoles in lieu of blouses, one patterned with red roses and trimmed with Habutai lace, the other less conservative in comparison, a sequined sheer black silk tank top.

"Hello," said Cameron. He shifted his eyes to each of the women, "Marie and Toinette."

"Mary," said red roses. "And Antoinette," corrected sequined sheer.

"Ah."

"Hello. Welcome to Dubai," said Mary, her voice that of a trade show hostess.

Cameron's eyes widened.

"You are surprised by my American accent, Mister Kincaid?"

"Should I be?"

Mary coyly lowered her green eyes away from Cameron to a solitary sugar cube plated before her. She playfully twirled the cube around the saucer with the end of her red enameled fingernail, "Some men are."

"I am not some men."

Mary flirtatiously tilted her head and eased a glance up at Cameron, "I am sure you are not."

"Yes," laughed Abbo. "Mary is from middle of America."

"I am from Belgium," said Antoinette, her green eyes

147

puppy wide, her long enameled nail pressing the edge of her lower lip.

"So then it is true," said Cameron.

"What is, Mister Kincaid?" asked Antoinette.

"Dubai is the land of many delights."

Abbo laughed deeply.

"That amuses you?" asked Cameron.

Abbo composed himself, "You are a man that appreciates fine things. Please be my guest and educate me in the designs of this menu," he paused and shifted his pupils side to side to each of the women. "And dessert is on me. What do you say?"

Cameron maintained an aloof tone, "I say let's order the first course."

CHAPTER 32
PARIS COUNTRYSIDE, FIFTEEN YEARS BEFORE

Christine peered over the crinkled road atlas into the withered brown field. "The farm is supposed to be right up here," she said. "That is an orchard."

"Where there is an orchard there is usually a farm house," said Cameron. "I'm sure the farmhouse is right over this rise." He wrapped his fingers tightly around the knob of the gear stick and lunged his shoulder forward. The gearbox of the old Citroen 2CV ratcheted loudly, resisting his effort. He nudged the shifter again. The car jolted forward, then the motor began purring smoothly up the hill.

"There, you see?" said Cameron.

Through the tops of the bare scraggly orchard trees, the crest of the hill revealed the weathered tin and shingle roof of a barn. Christine held the atlas tightly to her chest, straightened her back, and then extended her neck. The corners of her cheeks rose and she spoke with an elevated pitch, inhaling her words, "Oui, oui, that is the farm, Cameron."

As the Citroen topped the hill, the rest of the farm was

revealed. The house was attached to the barn. The aged stonework façade was intermingled across the two buildings. Christine began to tap her feet. By the time the car reached the small bridge at the bottom of the hill, she had started to slap Cameron's thigh to punctuate her remarks, "Look, look! See those little chocolate pooches in the yard. How cute!"

Cameron wheeled the Citroen into the pebbled drive of the farm and began the fight with the gear stick to shift the car into neutral. Christine did not wait for him to turn off the ignition. As soon as the vehicle slowed, she opened the thin door and made her way to the band of puppies frolicking in the yard. The gearbox quarreled loudly, yet above that were Christine's giggles and laughs.

Having successfully parked the car, Cameron opened his door and spun his feet out onto the stony driveway. He stayed seated for a moment, captured by the splendor of Christine rolling on the lawn with four puppies on top of her. Little chocolate labs near the same color as her long, now wild and sprawling, chestnut hair. Whimsically, she snickered and smirked. She communed with the small animals with quirky squeals and squeaks. Christine allowed the little paws of one to push her to one side and the muzzle of another to toss her onto her back. She let them bathe her face with thousands of little tongue kisses.

Cameron was mesmerized by the amount of joy these Labrador pups brought this innocent beauty. The image became interspersed with lightning flashes of chestnut haired children rolling across the lawn with their mother. Cameron saw himself there in the yard as well. In that instant, Cameron saw a possible future of a family in love and at play.

CHAPTER 33
ABBO'S HAREM SUITE, BURJ KHALIFA
LEVEL 104, DUBAI

Cameron stood at the corner of the glass walled suite, high above the city of Dubai. He peered into the vast blanket of twinkling lights that speckled far out toward the Middle Eastern horizon. Relieved of his Armani dinner jacket, he still wore his collared shirt and slacks. His tie was loose yet knotted. Mary had disrobed for him. He had smiled and then faced the window. Perhaps she thought him coy, playing a game, while ironically he was at odds facing her beauty, a beauty so reminiscent of Christine. Mary stepped up behind Cameron, seductive in her stride, and slowly draped her arms around his shoulders, resting her cheek against his back.

"You made a wise choice," said Mary. She pressed her naked body against Cameron.

"Did I?"

Mary held Cameron as Christine often had, her arms wrapped around his broad chest, her head resting on his shoulders, her pert breasts pushed into his back. Christine was most likely captive in the next room awaiting liberation from Abbo. In facing the window, Christine's memory had been invoked rather than defused. Cameron had a mission that Mary was part of, yet an act so natural as being with a woman, a woman devoted to indulging sensual pleasures, was at the moment the cause of mental duress.

"You know, Abbo is rarely so generous," said Mary, her nimble fingers worked the knot of Cameron's necktie, effortlessly loosening the silken material.

"Is that so?" He raised the end of the now loose tie and slowly pulled the thin piece of silk from around his neck.

"Well, he only shares me with very special men." Mary unfastened the second and third buttons of Cameron's shirt and then slid her hand beneath the tight fabric to slowly caress his flesh.

"He considers me special?" asked Cameron. He felt her sigh deeply behind him, quivering as her widespread fingers tightly strummed along his muscular chest. Cameron rested the lids of his eyes closed and allowed himself to release his restriction. In his lowered hands, he folded the long tie mid-length, then slid his hands to either end.

Cameron remained still, flexing his chest with deep breathes that further excited Mary and prompted her to eagerly unfasten the other buttons of his shirt, until his naked front was a field of flesh for her wide spread hands to soak in all at once.

Since Abbo had invited Cameron to 'try' Mary, Pepe and Alastair had maintained silence, all the while listening through his hidden mike. When Alastair spoke into his ear, he was not surprised. "You are special, Kincaid," said Alastair, mirroring Mary's sensuous tone. The levity was reminiscent to past undercover missions when Alastair would observe from a distance rooftop or darkened window. "Any sign of Christine?"

Cameron was not in a position to respond. With the silk tie firmly in his grasp, he slid his fingers over Mary's and entangled her hands into his.

"Of all those green eyed girls, you stood out," said Cameron.

Mary cooed, then said, "The sheikh like girls with chestnut hair and green eyes."

There was no visual component to the surveillance kit, only the earpiece and the microphone. Alastair and Pepe were not privy to what Cameron had seen. They did not see Mary and Antoinette at the table eighteen floors above, nor did they see the other women lounging half naked in the communal area of the harem suite. Abbo Mohammed had a deep fetish for women of a certain type and had built up a collection. Cameron painted a picture with the clues he dropped in conversing with Mary, so that they could understand.

"Oh my," said Alastair. "That is wrong."

"Cameron," said Pepe, "find her and get her out of there."

Cameron released one of Mary's hands to ease her around to the front of him in a way that allowed the tie to encircle her and then, his head bowed, he pulled the strip of silk to bring her against him, so that they pressed cheek to cheek. The heat of her breath burned into him. He slid his lips across her face and into her mouth.

Cameron kissed Mary deeply and she tasted sweet. His kiss excited her. She pressed herself into him, to devour him. She clutched the sides of his shirt and pulled. He tightened the hold of the tie around her upper shoulders to stay her arms. She fell to her knees and frantically positioned herself to take him into her mouth.

"Hold on," said Cameron. "Not too fast. Let me help you to the bed."

With a smile, Mary gazed up at Cameron and then rested herself into the slack of the tie. "You're the boss," she said. The tie became Mary's reins and Cameron held the ends tightly. Playfully, she maneuvered herself over to the bed. Cameron let loose the tie as she climbed onto the mattress.

Mary rose to her knees to where Cameron stood at the end of the bed.

"So how does an American girl end up in Dubai?" asked Cameron.

"I knew that enticed you." Mary clutched the sides of Cameron's open shirt again. She opened her mouth wide to fully kiss him, pushed her tongue against his chest, and then slowly raked her teeth closed, once, then twice, and then tilted her head up. "I was doing an escort trip with an older man, an American, to Kuwait city and one of Abbo's men discovered me."

"Discovered you? You were abducted?"

"No, silly, though that's kinky. I was offered a two year contract for more money than I ever thought I would see, and that was three years ago."

"A contract?"

"Sure, all of the girls here are under two year contracts. I am the exception. Not bad for a girl from Iowa."

"No, I suppose not."

Mary nuzzled against Cameron again, "I would do you for free though, even if Abbo had not asked. I have to admit I'm a bit of a celebrity groupie. A celebophile."

Alastair spoke in Cameron's earpiece, "I think I'm becoming ill."

"So nobody is here against their will?" asked Cameron.

Mary rested down on her shins and peered deep into Cameron. "Not at all," she lifted the silk tie from the mattress. "But, I suppose if you like your concubines tied," she wound the silk around her wrists and then raised them to Cameron, "we can play that game."

"That's not what I meant. Someone said something to me about the new girl."

"I assure you that little French whore got a great contract. She used to be a model, I think."

"Now, Cameron," said Pepe.

"Where is she, the new girl?"

"Why do you care? You have me."

Cameron lifted Mary close to deliver a passionate kiss. He inhaled as he kissed her, taking the air from her, causing her to swoon. He eased back. A faint plea of a breath slipped from her, his charm overwhelming. He lowered his voice, "I was thinking maybe…"

Mary was anxious, "Oh, you are greedy." She bit her lower lip and then said, "I'd rather have you to myself, but that could be fun. I have wanted to try her out since she came in. C'mon, let's go get her."

Mary spryly launched herself from the mattress, towing Cameron by his shirt.

"You know I interviewed her," Mary teased.

"What does that mean?"

Mary, comfortably nude in the dim light of the suite, glanced back at Cameron with a coy smile, "Wouldn't you love to know."

The hallway from the master bedroom led toward the center of the suite that sprawled almost the entirety of the floor. Mary walking naked through the corridor had no affect on the other tenants, all of whom were in different stages of dress, most topless in only panties, others fully nude.

"To interview means I look for what the sheikh likes and make sure flaws do not slip through. I have been with him the longest and know quite well what demeanor fits best."

They crossed the lounge area of the suite and entered the hallway leading into the other wing.

"So you actually interview?"

"In all kinds of places, all around the world. This is her room here." Mary knocked lightly on the closed door, "Babette, it's me Mary. I have a handsome present for you."

"Babette?" asked Cameron.

"Yes, I told you she is French, from Marseille I believe."

The door opened to a beautiful green-eyed girl.

155

"It's not her," said Cameron.

"Excuse me?" said Babette.

Cameron spun around and pushed open the door across the hall, startling a girl painting her toenails on her bed. "What are you doing?" asked Mary. Cameron continued down the hall, opening one door, and then the next, "She's not here. She must be upstairs."

. "Understood," said Pepe. "I am on my way."

CHAPTER 34
BURJ KHALIFA LEVEL 104, DUBAI

Cameron backed into the corridor, holding the door of Abbo Mohammed's 104th floor harem suite slightly open with the toe of his shoe. He slipped on his Armani dinner jacket, extended his arms, and then flexed his neck side to side. From the inside of his jacket, he retrieved two smooth stainless steel cylinders, the size and shape of cigar flasks. He twisted the metal dials affixed to the ends of the tubes to wind each counter clockwise and then held them up to ensure they were slowly spinning clockwise again. Cameron tossed each, one at a time, with a swift underhand pitch, back into the heart of the suite. From the door, the far glass wall lent a vastness to the space.

"These are going to be enough to gas the whole flat?" he asked.

From the tiny device resting inside of his ear canal, Alastair replied, "The compression on those canisters will disburse the gas across the entire floor. If you sent two cans into the central area, they're going to waft in an amnesia fog."

Pepe added, "In a few moments, they will never remember that celebrity chef Cameron Kincaid paid them a visit."

"Hmm," said Cameron. "Their loss." He smirked, and then gently eased the door closed with his cuff.

That part of the mission finished, Cameron snapped his fingers on both hands then reached up to fasten the knot of his tie, spinning on his outward foot toward the elevator.

In the center of the corridor, a muscular man in a dark suit was peering at Cameron. Cameron smiled at the man and sauntered past him to the front of the elevator, the whole while adjusting the knot of his tie.

"Excuse me, sir," said the man, now behind Cameron's shoulder.

"Yes?" said Cameron. He focused on his dull reflection in the stainless steel doors, and then quaffed his hair with the palm of his hand.

"What did you throw into that suite?"

"I'm sorry?" Cameron ran his index finger over his brows, indifferent to the man's inquiry.

"You threw something back into the suite when you stepped out. What was it?"

"Oh," Cameron gestured his thumb back to the door, "you mean when I...?"

"Yes, when you exited the door."

"Well, those were gas canisters. Like knockout gas, except those were for forgetting, kind of roofied them all at once, if you will."

The man drew a handgun from the inside of his jacket and directed the business end into Cameron's back. "Sir, you better step away from the elevator."

"Okay," said Cameron. He slipped one foot far to his side and then slowly began to drag his other foot to meet the first. The gunman's muzzle followed Cameron. Above them, the digital floor indicator dinged and the doors to the elevator began to slide open. The doors were divided no wider than a fist when the sound of two mosquitos whizzed past Cameron into the forehead of the gunman. Two men in technical service jumpsuits emblazoned with the swirling logo of the Dubai Fountain stood in the elevator. Each of the men wore a heavy utility belt, had a balaclava mask drawn down over his face, and held an MP-5 submachine gun in hand.

Cameron entered between the two and then spun around to face to opening.

"We done here?" asked Pepe.

"Yep," said Cameron.

Pepe and Alastair let go of the doors.

"You seem back in the game," said Pepe. From a duffel bag at his side, he removed another MP-5 and balaclava facemask for Cameron.

"Reluctantly," said Cameron, rapidly inspecting the weapon.

Alastair slid the keycard the Saudi had given them into the elevator console. "I never left," said Alastair. He tapped the numbers one, zero, and five and then punched the code, eight, two, and three.

"Going up," said Alastair.

The elevator floated to the next level in an instant. The interior console dinged with the same tone that the digital floor indicator had resonated in the corridor below. This time the doors did not separate. A thin crimson LED rectangle lit up high up on the console panel in front of Alastair's face. Within the rectangle glowed a crimson LED circle.

"I figure thirty seconds before downstairs looks in on us," said Cameron. He fit the facemask over his head.

"I wouldn't worry about the cameras. I was able to rig the elevator on a loop," said Alastair. He eased his head to the side to inspect the ocular scan from a different angle and then reached out his hand in front of Cameron. Pepe unsnapped the leather cover of one of the front utility belt pockets. From within he retrieved a hard sunglass case, a Ray Ban logo imprinted across the top.

Alastair saw the case in a side glance and then shifted his head around, "Oh, you didn't. I was looking for that.

That's my sunglass case."

"I had to put them in something safe," said Pepe. He flipped open the case to reveal a plastic baggy filled with ice and the two plump eyes of Taufiq Sawar. "This is a good case, strong."

"Just hand the thing over," said Alastair.

Cameron sucked in his chest as Pepe passed the cadaver specimen across the elevator. He curled his lip. He was not disturbed the two gruesome jelly orbs peering up from the case. Rather, he was displeased with Taufiq's fate.

"It was necessary," said Pepe. "You see that now."

Cameron cleared his throat and rolled his eyes to Pepe. "I knew that then. I don't have to like the situation."

Pepe was undeterred by his friend's suggestion of empathy. "Did I hear you correct that all of the women in Abbo's harem look like Christine?"

"This should do fine," said Alastair. He held the case up to the ocular scanner. The backlit LED circle and rectangle flicked from crimson to emerald.

"Yeah," said Cameron, "he has a fetish for caucasian women with green eyes and chestnut hair."

"Then I have no problem with the situation," said Pepe. "Get ready."

The elevator doors separated.

Outside of the elevator were two suit dressed security men, each with a hole in his forehead before he could draw his own weapon. With a mechanical rhythm stemmed from engrained training, Alastair stowed Taufiq's eyes, secured his duffel, and then entered the corridor. Alastair's comrades followed in fluent motion, Cameron holding left, and then Pepe squatted to drag his duffel out between the two dropped men. Pepe methodically sifted through the clothes of the corpses for radios and access cards. Alastair merely reached back to receive the coming bounty, his gaze fixed on the door of the 105th floor master suite.

Pepe finished rifling through the suited dead, set a charge beneath the sleeve of one, and then the three men edged toward Abbo's door.

It occurred suddenly to Cameron that after years of focusing on building a reputation as a restaurateur, he was now executing his second direct action infiltration and exfiltration in a week.

The three stopped at the door, each in position to charge and indiscriminately fire. Alastair pressed the muzzle of his MP-5 firmly against the surface of the door. He placed three fingers on the steel latch and between his index finger and thumb held the access card to the mouth of the slot. Calmly he asked, "Ready?"

The responses were as cool. "Clear," said Pepe.

"Clear," said Cameron.

Alastair slid the access card into the slot below the latch. The crimson LED on the top of the access reader blinked off and the neighboring LED lit bright emerald.

"Vive la Légion," said Alastair as he pressed down on the latch with his other three fingers and forced the door open with the muzzle of his MP-5.

CHAPTER 35
ABBO'S SUITE, BURJ KHALIFA LEVEL
105, DUBAI

The guard assigned to monitor the closed circuit video of the corridor outside of Abbo's 105th floor suite had his back to the door and his feet up on the small table that made up his makeshift security desk. Rather than watching the small screen in front of him, he was flipping through a comic book. He did not so much as flinch when Alastair forced the door with his MP-5. Too many years babysitting the secure suite had made the man complacent. Perhaps the guard thought one of the men from the corridor was coming in to use the restroom, or perhaps he did not hear the door as he was so wrapped up in the colored pictures of his magazine. Whatever the reason the guard did not bother to react did not matter. Alastair, Pepe, and Cameron would never find out. Before the door swung wide, the cheap pressed paper of the comic book was soaked with blood and brains.

In a mindful instant, the three men surveyed the hallway before them. The commandos had studied the floor layout from an acquired set of blueprints. Abbo's suite was supposed to mirror the harem suite a floor below and so far the entrance appeared as expected. They had entered into a hallway that opened to a larger central room. Along the hall were two doors. They expected one to be the bathroom and the other, they had decided, was a room for the guards. Cameron flipped off the power switch for the light. The other switches were at the far end of the hallway, past the doors, before the central room. Even Pepe, forced to wear glasses to read, was at home in the dark. The three edged forward. Light music rose from another far off room in the suite, as well as deep bellowing laughter, the unmistakable laughter of Abbo Mohammed. Cameron slipped into the first side door, a darkened bathroom, and then, confident no one was hiding inside, eased back behind Alastair. Pepe ducked into the room on his side of the hall and then returned with a nod designating that space also clear.

Each planted small charges along their path.

The three stopped at the end of the hallway. Mere meters away from where they stood, the edge of the suite met the Dubai night. The Middle Eastern horizon beyond was crystal clear from this height.

Cameron had already been through the harem suite below. Level 104 had not been modified from the layout they had read. Since the entrance hall and the two side rooms matched the plans, Cameron was confident that Abbo's suite would be similarly unchanged. From the blueprints, they learned that a central room encompassed a large area of the suite. To the left would be the kitchen, dining room, and a few small bedrooms, similar to where Mary led him to Babette in the floor below. Wrapping to the right would be another small bedroom, and then Abbo's master bedroom. The Burj Khalifa tower utilities and other elevators made up the rest of the floor on the opposite side of the corridor.

The number of guards in the suite was an unknown factor and a major risk. Striking the lights in the central room could signal additional guards and unwanted issue.

There had been no immediate response to the clack of Alastair's spent MP-5, loud even with the attached suppressor. That was a good sign, yet the burnt odor already filled the confines of the hallway and would shortly be spreading through the suite, demanding attention.

The bellow of Abbo's laughter echoed again. The warlord's laughter paired with images of Christine shot a pang through Cameron he did not recognize. He wanted to charge the master bedroom regardless of the plan.

A greater will seized him.

The tactician within Cameron introduced a scenario.

Cameron had deduced the warlord must be in the master bedroom, in the bedroom with Christine. That was the direction Abbo's laughter was coming from. Cameron had been in the master bedroom below with Mary. The room Abbo used on his visits to the harem. Cameron figured an easy gamble, for Abbo's own comfort, the harem suite and this floor, would share roughly the same decor. He tapped Alastair's shoulder and then eased himself as forward as he could without entering the central room. Directly outward from their position at the end of the hall the glass walls formed a corner. Relying on the reflective surface of the wall, they surveyed the room. From the reflection they could see two large sofas to their right.

Cameron's suspicions were correct.

Cameron calculated there would be at least one guard in that direction. Somebody more important than a guard, somebody Abbo could call on to fetch something. There had been a bodyguard in the restaurant, a dark Somali the size of a titan. Abbo had called the bodyguard Theal. That bodyguard had not gone down to the harem and was not one of those the three had shot upon entering the suite. Cameron tilted his head out a bit further, wary that reflections show two ways.

On one of the sofas, Cameron could see a man reclining, facing out into the night. A large black man with his eyes closed, possibly sleeping. The man was Theal.

Cameron signaled to Alastair. Alastair understood there was a man sleeping around the corner. Cameron also gestured to Pepe that he would march out around toward the kitchen.

The three matched eyes and nods and then flowed from the hallway. The three filed from out in a well-rehearsed formation, three bulldozers clearing the space. Alastair circled around Cameron to cover the right side of the room where the giant slept while Cameron launched from the shadowed hall into the opposite direction. Behind him followed Pepe, scanning from the left and then settling next to Alastair. They found no confrontation. The only guard in the central room was the man on the sofa, and he would never wake again.

Cameron continued to sweep his wing of the suite, the kitchen, dining room, and other bedrooms. All were clear, no guards, no Christine.

Christine was the woman in the master bedroom with Abbo.

Cameron spun back toward that end of the apartment, his MP-5 forward, his steps wide and swift. He recounted the rooms in fleeting checks, deck clear, walls clear, ceiling clear, check, check, and check. Departing gifts for each room, charge engaged with a twist, applied to the inside of the door jam.

Cameron's heartbeat was in his neck, closing his throat. His body and action were truly autonomous. He crossed the central room and pressed down the hallway toward the master bedroom.

Alastair and Pepe waited outside of the slightly open bedroom door, set to pounce.

The hallway was long and the last steps eternal.

From the bedroom Abbo laughed again deeply, sickly, and there was the sound of another, of a woman, breathing in heavy rhythm, fornicating.

Cameron's eyes were locked on Alastair and Pepe. Their heads subtly nodded in a rhythm to his steps, timing his entry, their launch.

The door burst open to let Cameron cross the threshold.

"Don't move!" screamed Alastair as he and the other two commandos stormed the room and surrounded Abbo, naked on the master bed, beneath the woman he was enjoying an instant before.

Abbo's bright white eyes beamed wild, practically lunging out of his skull toward the three invaders. Mounted on Abbo's groin, her back to the three, was a woman, naked and beading in sweat. His large hands firmly clutched the thin waist of the woman, almost encircling her, a Caucasian woman with long flowing chestnut hair.

CHAPTER 36
ABBO'S SUITE, BURJ KHALIFA LEVEL 105, DUBAI

Cameron, Alastair, and Pepe had long ago learned through early on that compartmentalization is the perfect unconscious psychological defense mechanism, used to avoid cognitive dissonance or the mental discomfort and anxiety caused by having conflicting values, cognitions, emotions, or beliefs. Perhaps that is why, when still physically and mentally acute, they mustered out. To scan a room out of the corner of ones eye and then, in less than a second, calculate the next action may appear an inhuman mechanistic ability, yet the judgment to make the instantaneous call, stems from the soldier's humanity.

Humanity was the reason soldiers were not sent on missions that involved them personally.

Soldiers could not be expected to compartmentalize a hostage situation involving their sister; at any point in the operation the risk was too high that soldier could compromise himself, could compromise the mission.

Yet there was no one else for this mission.

Perhaps Pepe had lost his edge.

Perhaps Pepe was merely a super soldier.

Pepe did not utilize his attuned peripheral vision entering Abbo's bedroom. When the door burst wide, he focused on those two bright white beaming eyes and in an instant he was directly over Abbo, the muzzle of his MP-5 thrust into Abbo's forehead.

The window of Pepe's mask revealing his upper face and eyes blazed varying shades of red. On no other mission had his blood burned. The rapidly forming beads of sweat appeared pink across his brow.

The muscles through Pepe's chest and upper body clenched and flexed tight as his arm extended forward, sinking Abbo's skull deep into the pillow. A vein shot up on Pepe's forehead and neck and, though anatomically incorrect, appeared to pierce right down into his hand, into the submachine gun, into Abbo.

Abbo cried out, a blood ring saturated where muzzle cut into flesh.

"Pepe," said Cameron.

Pepe did not respond. He leered at Abbo, into Abbo, he owned Abbo Mohammed.

"Pepe," said Cameron again. "It's not her. She's not Christine."

Pepe blinked heavy, his stare still given to Abbo, first one blink and then another, a wince, and then another.

"This isn't Christine," said Cameron, his voice somber.

Pepe's eyelids blinked heavy again, then again, meaty steaks slapping his eyes to attention, and then slowly he shifted his gaze up across the bed to Cameron and Alastair.

"Quoi?" asked Pepe.

"This is not Christine," said Alastair.

For the first time since entering the room, Pepe, the once super soldier trained to be mindful, to see all at once, looked into the face of the woman mounted naked on Abbo.

The woman was hyperventilating, crying, her cheeks streaming with tears. From far inside her throat, barely audible sighs and squeaks escaped in rapid burst. Her entire body quivered and she was barely able to hold herself up on the man she had been entertaining seconds ago.

"This is Antoinette," said Cameron.

CHAPTER 37
ABBO'S SUITE, BURJ KHALIFA LEVEL 105, DUBAI

Alastair removed the crumpled linen from the foot of the bed to drape the trembling woman's nude body. He tenderly placed his hands on her now covered shoulders and gently removed her from the groin of the titanic warlord. She let Alastair ease her to the floor. Her breathing, already elevated, increased, and her lower lip began to rapidly quiver. The subtle sighs and squeaks that had fought to escape her an instant before became squawks and caws as the woman, really not more than a girl, slipped into hysterics.

"Shhh," said Alastair. He held the girl's shoulders firm and gentle in his hands. "We're not going to hurt you. You're okay." He squatted to her height then matched his calm blue eyes to hers, "Breathe. You're okay. Breathe in through your nose, like this."

As Cameron watched Alastair calm the woman, he thought how different she was now from earlier in the evening, from the playful young woman at the table in the At.mosphere restaurant. The woman in the restaurant floors above had been flirtatious and seductive, but that had been before three armed commandos stormed the master bedroom and mentally overwhelmed her. She was now in shock and as a broken child.

"Out through your mouth," said Alastair, "there."

Her name was Antoinette.

"Again, breathe in through your nose, that's right."

Antoinette and the other girl that had been with Abbo, Mary, each had green eyes and wore their chestnut hair in the same fashion as Christine. That was Abbo's thing, his fetish. All of the women in the warlord's harem could pass for Christine, or sisters she never had.

"Okay, now, can you take a walk with me?" asked Alastair. He began escorting Antoinette out of the master bedroom.

Cameron had seen girls like Antoinette on countless missions. Things were going to get worse in her world before they got better. For the moment, though, she would be okay.

Cameron rolled his eyes back over to Pepe.

Pepe was calm now. The window in his mask was no longer the index shades of Dante's inferno. There had been a time when the stress of the moment would not have edged Pepe. Fortunately, his tactical training kicked in with a slight push from Cameron. Cameron had said his name a number of times before the outside world registered and then Pepe literally blinked himself back to the moment.

The muzzle of Pepe's MP-5 was still pressed against the warlord's head. Not with the same skull crushing force he applied during what Cameron could only define as a rage, yet with still enough pressure to ensure Abbo was not going to flinch.

Yes, that had been pure rage.

Cameron had recognized the fervor in Pepe's eyes. He had seen that same madness many times before on the faces of enemy combatants that fought with a cultish intensity beyond reason. He thought himself and his team above and immune to such irrational emotive drive. Yet this warlord, Abbo Mohammed, had hijacked a yacht with Pepe's sister on board. To liberate Christine, they had stormed the warlord's Somali compound only to discover Abbo had separated her from the other hostages. Christine was to have a role in his Dubai harem.

That was the intel they had.

Christine was their motivation, and each hour she was held hostage would push them closer to the edge. Cameron was not surprised by Pepe's reflex, entering the room to find Christine serving as a concubine to a warlord, to witness her act of forced fornication.

The woman in the master room was not Christine, nor was she engaged in the act of forced fornication.

Christine was not in the suite and she had not been with the harem.

Their self made mission had a primary objective of infiltration and exfiltration of one primary target, Christine Laroque. Now the mission had taken a turn.

CHAPTER 38
ABBO'S SUITE, BURJ KHALIFA LEVEL 105, DUBAI

Abbo Mohammed sat propped against his headboard. A crimson stream trickled from the center of his forehead where the muzzle of Pepe's MP-5 had broken the skin.

"What do you think you are doing?" said Abbo, the baritone of his voice resonating with contempt.

Cameron lifted a pillow from the side of the massive bed, "Here, you can cover yourself up."

"Does my manhood make you feel inferior?" Abbo shot Cameron a judging leer. "Good. I feel no shame. You should have shame. Thieves in the night, and you, Cameron Kincaid, I see you beneath your mask. You think you can steal from me?"

"We aren't here to steal," said Cameron. He dropped the pillow.

"No matter," said Abbo, his voice confident and deep. "You will not leave alive. My men will never let you leave."

Pepe had composed himself. "They are all dead."

"You think the men in other room and the hall are the only soldiers that protect me. You are foolish. I have men downstairs that will be arriving any moment to take your heads."

"Also dead," said Pepe.

Abbo furled his brow. "You play. You will see."

"The tall one, the two skinny men, the one with the scar? Dead, dead, dead, and dead, and your driver, too. Oui, he is also dead."

"That is impossible," said Abbo.

"No," said Pepe. "Far from impossible." He produced a knife from the inside of his jumpsuit. "I cut their throats one by one."

Abbo jolted himself from the bed, away from Pepe.

Cameron lifted his MP-5, "Ah, ah. Stay right there."

Abbo peered up at Cameron, judging the next action, and then relaxed back onto the headboard, his attempt to scramble failed.

"You are the assassins," said Abbo. He straightened his back and then cleared his throat. Abbo's head drooped around to Cameron, "You. You are a spy from the CIA, or one of the others from above, maybe?"

"No," said Cameron. "I'm just the wrong fella to mess with."

"Seems you hijacked the wrong yacht," said Pepe, "and took the wrong girl."

Abbo began to lean forward, "I don't know what you are talking about."

In a flash, Pepe raised his MP-5 high and then thrust his elbow back into the chest of the captive giant. The headboard cracked loudly as Abbo's weight burst back.

Abbo yelled up at Pepe, "What do you want with me?"

"Where is Christine?" asked Pepe.

"Who is Christine? I do not know who you are talking about."

Pepe's stout body twisted and his knee flew up into Abbo's chest, planting the warlord further into the bed.

Abbo lifted his hands to cover himself, his eyes wide, "Really, I do not know what you are talking about. I do not know about a yacht or this girl Christine."

Pepe swung the muzzle of the MP-5 back toward Abbo's face.

"Hold on," said Cameron. "We are talking about the Kalinihta. Demetrius Stratos' yacht you hijacked and took to your compound when you kidnapped his son Nikos and Christine, the woman that was with him. We have Nikos and we want Christine."

"You fools," said Abbo. "I did no such thing."

"What are you talking about?" asked Cameron.

"You have been deceived. Dada is the kidnapper. It was him that kidnapped my son and took him to this compound you speak of. The compound belongs to Dada."

"What are you saying?" asked Pepe.

"I have nothing that far north. Dada took that compound from the Merca when he drove them out. Why would I hijack that yacht? I have no quarrel with Demetrius Stratos. I have been dealing with him for years."

Cameron shook his head, "You're lying."

"No, no," said Abbo. "This is about money."

"What money?"

"The waste disposal money. That is what Dada wants. Demetrius charges one thousand euros per ton to dispose of toxic waste created by companies across Europe. For five euros per ton, the National Volunteer Coast Guard allows his ships to dump millions of tons of the waste. They dump far out in Somali waters. Demetrius pays me, and then pockets the difference. Why would I ruin all of this?" Abbo gestured his hand around the suite. "This is that scheming Dada. Dada is in London to rework the deal for the Somali Marines."

Alastair had returned and was at the foot of the bed, "He is lying to save himself."

"I am not lying. Dada has made a fool of you to win the deal with Demetrius and to take me out at the same time. My spies tell me he tries to get double increase. He wants everything. He is the one that sent you, is he not?"

"Why do you say that?" asked Cameron.

Wounded, Abbo lowered his voice, "Maybe you work for Dada? Maybe you were the ones who took my son? What have you done with him? Have you killed Feizel, killed my son?"

"He's lying," said Alastair.

"He's not," said Pepe.

"When is the last time you saw your son?" asked Cameron.

"I have not seen my son in weeks. He is not content to stay here. He is young and travels through Europe with the young people, where the young people dance. He was last in Ibiza when I spoke with him, then he disappeared."

"Disappeared? What do you mean?" asked Cameron.

"We always talk, every few days. Then nothing. He did not use his credit cards. No one had seen him. I was told he had been kidnapped and taken to the compound in Kismayu. By the time my men were able to get there, the compound had been burnt to the ground. Was that you?"

"Yes," said Cameron. "We liberated Stratos' yacht and crew from the compound."

Abbo stretched his neck tall, "Did you see my son? Do you know what that dog did with him?"

"Not everyone was there," said Pepe. "That is why we are here."

"Then I must go to London," said Abbo. "I know now what he is up to. I will set things right with Demetrius and I will torture that dog Dada to find out where my son is."

"Your son is dead," said Alastair.

"What?" asked Abbo.

"Feizel was in on the deal to screw over his old man," said Alastair. "The heir to the throne. Just didn't play out like he thought."

Abbo's eyes began to blaze red, "Now you lie!"

Alastair continued, "He had a gun when we arrived. What kidnapper would give their hostage a gun?"

"Where is he? What have you done?"

"He is dead," said Alastair. He nodded toward Pepe. "My friend shot him in the head."

Abbo shouted a guttural scream, "No, this cannot be!" He threw his outstretched hand up toward Pepe's neck, his wrists and fingers gnarled in the air, prepared to mangle. Pepe's knees buckled as he dropped back to dodge the lunging warlord. Pepe squeezed his trigger as the warlord soared toward him.

Abbo convulsed in the air, riddled by the stings of the MP-5 submachine gun, before falling twisted on the bed, less half his skull, which now plastered the face of the headboard.

"Why did you have to go and say that?" asked Cameron.

"You really think he was going to forget about us?" said Alastair. "He was going to hunt us down for what we did today alone, and once he found out the truth about Feizel." Alastair shrugged, "Well."

CHAPTER 39
ABBO'S SUITE, BURJ KHALIFA LEVEL 105, DUBAI

The door of the suite boomed in thwacks and thuds, the hollers of the men on the other side escalating in accordance with their impatience.

"Sounds like they really want to get in," said Cameron.

Alastair was stowing all of the loose gear back into the duffels. He glanced out into the night past the glass wall. "We have less than a minute to wait for our cue."

Pepe was setting the final charges around the edges of the glass. "Will that be enough time? As soon as Abbo's men figure out the card reader's shorted they are going to take that door."

"They will have to have great luck trying," said Alastair. " I checked the lock when I sent Antoinette out to the corridor, that door should hold."

Cameron zipped the front of his jumpsuit, "This fits, and I get a logo as well."

"They came in a set," said Alastair. "You know, Pepe, if you would have really killed all of his downstairs men like you told him we would not be in a rush."

"I would have enjoyed the task," said Pepe. "You were the one that said we should minimize risk by manipulating the camera system. You should have started the fountain sooner."

Alastair stopped and shifted his gaze to Pepe. "I triggered the remote as soon as I bloody well could, thank you. I think all of Dubai is going to appreciate this unscheduled performance." Alastair resumed zipping the duffels. "You should take a look down at the extravaganza."

"Hmm," said Pepe. "Magnific."

"You're damn right," said Alastair. "They haven't used those extreme shooters since the opening ceremony."

"They really shoot the water fifty stories in the air?" asked Cameron, adjusting his harness.

"With percussion as loud as thunder. When those babies go off this whole building, that entire mall, hell, the whole city, is going to shake. It will be great. Except..."

Pepe was adjusting his harness as well. Without looking at Alastair, he asked, "Except what?"

"I said they haven't been used since the opening ceremony."

"So?" asked Pepe.

"When I went out on the lake this afternoon to calibrate them, they registered as engaged on the control screen."

"That's fine then," said Cameron.

"Well, that only means they are calibrated for the performance and registering. If they are not set up to receive pressure or something goes wrong, this may not work."

"So then the world knows we are here?" asked Pepe.

"We reduce the element of diversion," said Alastair.

"No matter," said Cameron, "we're leaving. Do you hear them out there? They're rabid."

"No worries. There would have to be—" Alastair abruptly paused as the yelling suddenly escalated, flooding the suite beyond the master bedroom, "A secondary mechanism. There would have to be a secondary mechanism. How did we miss that?"

"We need to go now," said Cameron. "The bolts on this door won't hold them long."

Abbo's soldiers began thumping the bedroom door.

"All good," said Alastair. "The music is about to crescendo and then we make our exit. Three small percussions, then the two larger ones. Ready yourselves."

"What music?" asked Pepe.

"You cannot hear the music from here?" asked Alastair. From beyond the glass wall, they heard a muffled boom. "That's one. You'd better back up."

From inside the suite they heard furniture now thudding against the door.

"That's two."

Pepe held the trigger in his hand.

"And three, get ready, Pepe."

The panels in the center of the bedroom door began to break inward, yet the door stayed secure in the frame.

Alastair's focus was intense. His eyes went vacant as he distinguished the outside concussions from the rounds the men beyond the door were firing into the locks.

Alastair yelled, "Now!"

Pepe flipped the charge in sync with the sound of thunder from the extreme shooters of the Dubai fountain below. The glass wall disintegrated into the Dubai night, high above the lake.

At that same moment, Abbo Mohammed's men broke the door to the master bedroom free from the reinforced bolts.

Pepe, Cameron, and Alastair thrust themselves into the void adjacent to the tower As Somali soldiers poured into the dead warlord's room.

Pepe, Cameron, and Alastair separated quickly on launch, then tossed their chutes out, their canopies pulled up and open. The soldiers raced to the perch of the now open level. Alastair's voice tinned in Pepe's ear, "Now, Pepe."

Pepe squeezed the second igniter.

To the left of the three commandos, eruptions of fuchsia hued water towered upward, high above the other buildings around them, accompanied by thunder. The series of charges set throughout the suite during the sweep exploded in a cascade, propelling the unprepared soldiers from the open ledge.

Alastair pointed a green laser toward a darkened parking area to the far right of the fountain spectacle. As the three drew closer, a fluorescent green glow stick appeared, first waving, then still. Using the light of the glow stick as their guide, the three honed on their target.

The heat of the desert enveloped Cameron.

Though the next steps were clear—go to London and to Dada—that left little relief. Their plan was to BASE jump with a fourth. A fourth that was supposed to be held by Abbo Mohammed, and she wasn't here.

Cameron adjusted the lines of his canopy to swing himself around and into alignment with the green glow stick. Cameron heard a whizzing close behind, another, and then two concussions filled the air. Hundreds of amber and indigo lights filled the heavens above him.

"What the hell," said Cameron.

Into his ear, Alastair responded, "The fireworks are beginning to erupt."

"Fireworks? Are you nuts?" Another whiz shot behind Cameron, followed by another pop, resulting this time in a magenta sky.

"I didn't think they would turn on," said Alastair. "I didn't put them in when I created the show protocol. There must be an automatic override."

"An automatic override?" asked Cameron.

"Don't worry. They're farther away than they seem and we are about to touch down."

The next rockets went up with a swish. "Oh, dear,"

said Alastair.

"Is that what I think?" asked Pepe.

"Hold on," said Cameron.

The sky above lit amber again, this time to the sound of popcorn popping, and then the rain began. Surrounded by the pouring lit remnants of giant fire blossoms, the three were ready for the silks to degrade and for airspeed to rapidly increase. None of those things happened. The lightshow was farther away then they perceived, an illusion.

The dim parking lot became illuminated as they dropped close. The only vehicle, a vintage VW van, was parked to the side. The three touched down as they had countless times before and in the same motion, began to gather their gear. Rehan, the twelve-year-old boy from the Marmoom Camel track, was waiting next to the open doors of the van. He scurried over to the center of the parking area, scooped up the glow stick, and then buried the light in his pocket. Rehan then ran over to Pepe and, with two hands and a heave of a lift, clutched his duffel. "Let me help you stow everything in the lorry, Sayyed. I have the water and food you requested. Where is the other?"

"We have to make another stop," said Cameron. "C'mon, let's stow everything into the van and get out of here."

CHAPTER 40
PARIS COUNTRYSIDE, FIFTEEN YEARS BEFORE

The voyeuristic glances of Christine, stolen through the Citroen's rearview mirror, pleased Cameron. In the backseat was innocent bliss. She had wrapped the chocolate lab in her scarf, cradling the puppy as she would a baby, and now soothed her tiny brown bundle with a maternal voice.

"You are such a cute baby," said Christine. "Are you a cute baby? Yes, you are."

The miniature muzzle poked up to reach Christine's chin, so she folded herself toward him, giggling while his tongue basted her neck. "Such nice kisses. You are a darling little one." Her words appeared to encourage him to eagerly devour his new mistress with a tongue lapping that paired with her further laughter.

"You have a new love," said Cameron.

"Isn't he beautiful? What should we name him?"

"What would you like?"

"Oh, I already love him so much," said Christine. "Maybe little Cameron."

"Are you serious?"

Christine shifted her eyes up from the pup to the mirror, "Don't sound like a grump. You will hurt his feelings. I would not name this little darling a grumpy man's name."

"Hey, I am hurt."

"You are not. Besides, I want him to keep me company when you are away, not remind me of how much I miss you."

Cameron had no response to this. His time between missions had diminished with each assignment. His career was unique, allusive, and one he was unable to share with Christine. He could not fool himself. Not too much time would pass before two to four week stints would turn to three and then six month operations. There were operatives he was aware of that had been in the field for years. His special talents had advanced him beyond one and done direct action missions. Christine's opportunities were advancing as well, having traveled twice to Asia and once to Mexico already this year. A time would soon come when the few brief, fleeting days of the calendar, days when the two lovers could be together, would no longer intersect.

"I know," said Christine. "He looks like a Moby." She dipped her chin and the lab lapped at her again. "You like that name? Moby."

"What is a Moby?" asked Cameron.

"He is a Moby."

"Doesn't Moby mean immense, enormous, like the whale?"

Christine pushed her nose down into Moby, "Vous avez un immense amour? Yes, you do, a Moby heart." Christine glanced up to where Cameron's eyes would meet her, "He has an immense love like you."

Whether the warmth came from her green eyes or from the words she chose, Christine stoked a fire within Cameron's core that burned throughout his limbs and straight up the back of his neck, stiffening his skull with the anxiety of a small boy. She dropped one brow ever so slightly. A quiver shot through him, a nauseous jolt that forced Cameron to widen his eyes and pull his attention toward the road.

"We may still have some luck," said Cameron. He lowered his head to look out and beyond the bonnet of the Citroen. "The sun has broken through."

"Marvelous, we can still have our picnic."

EPISODE III

CHAPTER 41
THE MAY FAIR HOTEL, LONDON, MAYFAIR

Pepe's eyes fixed on his reflection in the stainless steel of the service lift doors. He extended the back of his neck to lengthen his height and then pulled in his gut. He frowned at the result.

"You're just now noticing," observed Cameron. He peered at his own reflection. He raked his fingers above his ears through the wafts of hair that appeared to hold more grey than when he had left New York only days before. "We're all getting older."

Pepe slid his hands to the inside of his grey sport coat. He hoisted his trousers and then smoothed his maroon mock turtleneck above his waist. He patted his belly in place and then smirked at his faux thinner appearance. "Speak for yourself."

"I'll have you know I run every morning and hit the gym every night," said Cameron. "I have to be in shape for the cameras, at least. You can't tell me you still run."

"I am as fit as ever," said Pepe. "No, I don't run. I

still do my katas though, and yoga now, too."

Cameron lifted one brow. "You do yoga?"

"Yes, yoga," said Pepe, indifferent to Cameron's skepticism. "Keeps me limber," he paused, then added, "For the ladies."

Cameron grinned.

Pepe shrugged. "Too much food on the plane is all. Every plate is served American now."

"Now that is cognitive dissonance."

"Guh," said Pepe. "You know, I think he should have come anyway. His connections here in London could have been useful."

Cameron flexed his head to one side and then to the other. "I would have liked Alastair to come as well. Heading back to Kenya was a good idea, though. He can work with Eazy to trace back the satellite imagery from the time of the hijacking. If we would have done that rather than following the false intel we would—"

"I know," said Pepe. "We would have her by now."

"Besides, Alastair is Kenyan. We have as many connections here as he does, easily. We have all of the connections we need." Cameron readied the SIG P226 9mm hidden beneath his jacket, making sure not to reveal the handgun to the camera in the upper corner of the cabin. "We are almost there."

"I'm ready," said Pepe. He hoisted the small black nylon duffel from the floor between them, swinging the bag up to his side to swallow his other hand.

The doors to the service lift opened onto the fourth floor, the luxury level containing many of the May Fair Hotel's illustrious suites. The two were explicitly there to revisit the Amber suite. Though the décor of the May Fair corridor was the same as their last visit days before, the same carpet, same wall covering, same indirect artificial candlelight, their intent brought a new vibrancy to the place. Abbo Mohammed's last words were that Ibrahim Dada was behind the Seychelles hijacking of the Kalinihta, behind Christine's abduction. If what Abbo told them were true, then this visit would play out much differently than the last.

The service lift opened to a hidden alcove near the stairwell at the end of the corridor. The lift bay for the hotel guests Cameron and Pepe had arrived in on their prior visit was at the opposite end of the hallway and from there, halfway down the adjacent corridor, was the Amber suite.

Cameron and Pepe acted with a sense of urgency, their strides rhythmic and their motion direct. Hammers ready to strike nails.

As they rounded the corner of the corridor, Cameron removed the Sig P226 from under his jacket. The same titan was guarding the suite, his posture impressively statuesque, unwavering. Cameron was impressed that the mammoth man, after peripherally dismissing their first steps, snapped toward a defense pose with such immediacy. The nimble sentinel appeared more machine than organic. The guard's impressive defensive move was no matter, however. The micro second hesitation was enough for the MP5 inside of Pepe's nylon duffel to release two bursts. The massive bodyguard slammed to the carpeted floor before gaining his stance.

Crossing the front of the door without losing stride, Pepe slapped a sticky charge on the area where they had seen the added interior locks. Stopping short of the door, Cameron slipped his forged keycard into the lock slot, and then added a second sticky charge below. Both men pressed their backs firmly against the wall and glanced away. The sides of the door above and below the lock slot disintegrated in a loud thud. Cameron pulled the security keycard back out of the lock slot. The small scarlet LED blinked out, the emerald light went on, and no alarms were triggered downstairs.

Pepe threw his hand down on the latch. Cameron swung a barrelhouse kick into the door.

There was a loud crack and then the sound of thunder.

The door bluntly slammed onto the second titan, forcing him back into the wall. The sawed off shotgun he held met his chest, and erupted into his shoulder.

The large man howled.

Pepe immediately took his place to the front of Cameron. He was well past the door when, still pinned against the blood-spattered wall, the giant's body buckled. As Cameron passed the mangled guard, his sinuses filled with the hot metal odor of the newly spent shotgun shell, and the pungent urine soaking the whimpering man's clothes.

Cameron jabbed the door again. With another howl, the giant collapsed to his knees.

For the second time, Pepe and Cameron entered the heart of the large beige and brown luxury suite. The objects d'art and many amber lamps in the room were still the same, yet as the corridor, the Amber suite had changed.

In the center of the large L-shaped amber plush sofa sat Ibrahim Dada, in his impeccable Savile Row tailored suit, appropriately the centerpiece of the room. Despite the shotgun blast and howls from the hallway, the well-groomed dark African again appeared indifferent to Cameron and Pepe entering the room. A football match, different teams from the last visit, was in play on the plasma television.

Apart from Dada, the room was clear. Pepe and Cameron were silent, their weapons drawn toward the warlord statesmen.

A long moment passed and nothing happened, not even on the screen. The players volleyed the ball to and fro and nowhere, meandering around the field.

From the couch came a long tired sigh, almost a yawn, yet somehow more polite. Then Dada carefully pinched the knees of his trousers and lifted himself from the sofa. He slowly turned from the television to Cameron and Pepe and said, "A dull game, really, wouldn't you say?"

Cameron and Pepe said nothing.

"Gentlemen, there was no need for all of the fuss. You are welcome here, particularly since I seem to be in your debt."

"We wanted your attention, Mister Smith," said Pepe.

"Or should we call you General Dada?" asked Cameron. "Or do you go by Admiral now?"

"Well, many titles, actually. As I mentioned to you the last time you visited, I am in this country on diplomatic status. Anyway, as we appear to know each other now, let's say we cut the formality, Mister Kincaid. May I call you Cameron?"

"Kincaid will be fine."

"Then call me Dada."

CHAPTER 42
THE MAY FAIR HOTEL, LONDON, MAYFAIR

Pepe and Cameron were in a state of war. They were on a mission. The mission was direct action infiltration and exfiltration, objective one being to secure and rescue Christine Laroque, and if she was not in the suite, then objective two was to identify her location.

Neither Cameron nor Pepe were pure soldiers anymore. Neither lived the constant rigor that was a lifestyle yet also the mental fortification that kept them bound to honor. Since neither man was as they once were, each was beginning to deal with the toll of the last few days in a different way.

Cameron kept using the crutch of rationalization for his actions and he was well aware that his old friend Pepe was becoming a new man altogether. Pepe would not be burdened with rationalization and that would ultimately lead to something vacuous, of pure blind intent. Cameron understood that Pepe was distinguishing civility from direct action less and less by each hour, becoming an untempered lethal force that would not hesitate to consider anyone in the way of his mission expendable or collateral damage. They had both been trained to know when to put blinders on and when to create a two-color world. Cameron was not compartmentalizing when he took his blinders off and Pepe was leaving his on. Cameron and Pepe needed to find Christine soon, for their sake as well as hers.

Before Cameron and Pepe was Ibrahim Dada, deceivingly groomed in the fashion of a wellborn patrician, far in manner and creature comfort from the pauper fisherman that had turned to fighting early in his country's civil war. Appearing calm, cool, metered, and indifferent, Dada was as deceiving in manner as the whole of Somali piracy. No wonder that no westerner understood the core of Somali piracy, marketed to the western world as simple-minded marauders driven by greed.

There were those evil men, simpleton thugs and rapists, abducting tourists and aid workers for unheard of ransoms. They were gangsters no different than the kidnapping bands of thieves of South and Central America, or the street clans that owned the shadows and slums of every global city.

True piracy was something else, something so much larger, on a far greater scale. Men such as Ibrahim Dada did not conduct their business alone. They held seats at the table, with men and women educated at Harvard, Oxford, Cambridge, and Yale. They parleyed with officers of major corporations and financial institutions, modern day corporate aristocrats that by all but description were pirates themselves. Men such as Ibrahim Dada held court with those that shared a vision, a grand vision. In them, he saw himself grand, immaculate, impeccable, and though that is how Ibrahim Dada portrayed himself and believed himself to be, to Cameron he appeared otherwise. As through the psychologist's Johari window, where part of the subject is hidden to himself and revealed to others, Dada appeared to

Cameron as the true sociopath he was, a psychopath without empathy, remorse, or trepidation. The flawless Savile Row suit tailored to fit Ibrahim Dada clothed a monster, not a man.

"You wasted no time coming from Dubai," said Dada. "You must be thirsty."

Dada walked slowly to the side bar. "I would offer you food as well," he gestured toward the hallway, "but unfortunately I am a bit understaffed at the moment."

"It was you that hijacked the Kalinihta," said Cameron.

"Now, let's see," Dada clasped his hands together, "what do we have? Honestly, I have not had to make a libation for myself in quite some time."

"Why did you lie to us?"

"Here we go, what would you like? Gin, whiskey, American bourbon, perhaps?"

The black nylon duffel let loose a short burst.

The lamp at the end of the sidebar shattered.

"We are not here to drink," said Pepe.

A veteran of combat, Dada did not flinch. "Your choice," he said. "I will have a bourbon." Dada lifted a rectangular crystal container from the back of the side bar and removed the cork. "I am not so much a practicing Muslim, really."

"We have an idea of what's going on," said Cameron. "We wanted to hear it from you."

Dada faced them and lifted his newly poured rock glass to his chest, letting the index finger of his other hand lightly surf the rim. He sighed, then said, "What is going on? I tell you, more than you can imagine."

"The girl from the yacht," said Pepe. "You knew we would come for her, now where is she?"

From behind Cameron and Pepe came a deep recognizable voice, "She had a lovely scream, musical."

Cameron and Pepe spun to face each other. They and Dada were still the only three in the room. The voice had come from Pepe's right, through an empty open door in the far corner, behind the long glass-topped dining table. They each eased back toward the walls behind them, Cameron toward the inner wall, still covering an indifferent Dada, and Pepe, backing to the outer wall, focused on the open doorway. When Pepe reached the far wall, he flashed a subtle finger gesture to Cameron to signal that his line of sight through the open door was clear. The owner of the voice within the next room of the suite was behind the wall.

"You remember Colonel Tijon," said Dada. "You have met before."

Cameron was bitter. "We were never properly introduced."

"So beautiful, that one," bellowed the voice. "Trembling and quivering." From the adjoining room the tall bald man, dressed again in his fine white suit, crept partially into the frame of door, his head tilted to the side to make him fit. "I do not know if she had ever seen a black man so large before."

Pepe's lip curled, "You bastard." His right arm shot erect, the black nylon duffel almost falling away. A rapid cascade of holes appeared in the plaster above the incredibly nimble Colonel Tijon as he dove behind the long dining table, his own submachine gun in hand.

Pepe trailed the flying white suit with another immediate burst while simultaneously Tijon sent a volley of bullets up from the floor. Assailed from two directions, the thick lead glass tabletop disintegrated. Pebble sized glass fragments sprayed the entire end of the room.

The P226 in Cameron's hand, unable to target, hovered in an uncertain circle toward the floor behind the table, while Cameron flashed his head over to Dada, and then to Tijon again.

The MP5 extended in Pepe's arm appeared to lead him in a march around the end of the topless table.

Cameron moved toward the table from his side of the

room.

In a surreal gymnastic maneuver, Tijon launched a chair toward the MP5, using the momentum to bring himself to his feet. The MP5 dislodged from Pepe's grip. Pepe threw his weight toward the rising man, skullcap first. They connected head to shoulder. Tijon's height and Pepe's girth collided, and both men spun at the opposing force.

Cameron lifted his hand to fire. In his peripheral, Dada was moving away. He spun back toward Dada, who was briskly making his move for the master bedroom.

"Hold on," said Cameron. He bolted behind Dada, not wanting to shoot him. Dada reached the master bedroom. The door swung toward Cameron. His arm extended, Cameron lunged to catch the door, but failed. The door slammed his fingertips. He could hear the metal engage and then click inside of the frame. Cameron still attempted the latch. He thrust his shoulder into the thick solid wood. They had brought no more sticky charges.

"Cut him off, he is going out into the hall," shouted Pepe.

Cameron spun back toward Pepe and Tijon. Fists raised, they were now trading punches. A clue Tijon was educated abroad was that he held a traditional boxing stance. His form was rigid and predictable. Pepe was trained in a variety of martial arts—Taekwondo, Kung Fu, Karate—and he was a Judo master. Pepe had an array of techniques at his disposal, and of the many, he chose to mock Tijon with the Wushu form Zui quan, that of the drunken boxer. Tijon continued to throw blows that could not connect. Even when Tijon dared to be creative, stout Pepe easily out maneuvered him. Pepe dodged an elbow strike that cratered the sidewall, and then returned with a solid uppercut.

Pepe was faring on his own. Dada was the priority.

Cameron realized that of course Pepe was right. Dada would only have gone into the master bedroom if there were a way out, an escape route. He let his brain go calm and hurried to the hallway. The steel doors of the guest lift were already sliding shut.

CHAPTER 43
THE MAY FAIR HOTEL, LONDON, MAYFAIR

The large carcass outside of the Amber suite door reeked from loosened bowels. The sides of Cameron's sport coat spread away from him as he launched over the corpse into a full run down the fourth floor corridor. He did not slow for the corner, or to mess with the guest lift, rather he burst directly through the door of the stairwell and leapt over the steps to the landing below. Cameron took more time spinning around the half flight landings than the short bounds across each set of steps.

At the lobby level, he thrust himself through the stairwell door into a calm and empty hallway. The serenity struck him hard and sent him reeling back to the near wall. He was holding a handgun in a country where he should not have one, and the cameras had only been rigged for the fourth floor. He stilled himself. He remembered stealth. Nonchalantly, Cameron straightened his posture. He slid the P226 beneath his coat and then, with a brisk and study stride, made his way toward the lobby.

Apart from the Clef d'Or concierge, the lobby was empty. The dull grey light of dusk poured in from the street onto the ruby-laden Baccarat chandelier and surrounding eclectic objects d'art transforming the lobby of the finest hotel in London to a sleepy Tuesday evening gallery.

There was no sign of Dada.

Cameron moved first one and then his other foot back before spinning toward the direction he came. He quickened his stride and then with a glance back to ensure no one was watching, eased up to jog the few steps to the stairwell.

Before the stairwell door closed, Cameron propelled himself inside, scrambling from landing to landing, down to the lower level. He suspected he could access the secret sublevel parking structure that he and Pepe had discovered days before from here. The humid service floor was eerily vacant. Giant tumbler dryers whirred around him. Cameron raised his weapon and began to prowl through the narrow spaces between the tall laundry machines.

From the corner of the room he heard the clank of a metal door closing.

Cameron marched toward the corner. He found a door behind one of the mammoth industrial dryers. He loosely clutched the latch, pressed his shoulder to the door, and readied his P226. He began a mental four count and on two, he pushed and released the latch while forcing his shoulder into the door. The door flung open to the garage and found two young men dressed in the garb of May Fair service staff, one holding a spliff, the other a lighter. Their eyes went wide and mouths agape.

"We're on break," said the one holding the spliff.

Cameron's P226 was still raised high. He shifted his eyes from the boys to the expanse of the garage and then back. Both of the boys were fixed on his weapon.

"Maybe our break's over," said the young man holding the lighter.

"Yeah," said Cameron. "I think so." With a side step, he pushed the door open further. He flicked his head at the two and then added, "We have a security issue. You'll be safer inside."

The boys looked at each other. "Safe is good," the boy with the lighter said to the one with the spliff. They nodded at Cameron and then scurried past him into the safety of the laundry room.

Cameron slowly stepped away from the door. He peered deep into the underground garage, this time detecting movement on the far side near the exit. The shining white bonnet of a vintage white Bentley skimmed above the tops of the newer luxury cars in the lot. The car was surely the same vintage white Bentley Cameron had seen on his last visit below the May Fair. The same Bentley he and Pepe thought belonged to the tall bald man and, by relation, to Abbo. Moments ago, he had met the tall bald man, Colonel Tijon, which meant the Bentley belonged to Dada.

Outside, somewhere on the street, was the driver Pepe had hired on their last visit, yet no backup car had been parked underground. They had not missed the detail. They had decided that the budget was light for an expense that, ironically, they had agreed was of unlikely use.

Boosting a car was an option, though that could draw too much attention and odds were that the vehicles parked in this secret lair would all be easily traceable through a LoJack system or, like Cameron's own Mercedes, would simply shut off once reported stolen. He could contact their driver to follow Dada, though that would not really be necessary. There was another way to track the warlord. Pepe's local contacts had access to the London closed circuit camera systems, the London CCTV. To find a vintage black Bentley would probably be close to impossible. Finding a vintage white Bentley in the London vicinity would not be so tough.

Rather than return to the stairwell, Cameron went to the lift. He slid in his keycard to return to the fourth floor luxury suite lrbrl. The depth of the sublevel made his earpiece inefficient, silent, so he did not attempt to speak to Pepe until the lift was clear of the lobby.

"I am on my way back," said Cameron. "Are you still in the suite?"

No answer.

Cameron waited for the slow lift to climb another level to speak again, though he was sure the tech was well clear for reception.

"I'm forty-five seconds out," said Cameron. He was confident that Pepe was still in the suite. Pepe would respond if he had gone to the street. For some reason Pepe was silent.

The P226, having dodged the cameras of the lift, was again in Cameron's hand as the metal doors slid open. Halfway down the silent corridor, the corpse of the massive guardian remained twisted in the same collapsed pose. There were no alarms, bells, or whistles, emanating from the small camouflaged boxes mounted on the ceiling and walls. Only the subtle roars of the football match flowed from the Amber suite.

CHAPTER 44
THE MAY FAIR HOTEL, LONDON, MAYFAIR

The stench at the entrance of the luxury suite was far worse than it had been minutes earlier. The giant behind the door had bled out from his self-inflicted wound and, in course, had released his innards. In the brief instant Cameron took to cross the threshold, his eyes flooded. He made a note to himself to leave through the bedroom as Dada had, and then, remembering that the door was bolted, scrunched his face. Cameron stopped in the hall, his P226 ready to fire and his stomach ready to vomit from the smell of putrid sweet sewage at his back. He mentally repeated the mantra, *In through the mouth out through the nose.*

The roars of the crowd emanating from the surround sound system had escalated due to some play or maneuver Cameron could not see. He gleaned for any sound other than that from the match—walking, shuffling—yet there was nothing.

Pepe could be beyond his line of sight, yet so could Tijon.

The odor behind Cameron was unbearable. His stomach knotted and he caught a wretch in the back of his throat. He had to move. Led by his weapon, he entered the main room.

The room was empty, no Pepe, no Colonel Tijon.

To Cameron's right, the door to the master bedroom, the door Dada used to escape, was closed. To his left, a haze of dust floated above the remains of the dining table and an array of bullet holes and cracked plaster bordered the door from which Colonel Tijon had entered. The carpet between Cameron and the doorway was matted with countless fragments of broken glass from the disintegrated tabletop. He crept toward the open door with all of the stealth he could muster, unable to silence the glass crunching beneath his feet.

Cameron froze, the doorway a mere step beyond.

The adjoining room was quiet. Cameron raised his foot to take another step. Mid-step he heard an abrupt smack of metal slapping against a surface. Far inside the room, something had dropped onto a tabletop. A slow rickety creaking followed. The unmistakable creak of an old desk chair, taking the weight of a stout man, or a tall one.

In a sleek move, Cameron let himself fall forward into the doorway, so that as he spun toward the far side the room, his body was lower than a predicted line of fire.

No weapons were fired.

The walls were marred with blood and indented by strikes from the room's lamps and side chairs, the remnants of which were shattered across the floor. There was a man seated at a desk as Cameron had deduced, Pepe. Colonel Tijon was standing next to the desk, facing the wall. Not standing, Cameron realized, as much as being held upright by his head, which was lodged into the wall. The chair was bent unnaturally back, threatening to collapse under Pepe's weight. Pepe reclined further, twisting the chair to face Tijon. Pepe's sport coat was on his lap, ripped and tattered.

He did not appear to have any cuts yet his knuckles, forearms, and face were scarlet, coated with blood, blood that was not his.

Cameron spoke softly, "We need to get out of here. We have to put a trace on Dada's car."

Pepe did not shift his body or veer from his gaze. He too spoke quietly, "I found a computer." On the desktop next to Pepe was a silver metal laptop, the source of the slam on the desk.

"You need to see the look on his face," said Pepe, "the man that took my sister."

"I think we better just go. I'm surprised no one is here yet."

"We will, first go into the bathroom and take a look at him."

Cameron raised his voice to a strong plea, enunciating his friend's name, "C'mon, Pepe, let's go."

Pepe spun his head toward Cameron. "Kincaid," he screamed, "look at him."

Stunned, Cameron decided that he best do what his friend of many years had requested. He nodded and then stepped into the small bathroom. He was prepared to see Colonel Tijon mounted on the wall, his head the protruding bust of a trophy animal. What he did not expect to see was a bludgeoned, beaten, and swollen mass. After Pepe had thrown Tijon through the wall, he had continued to beat him past the point of death. Cameron surmised Tijon might not even have been conscious to receive the final deadly blows.

Cameron left the bathroom. Pepe had risen from the chair. In one hand he held his black nylon bag, the end torn from the MP5. His jacket was tucked under his other arm, above the computer.

Pepe spoke softly again, "You're right, we should go. I am a mess."

Cameron faced Pepe, a man becoming twisted in

pursuit of his sister.

"What did you do to that man?"

"I gave him," Pepe paused, "I gave him some of what he deserved."

"In the Legion," said Cameron, "we were trained with the highest code. 'In combat, you act without passion and without hate, you respect defeated enemies'. What did you do, brother?"

Pepe tilted his head slightly to the side. His face was blank. Cameron saw no recognition in his friend's eyes, for him or the words. Then Pepe spoke, "Cameron, of all people, I think you understand. They took Christine." Pepe nodded toward Tijon's lifeless body. "That man took my sister."

"I know," said Cameron. "But we took an oath. We are better than them."

"Kincaid," said Pepe. He paused, shifted his gaze to the floor, and then back into Cameron's eyes. "We are not in the Legion anymore."

CHAPTER 45
THE MAY FAIR HOTEL, LONDON, MAYFAIR

Cameron guarded the door of the lobby restroom to ensure no innocent passerby would enter to witness the deluge of blood-mingled water. Pepe was methodically expedient and efficient in scrubbing the sticky sap from his forearms, hands, and face. The brisk water also appeared to calm and rejuvenate him.

"Careful not to get any blood on that counter," said Cameron. "That white marble doesn't look very sealed."

"You really think you need to tell me how to wash away blood?" asked Pepe.

Cameron did not respond. He wanted to forget what Pepe had said upstairs about disregarding the Legion. They would always be associated with the Legion. They may not be active, yet the Legionnaire's Code of Honor forever bound them. They had made a commitment to live life a certain way. To follow a code that adapted to the world in or outside of the Legion. Honor and fidelity was the way of the Legion, and faithfulness to honor, a portion of that doctrine. Cameron could no more believe that Pepe had resigned his loyalty to honor as he would believe that Pepe could desert him, regardless of a few harsh words.

They had been stalwart members of the Green Dragons and the loyalty Cameron dedicated to his friend, his brother, was mutual and absolute, and could not be abandoned. He had to allow for time and conditions, their vow to fight without passion and hate had come years before the men in the suite had taken Christine. He would have to forgive his friend for a moment of frenzy.

Then Cameron was struck with a moment of clarity. He awakened to a revelation that the absolutes placed on faithfulness and honor were not the true cause of this trepidation. The true cause was not so black and white. In the darkness loomed the greater picture, the extraordinary violence, and an unnecessarily high body count. He realized he had been ruminating the last few days. That he could not quiet his mind irritated him. Legionnaires learn that some people could die, and that some indeed should. They learn not to hesitate, for some people warrant action, the bad people. The events of the past few days, the past hour, though extreme and unorthodox, should not have bothered him. Cameron was in an unexplored space, and Pepe, he feared, was cracking, or had already cracked. They were confronting cartel leaders and killing them off like bugs; repercussions were inevitable.

Pepe had finished scrubbing. As Pepe dried his hands, he peered questionably into Cameron's eyes.

"Did you go somewhere?" asked Pepe.

Pepe's jovial tone and expression had returned. The presence of a familiar Pepe snapped Cameron back from distraction. "Huh, yeah. I guess I wandered off."

Pepe smiled and then patted Cameron on the shoulder. "Well, stay close my friend, I need you near me."

From within the black nylon duffel Pepe retrieved a dark grey long sleeved shirt similar to the bloodied maroon one he had folded into his sport coat.

"You brought a change of clothes?" asked Cameron.

Pepe laughed. "No, of course not. This shirt was in a package in one of the bureaus." He pulled the shirt over his head and then pulled the waist in place. He patted his stomach and curled the side of his lip. "Must have been purchased for one of his men," he said.

"Hey," said Cameron. "You look fine. Now let's get out of here. I want to check with your friend to see where the Bentley has gone off to."

"Of course," said Pepe. He gathered his jacket with the bloodied shirt tucked neatly inside, the computer, and his black nylon duffel. The two exited the restroom and slid out the first side door as incognito as possible.

"Taxi, gentlemen?" asked the curbside doorman.

"No, thank you, we are walking this evening," said Cameron. The two began to make their way down Stratton toward Berkeley Street.

Pepe held the nylon duffel out to Cameron. "S'il vous plaît."

Cameron took the duffel from Pepe, who began digging through his front pocket for his mobile phone. He fished out the device, perused the screen with his thumb, tapped a name, and then put the phone to his ear.

Cameron tilted his head toward Pepe. "I have been meaning to mention. I noticed you finally gave in on a new phone."

Pepe smirked. "They forced me by discontinuing service on my old one." He nodded his chin toward the device. "This girl, Kincaid, she will know where the Bentley is, guaranteed, and if Dada has left the car, she will know too. She is tuned in to the closed circuit with her computer. Magic is what she does." He raised his arm holding the laptop and made a waving gesture as they crossed Berkeley Street. "Probably watching us now."

Cameron raised a brow. "One of your ladies maybe?"

Pepe raised his brow in return. "My cousin." The tone of Pepe's voice abruptly changed, "Victoria, bonsoir." Cameron and Pepe turned to walk down Berkeley Street. Pepe continued, "Bien, bien." A pause. "Oui, blanc Bentley." Another pause, "Aha, oui." The two men stopped to the side of their waiting car, the black Bentley Pepe had arranged for them on their last visit. Cameron opened the rear door and bowed his head to move inside, and then Pepe stopped him. Cameron straightened and then turned back to Pepe to see why his friend was holding him by the arm. Pepe had the mobile phone between his shoulder and chin. "Oui," said Pepe again softly. He released Cameron's arm to point across the street. Cameron followed the gesture to Pepe's target and there, parked halfway down the block in front of the May Fair Hotel's Palm Beach Casino, was the white Bentley.

"Oui. Merci. Ciao," said Pepe and then he pulled the phone from his ear.

"That is our white Bentley parked outside of Palm Casino?" asked Cameron.

"Yes. She said the car drove around the block to the front of the casino."

"And Dada?"

"She has access to the cameras inside as well," said Pepe. "Dada is in the VIP room in the Palm Beach Casino."

CHAPTER 46
THE PALM BEACH CASINO CLUB, LONDON, MAYFAIR

With the light of day past, the tourists of the Mayfair district had departed. A sparse number of denizens quietly darted up the walk, en route to supper or cocktails. A sconce lit canopy near the back of the May Fair Hotel denoted 'The Palm Beach Casino Club.' Cameron stopped short of the art deco glass doors to glance across Berkeley Street, back toward the Nobu restaurant. In front of the restaurant, parked between a Ferrari and a Maserati, was the Bentley Pepe's friend had arranged a few days prior.

Unable to see into the car, Cameron nodded. "I heard you," he said. "My earpiece is working fine. You can hear me all right, then?"

From the backseat of the Bentley, hidden from Cameron by shadow, Pepe responded, "Loud and clear."

"Okay, here we go," said Cameron. "Let's see if I am remembered."

"The way you part with money, I doubt they would have forgotten the Dragon Chef."

"You don't tire of saying that do you?"

"The phrase pleases me," said Pepe.

Cameron reached for the door. Before he could grip the long handle, the tall glass door began to open. Inside the vestibule, a doorman spread his free arm up to gesture Cameron inside.

"Welcome back to the Palm Beach Casino, Mister Kincaid."

"Thank you," said Cameron as he walked into what once was the grand art deco ballroom of the May Fair Hotel and had since become the most exclusive casino in London.

Comfortably spread out across the room were at least ten roulette tables, a small casino as gambling houses go. Light hued wood, indirect artificial candlelight, a few other games, and some festive gamblers created an effervescent atmosphere.

A second man greeted Cameron as he entered the room. "Welcome, Mister Kincaid," he said. "We are so pleased to have you back."

"Thank you, I'm sure," said Cameron.

A light chuckle resonated in Cameron's inner ear.

"I remind you the maximum bet on the floor this evening is one thousand pounds. What game would please you, sir?"

"Is the Gold Room open?" asked Cameron.

"Excellent, I was about to suggest that. We do have some VIP guests such as yourself in the Gold Room and you are welcome to join them. The game this evening is blackjack."

"That would suit me fine," said Cameron.

"Very good, Mister Kincaid," said the man at the door. A young beautiful brunette woman approached. She was attired in an indigo cocktail dress that appeared more sophisticated than usual for a member of the staff. "Please escort Mister Kincaid to the Gold Room."

"Certainly," said the young woman. She then gave

Cameron an endearing smile. "If you can follow me, Mister Kincaid."

Cameron followed the young woman toward the casino floor. His first step onto the spongy carpet caught him off guard. Cameron sometimes ran on a track at the New York East River Park. The surface of the running track had the same floating push and bounce. He oriented himself, peering around the room, his mindful habit. He glanced to the electronic slot machines lining the outer edges, counting them. There were never more than twenty slot machines in a London casino, a gambling law. They neared the round floor in the center of the room, home to one of the ten roulette tables.

The croupier spun the ball and at the same moment called, "No more bets."

A few young players dressed in high priced jeans and pressed collar shirts continued placing bets even when the ball was rolling. The croupier appeared not to mind. Cameron passed the door to the Poker Room. In the Poker Room, the tables below the palm shaped crystal chandelier were busier than those on the central floor, even busier than the craps game. When they reached the door to the Gold Room, Cameron glanced back across the casino. Something had changed since his last visit.

Cameron mentioned his observation to the young woman. "The baccarat tables that were on the central floor?"

From in his ear Pepe asked, "Is that where you left your money?"

The young woman leaned into Cameron. "Our apologies, Mister Kincaid, games rotate through the casino," she said, and then extended her arm to open the door to the VIP room. She did so in a purposeful maneuver that slid her breasts above the top of her blue dress to his attention. "Can I start you with a beverage?" she asked.

Cameron did not let his eyes fall from hers. "Seltzer

would be nice, with a slice of lime, if you have it."

"Certainly, Mister Kincaid. Would you like me to introduce you to the other guests?"

"That will not be necessary," said Cameron. "Thank you."

Cameron entered the VIP lounge, a smaller room in the fashion of one of the May Fair signature suites and finished with the same light woods as the central casino. There were not many guests in the room. He recognized the two young men on the sofa and the young woman that sat between them; one was a British musician, and the other two were actors. They were drinking pints of lager and watching a football match on the muted plasma television, the same Bang & Olufsen model that Cameron had seen in the Amber suite. In a lounge chair in the corner of the room, a middle-aged man he did not recognize tapped away in a binder, a keyboard and tablet combination. Perhaps the man was a manager to one of the other VIP guests, or merely wealthy.

At the table to the side of the room, a dealer was presenting cards for blackjack. Three of the four seats were filled. Cameron recognized all three of the players, a scruffy British musician from the nineties in mirrored sunglasses, from Manchester if he recalled correctly, an actor from a popular BBC science fiction show, and seated to the side by himself, another man. Ibrahim Dada in his impeccable Savile Row tailored suit gently touched the table to accept or pass cards as they were dealt. Cameron slid the empty chair back enough to sit. Neither Dada nor the musician acknowledged Cameron. The actor met Cameron with a toothy smile. "Hey there," he said. "Yes, do have a seat." The actor then turned back to the cards in front of him and raised his eyebrows. "No need for us to be miserable alone."

"Thank you," said Cameron. "Looks like a good game." A code to Pepe that Dada was at the table as they were told he would be.

"A fourth," said the musician without looking over. "Bloody marvelous, maybe you can change the luck of the table."

Dada said nothing.

The dealer raked in the cards. "Chips, sir?"

Cameron held up his hand spread wide.

"Very good, sir, I can handle that for you," said the dealer. He dropped his arm beneath the table and retrieved a tray of chips with blue and yellow markings along the edges. He rapidly brushed his index finger across them away from his thumb, a bit of motor memory, and then lifted exactly ten chips from the tray.

Cameron placed the stack on the green felt in front of him. "I take it the bet is five hundred?" he asked.

"That is correct, sir," said the dealer.

Each of the others tossed in a chip and the dealer began to place the players' cards face up.

Pepe spoke into Cameron's earpiece, "I have not heard him."

Cameron made a mere grunting noise. The other players paid no notice as the reaction was appropriate, the cards dealt to each totaled to two eighteens, a nineteen, and a twenty. The dealer showed a ten. All four stayed and added another chip, money not being a consequence. In a blink, the table held four thousand pounds of the players' money and still the game was not that interesting. The dealer flipped his hidden card to reveal a three. He drew another card, a king to bust.

"You did bring some luck," said the musician. "This guy has been raking us all night." He gave a nod toward Dada, "Except him."

The actor, jubilant with a win, let the four chips drop onto the felt in front of him in a trickle and then, with his new found luck, immediately tossed two to his betting square.

Cameron tired of Dada's indifference. Less than an hour before, he and Pepe had made mayhem out of Dada's suite upstairs and though the Metropolitan Police sirens had not yet begun to echo through the quaint upscale district of Mayfair, Cameron was certain they would soon. He leaned to Dada and spoke under his breath, "And you, Dada. Do you feel you have luck on your side? The hotel is about to become very hot."

"I do like to gamble," said Dada. "However, I am a diplomat." He flashed a leer to Cameron, "Remember? And this hotel expresses," Dada raised his eyes to the dealer, "the utmost discretion." The dealer peered back knowingly, and then shifted his attention to the deck. "My rooms, I am sure, will be in full repair on my return."

Pepe was noticeably angered, "Listen to him gloat."

"We don't care about your other business or what your," Cameron sucked in a breath through his nose, "*cartel* is doing in London. We want the girl, Dada."

The cards shuffled, the dealer prepared to send out a new round. Dada raised his hand to the dealer. He waved his finger in a circle toward the tall stack of chips. The dealer nodded and then Dada rose from his seat.

"You're leaving so soon?" asked Cameron.

Then from the voice in Cameron's ear, "Let him go. I have his calendar on the computer."

This needed to end now. Ignoring Pepe, Cameron raised himself from his chair, "You really should stay."

"No, Cameron," said Pepe. "He was waiting for reinforcements. Two more sedans have arrived, four men in each. I believe Dada and Abbo recruited every tall man in Somalia."

Dada slowly turned away from the table to Cameron. The warlord's skin was so dark as to be a perfect mask yet his bright eyes, so revealing, made clear his revel of Cameron and the circumstance. "Another dull game," said Dada. "Wouldn't you say?"

Daniel Arthur Smith

CHAPTER 47
CHANNEL TUNNEL, FOLKESTONE, KENT

A blanket of blackness abruptly cloaked the Eurostar cabin car. The English morning was no more. Pepe took no notice, nor did he waver from his task. With the window beside him now gone dark, the train car interior was illuminated by a methodical patchwork of soft hued lights. Pepe appeared frozen against the tall tan leather headrest that spanned the top of his chair. On the small table in front of him, two MacBook Pros traded images, the actions reflecting on the lens of his glasses. One computer was his and the other was from Dada's suite.

Cameron sat across from Pepe in the aisle seat. Their four-club table was the first in the cabin. He leaned to the aisle side of his own cushioned chair so as to split his view between Pepe and the other first class occupants. He stared at the cover of the paperback on the corner of the table. The book he had found at his seat was titled Agroland. The synopsis intrigued him, horror in the Jordanian desert, yet he was too anxious to read. He rested his hand on the cover of the book and then ran his fingertips lightly across the surface in a rapid succession, two then three times, and then recoiled his hand to his lap. He shifted his view to the monitor's reflection in his friend's glasses, admiring Pepe's diligence.

"How many times have you gone through the files on that thing?" asked Cameron.

"A few, we have twenty minutes more in the tunnel and then less than two hours to Paris," said Pepe. "I will keep looking until I can find a clue as to where he is staying, or at least where he is holding her."

"Hmm," said Cameron. He tilted his head toward the aisle and ran his eyes the length of the cabin car. "Any chance he is on the train?"

Pepe dropped his head slightly to peer above the rim of his glasses.

"Only asking," said Cameron, still scanning the occupants of the cabin not hidden from him by the large luxury seats. "He is obviously not here in business premier." He allowed a sneer to push his lips to one side. "I cannot imagine a man like Dada riding coach."

Pepe had returned his attention to the computers, his hands drifting from one to the other as he recorded any findings from Dada's into his own. "He has two entries for today, Eurostar, and dinner in Paris, and for the day after tomorrow lunch at La Closerie de Lilas."

"Times would have been helpful."

"He did not use the calendar program," said Pepe. "The document is an itinerary really, with this week's dates, and those few entries."

"Hmm."

"Besides, he could be on any train," said Pepe, his eyes unwavering from his task, his tone flat. "Or he could have taken the shuttle with his Bentley."

"That's a thought," said Cameron. "Would be a bit easier to find him in Paris." Turning toward Pepe, Cameron straightened a bit. "Speaking of which, do you have any cousins in Paris that have access to the closed circuit camera system?"

"Like in London? No, I do not. Paris is somewhat dark to us in that way. We will have to rely on the street. I have many cousins there."

"Yeah, I remember," said Cameron, settling back to his former position. "I'm sure that'll be fine."

Cameron continued to peer down the length of the aisle at everything and nothing in particular, pensively nibbling his lower lip. The glass door at the opposite end of the car slid silently open, allowing a young blonde woman in a tight fitting Eurostar service uniform to enter pushing a small food and beverage cart. The steward prepared a tea service and then began to offer passengers refreshments. Each time the young woman leaned into a club table or side chair, Cameron lurched a bit to see if the occupant of the seat had changed since he had walked through the car moments before. Of course, the occupants were as they had been, the older couple by the door, the German family at the four-club, and the array of middle and senior managers with their laptops open. Each kind service the same, a recognizable face, the tea and biscuits, and then on to the next, accompanied by a jolt from somewhere within.

Pepe did not need to move his eyes away from the tabletop to sense Cameron's uneasiness. "What's bothering you, mon ami?"

Cameron was quick to respond, "About last night."

"What about last night?" asked Pepe. "She was not there. She will be with him." Pepe's fingers began to rapidly tap the keyboard of his MacBook Pro.

"A bit extreme, don't you think?"

"Oh, the Colonel," Pepe cleared his throat, "Oui." He kept his gaze fixed forward and continued his quest through the computer folders.

"Yes, the Colonel," said Cameron, "the hotel, the hotel

in Dubai, we aren't soldiers anymore."

"I think we did fine," said Pepe. "Maybe you are getting slow."

"That's not what I mean. I did my stint. I live a different life now."

"Maybe you are getting soft."

"Maybe," said Cameron.

"What do you want?" asked Pepe. "Do you want to go back to New York, to your Green Dragon restaurant?" Even with this, Pepe did not make eye contact with Cameron. "Fine, fly out of De Gaulle."

"That's not what I am saying either." Cameron leaned into the table and in a softer voice said, "Pepe, we are not mere killers, we are men of honor."

"Ah, you are still upset about our conversation in Dada's suite," said Pepe, and then he enunciated each of the next words he spoke with a deliberate pause between each, "You are getting soft." Pepe tapped out a few more keystrokes and then in a droll tone added, "Yes, we took an oath. Yes, we are better than them, and you and I, and the others, will always be Dragons together." He slipped off his glasses and gazed kindly at Cameron. "Are you pleased now?" he asked. "You should not have tried to make such a silly point right after I mounted that monster to the wall."

Cameron rubbed the side of his jaw and then squeezed his fist around his chin. "I sound like an old man?"

"You do," said Pepe. He fit his glasses back to his face and returned to the keyboard.

"What are you typing up?"

"I have found spreadsheets with ships and manifests."

"And currency amounts?"

"Neatly beside each ship," confirmed Pepe. "Some in pounds, some in dollars based in percentage by tonnage."

"So it seems that Abbo was not lying about the toxic disposal in Somali waters," said Cameron.

"So it seems, and these numbers add up to large sums."

Pepe spun the computer to Cameron. "Here is another spreadsheet. Does the list look familiar?"

"Yeah, I recognize most of the names, those are the hijacked ships we read about on the way over from New York. This is robust, names, flags, crew complements, cash sums, everything you would need to know to—"

"To hijack a ship," said Pepe.

"Yeah, to hijack a ship. I wonder, do the coordinates in the second column and the dates in the third and fourth column matchup with the hijackings."

"Look at the SS Oceana."

"SS Oceana, here she is, dated—"

Pepe spun his laptop around beside Dada's so that Cameron could see what he had brought up. On the screen was a news article. "Dated yesterday," said Pepe, "The SS Oceana was hijacked yesterday in the Gulf of Aden at the coordinates listed on the spreadsheet."

Cameron pulled Dada's computer closer. "This is list is ongoing. The next ship is dated a few days from now and the next two the week after that."

"The date on the file precedes the date beside the first ship," said Pepe.

"Excuse me?"

"This spreadsheet was made before any of these ships were taken," said Pepe.

"That means—" Cameron rolled his eyes up to Pepe.

"That means all of those ships were scheduled to be boarded," said Pepe. "The dates in the fourth column the planned release date, and the sums in the fifth the prearranged ransom."

"All held for different times and different amounts."

"Insurance limitations, I suppose." Pepe tapped two fingers to the top of the monitor. "I found another spreadsheet that list manifests, arms, chemicals, drugs, all there."

"Dada has come a long way from hoarding

international aid. I am surprised he left the May Fair without this."

"I'm not," said Pepe. "The files were in folders that sync with a mobile device. He probably does not realize these were left on this machine."

"So Dada is running the naval operation with a mobile," said Cameron.

"Apparently," said Pepe. He hooked his monitor with his finger and drew the computer back to him. "In the luxury of London. I'm sure Abbo was doing the same."

Cameron tossed his head back onto the leather pillow of the chair. He gazed up at the ceiling. "Dada wasn't even muddled in the casino. He sounded so sure that the rooms would be in order on his return."

"Well, he is a diplomat. I heard him remind you."

"Still, the fact remains that the hotel, or whoever, is in compliance." Cameron slowly shook his head side to side.

Pepe peered over the rim of his glasses again. "And we have never been followed by a clean team?"

"I know, I know, but that was different, those jobs were sanctioned." Even as the words left Cameron's mouth, he realized the hypocrisy. Pepe subtly nodded.

CHAPTER 48
PLACE DAUPHINE, PARIS

The Renault taxi stopped short of the famed restaurant, Caveau du Palais, one of Cameron's favorites in Paris. Cameron stepped to the curb and let Pepe pay the driver. From the inside of the café, the tinny voice of a radio announcer carried out to the street. Over the top of the cab, Cameron could see locals playing pétanque on the sand gravel square among the chestnut trees. In turn, they tossed metal balls toward a wooden one, half the size. Cameron remembered the name of the little ball was the cochonnet, or the piglet. He had played himself in his early days in Paris, and in Corsica where some of the men called the game bouchon.

In the days of playing pétanque, Cameron had not resided in upscale Place Dauphine. He and Pepe had shared leave in a small hotel outside of the city center, in the suburb of Asnières-sur-Seine. At the time, Asnières was still predominantly populated by Pieds Noirs, those French citizens that had lived in northern Africa before the wave of independence. The hotel proprietor, Absolon, had been a Legionnaire as a young man and had then stayed on in

North Africa to build his fortune as a colonist. He was sympathetic to Legionnaires and they received a hotel rate fitting of young soldiers. The constant presence of the young Legionnaires in the hotel reminded the older man of the finer days abroad. Over dinner, the nostalgic hotelier would inevitably switch from wine to cognac and begin to share stories of the Algerian golden era, often crowning the evening singing the unofficial anthem of the Pied Noir, Le Chant des Africains, The Song of the Africans.

In those early days, the young soldiers had caroused through Paris with Pepe's sister Christine and her entourage of friends. Later, when Christine and Cameron became entwined, he shared her small romantic flat near the American University, steps from the Eiffel Tower.

Cameron absently glanced over his shoulder, expecting to see the Eiffel Tower of his youth, only to see the restaurant front of Caveau du Palais.

Pepe exited from the other side of the taxi and faced the square. Before joining Cameron on the curb, he set his duffel on the ground, slid his hands into his pant pockets, and stilled himself in the middle of the street so that he too could take in the Parisians. The moment was picturesque to Cameron; Pepe was standing with his back to him, his satchel squeezed tight under the arm of his sport coat, his duffel beside him, a man returned home. Cameron was unsure what Pepe was thinking for that long moment alone in the street. He imagined his friend was also reminiscent of time spent with Christine. Awake from his brief spell, Pepe slowly joined Cameron at the curb. Without looking back at the square, he said in a low monotone, "You know Place Dauphine has always been my favorite square in Paris. Come, let's have a coffee."

"A pied-a-terre in Place Dauphine among Paris' most beautiful townhouses," said Cameron. "I had no idea you were doing that well."

"Like most here, we inherited a family flat. My aunt

had no children of her own. It is Christine's flat really."
Pepe clutched the top of a café chair of the nearest sidewalk
table. "Let's sit. You will like the espresso. The food and
wine is also excellent. No need to come here if you can't get
a table outside, though."

Cameron inhaled deeply through his nose. That
Christine would live here made sense to him. She was, after
all, a top model with her own wealth. "I would rather go
right up if you don't mind."

Pepe released the chair and raised his brow. "Sure
thing. Let's get right to business." He subtly nodded his
head. "Give me just a moment, I will get the keys and have
them send up some soup and croissant."

"Thank you," said Cameron.

Pepe went to the counter of the café, spoke quickly
with the host, and then rejoined Cameron.

Pepe bent his head back slightly, gesturing to a building
to the right of the restaurant.

"The flat is in the building over, above the gallery."

"Her roommate is expecting us?"

"I spoke with her briefly," said Pepe. "She is on a
shoot in Jakarta."

"She is also a model?"

"Oui," said Pepe. He led Cameron to the forest green
double doors. From his pocket he pulled a key ring. He
stuck an odd shaped key into the lock, sending the door ajar.
With the next key, Pepe unlocked the interior door, a
frosted glass pane etched with an elaborate floral design and
bordered in polished oak. The two proceeded into the small
marble floored lobby. To their right was a set of eight
mailboxes and in the rear, the door to the gallery, a spiral
stairwell, and an open-air lift. They took the stairs to the flat
three stories above. On each landing they passed were three
matching doors, wooden and frail with age. At the top of
the stairs, unique from the others below, was a single dark
saffron metal door. Three shining brass deadbolts lined the

edge. Pepe shook the key ring open into his palm so that the keys to the deadbolts would reveal themselves, and then he methodically unlocked each one.

CHAPTER 49
PLACE DAUPHINE, PARIS

The door to Christine's apartment opened to the bright glow of daylight, enhanced with the contrast of the darkened stairwell. The design of the apartment, far more than a mere pied-a-terre, spoke of Christine. The large flat had been redone in recent years, the smooth ivory walls showed no signs of age and the furniture was new and modern, with the exception of a few choice pieces such as the stuffed tan leather chair and an antique lamp with a Tiffany type art nouveau colored glass shade. The tall, sheer, cloud white panels that draped the windows brought a glow into the room, revealing far behind them the sparse tops of the chestnut trees in the open square below.

The two set their bags near the stairwell that led to the top floor bedrooms. Then Pepe removed the satchel that held the laptops from his shoulder and placed the bag on a small black lacquered table at the end of the sofa. Cameron paced slowly into the vast room. On the sidebar near the door, a piece of china, the pink landscape pattern ancient and dulled, held some euros, a keychain, and a few small folded sheets of paper, pocket worn and discarded, fragments of Christine's day-to-day life. Across the room was a gas fireplace framed with a lacquered cabinet and mantel in fashion with the side tables. A picture atop the mantel caught Cameron's eye. He moved closer; it was a photograph of Pepe and him when they were very young, and each with their arms around a younger stellar beauty, Christine. The three were smiling.

"I remember that day," said Pepe behind him. He was in an open closet reaching for something up top. "That was the day you took her to get the hound. What was that dog's name?"

"Moby," said Cameron.

"Oui, Moby. A silly name for a dog, the name of a whale."

"Immense amour."

"Qua?"

"Christine said the puppy had immense amour, a Moby heart." Cameron lifted the photo from the mantel then glanced up toward Pepe. "She said the dog had an immense love like me."

Pepe nodded solemnly, then raised a hard plastic case he had retrieved from the closet. "Come with me to the table."

Cameron returned the photograph home to the mantel, peered into the picture one last time, and then joined Pepe in the next room. Pepe had placed the case on the table and was working a combination to unlock the lid. Cameron knew what the contents of the case would be and was not surprised when Pepe removed two pistols.

Pepe held one of the handguns out to Cameron. "If I remember, you like a Ruger," he said.

"What's not to like," said Cameron. He pulled the slide back to inspect the P95 and to ensure the chamber was clear. "Center fire, balanced to be ambidextrous," he tossed the Ruger from one palm to the other. "A fine weapon overall." He then picked up the two Ruger magazines bound together by a rubber band and inserted one into the grip. "Besides, I don't think I have much choice. I can't imagine you would give up your M9."

Pepe was inspecting the Beretta he held with the same expedient efficiency as Cameron had with the Ruger. "I also have a SIG 9 in the bedroom closet if you prefer."

Cameron squinted, "You know, I keep only one of these around. In my safe, no less, you seem to have access to a private armory in every western country."

Pepe pulled the slide of the Beretta. "Of the many things a man can do to excess, he can never be too well armed." He handed Cameron a knife from inside the case and then headed up the stairwell. "I will get the SIG."

The intercom near the door buzzed.

"Can you get that?" Pepe's raised voice carried through the flat from the upstairs bedroom. "I am sure that is the food. They were to send up mushroom soup and lamb. You will enjoy the soup."

"And the lamb?" asked Cameron as he went to answer the intercom.

"You will especially enjoy the lamb."

On the black and white screen of the intercom, Cameron watched the slightly doubled image of a young man lift the bags of food up to the camera. Cameron tapped the button to grant the deliveryman access, opened the steel door, and waited for the food to make the journey up the stairs. The echo of the young man's rapid steps shot up the spiral stairwell. He reached the floor in seconds. The deliveryman nimbly stepped across the landing to the door, his thin frame almost swaying from his expedient momentum. Cameron exchanged the euro bill he held out between his fingers for the delivery.

"Merci," said the young man, before spinning around to depart as rapidly as he had arrived. The deliveryman was already a lean shadow descending the first few steps of the spiral stairwell before Cameron was back into the flat.

Cameron walked the box and two large bags over to the table. "What all did you order? This is heavy."

"Must be the wine," said Pepe returning to the table. "They are also very generous."

Pepe opened one of the bags and removed two small paper cups. "Here, have an espresso."

"Thanks," said Cameron. He popped the plastic cover from the lid and then went to the window to again gaze at the square. He sipped the coffee and allowed his eyes to wander from the trees of the square to the street below. "I don't believe this."

"I told you the espresso was good."

"No, yes, but no," said Cameron. "That's not what I meant."

"What is it?"

"There is a white Bentley parked outside."

CHAPTER 50
PLACE DAUPHINE, PARIS

Pepe continued to remove items from the bags. "That has to be a coincidence, we couldn't be so lucky," said Pepe.

"You're right," said Cameron. "How could Dada find us? He could not have followed us all the way from London. Unless." Cameron swung his head in the direction of the satchel. "Could that laptop be bugged?"

"Not really," said Pepe. Then he stopped sorting through the bags and fixed his eyes on Cameron. "Unless it is, location software is standard on Macs."

"Location software?"

"Yes, it is called 'find my computer or phone' or something. That is why I had the old phone you joke about." Pepe shook his head and went back to the bags. "The computer would have to be open though. That is not Dada."

"Unless he followed us," said Cameron.

"You said yourself he could not have followed us from London. Ridiculous." Pepe opened a piece of foil revealing four warm loaves and held them close to his face to take in the sweet scent of the warm bread.

"He could have followed us from the Gare du Nord when we left the Eurostar," said Cameron. "You had the computer open on the train."

Pepe lowered the foil-covered loaves and peered up at Cameron. "They could have done this, yes. Tracked us the entire journey with the software and then waited for us at the train station." He shook his head. "It is not them though. We have only arrived."

"They're driving away," said Cameron. The side of his upper lip went up in disgust of his own paranoia. He tilted the paper cup up to pour the rest of the espresso down his throat.

"I told you. Not as many Bentleys in Paris as London, yet still a few." Pepe held his hands above his shoulders. "I asked them to send up some wine. There is no wine here."

Cameron set the paper cup on the table. "I want to stretch my legs anyway. I'll run down."

"Fine," said Pepe. "I will get the plates from the kitchen and you can go downstairs to get the wine. Vin rouge s'il vous plait."

"Of course," said Cameron.

Cameron picked up the SIG Pepe had set on the table and tucked the pistol into his waist opposite the Ruger. "I will be right back," said Cameron. He flashed his brow at Pepe and his old friend returned the gesture.

"Go then, be quick," said Pepe. "Once I open the box the lamb shanks will be cold."

Cameron slipped down the spiral stairwell with the same speed as the young man and was almost to a run exiting the lobby. He caught and composed himself before putting foot on the sidewalk. The white Bentley that had been parked near the restaurant was now nowhere in sight. As he walked the few short meters to the restaurant, Cameron focused his memory on the Bentley. In his mind, he created a still photograph. Cameron studied the picture. The occupants had been out of view from the window above. He ran his eyes along the side of the vehicle and let them rest on the license plate. The country of origin was the UK. Still, he was not sure if the id on the plate had been Dada's. Cameron had been quite far away. He sucked in a deep breath to release the thought, a confused fixation, and made his way through the tables toward the host.

The host recognized Cameron immediately. "Votre ami a oublié le reste de la nourriture," said the host.

"What do you mean my friend forgot the rest of the food?"

The host held up his hand, "Un moment." He stepped over to the counter and returned with two bottles of wine in one hand and a small box in the other. "The young man did not take the lamb." The man smiled as he held the bottles out for Cameron. "I tried to catch him but he was back in the auto and vroom."

Cameron's adrenalin pumped up. "What auto?"

"You did not see?" The host looked confused. "Your young friend has a nice white Bentley, antique I would guess, I tried to get his attention, then vroom." He raised his brow apologetically then again offered the wine and box of lamb. "Your food."

"Merci," said Cameron. Cameron spun around, intent on notifying Pepe back in the flat. Behind him, the further confused host raised his voice, "Your food."

Cameron yelled without glancing back, "Un moment." The Bentley did belong to Ibrahim Dada, there was no doubt, and whatever was in the box under the bags was imminent danger.

The bomb that had been delivered to the fourth floor ignited before Cameron reached the building.

A firestorm bellowed out of the windows of Christine's apartment.

Objects and flame shot out onto the street and into Place Dauphine. The glass of the windows above and below the fourth floor shattered, as did the huge street level pane of the gallery.

The blast was strong enough to disorient Cameron four floors below and threw him into a spin. He landed backward onto the curb to brief silence.

Cameron was in disbelief. People ran out of the Caveau du Palais to the commotion. The street side café was in disarray and the patrons that had been sitting on the walk crawled or hid among the tables and tossed chairs, confused and in shock. A woman was screaming, yet her hysterics were muffled and far away.

The air flooded with rancid smell of the burning building.

Pepe was not running out. Pepe would not be running out.

Years of training kicked in. Stunned and unaware of his own actions, he clutched the Ruger that had fallen to his side, unaware if anyone had noticed. He was unsure how long the 9mm was on the curb, seconds or minutes. Cognizance began to return swiftly with the full caliber of the sounds and smells around him. Cameron scooted himself to his feet. The sirens were very close. Cameron remembered, the police, the hospital, were all only a street or two up the island. He realized he could not be seen there, someone would recognize him in too short of time. He slid the pistol into his jacket and began to casually walk across the square.

CHAPTER 51
PARIS, FIFTEEN YEARS BEFORE

Pepe was elated to see the wee chocolate lab rolling on the blanket next to Christine. He did not bother to acknowledge Cameron or his sister and instead immediately knelt down between them and planted his face close to the frolicking puppy. Moby responded to Pepe as well, leaping toward Pepe's shaking nose with little tiny paws and a nipping jaw.

"He thinks your face is a toy," said Christine.

Pepe behaved no different than Christine had with the small animal, speaking in a childlike way as if Moby were a human baby and not a puppy, "You're a cute little one. Oui, vous êtes."

"How did you find us?" asked Cameron.

Pepe answered Cameron with the same cooing voice, aiming the words at Moby would. "I went by the flat on Rue de l'Exposition and you two were not there. I knew you would be over here at the Champ de Mars, off the field in your spot."

"So I guess there is no hiding from you, mon ami," said Cameron. He rolled back, propping himself up from behind with his elbows. He peered up at a nearby treetop capped with the peak of the Eiffel Tower. The Tower, halfway down the field from where they picnicked, did not appear as large as when viewed from other parts of the city.

Christine gently placed her hand upon the lab's neck. She caressed his delicate shoulders, prompting the puppy to curl into a tight ball. His eyes closed and he appeared to drift to sleep.

Pepe pushed his hands into his knees and straightened his back. "You seem to have a special touch. I think maybe my neck is tight as well." He twirled his head to adjust his neck. The muscles in his upper arms slightly rippled, swelled, and fell with his motion. "Could I be next?"

Christine giggled softly. "You are a big pup yourself, maybe?"

"Really," said Pepe, now exaggerating stretches from his shoulders, "I could use a massage." His tight grey t-shirt accentuated his muscular upper body.

"Then I suggest you go get one," said Cameron.

Pepe stopped his stretching. "I think I will stay. Would I be correct you have some vin rouge in that basket? Maybe some bread?"

"Sure," said Cameron. He lifted the basket over to the side of the blanket where Pepe knelt.

"You are always eating," said Christine. "You should be careful you do not become a huge plum."

"Nonsense," said Pepe. He tore off the heel of a small loaf of bread. "Un quignon de pain ne va pas me faire de mal." He ripped away a piece of the heel with his teeth and then reached into the basket for one of the small bottles of wine to wash the bread down. With a full chewing mouth he said, "I will always be thin and strong." He puffed out his chest and smiled widely, the chunks of bread in his mouth pushing out his cheeks.

Christine laughed aloud.

Pepe shuffled through the basket to find what other

treats were hidden inside. He brought out a silver camera and pointed the lens at his sister. "Let me take your picture." Cameron and Christine leaned into each other. Christine assumed a trained pose and Cameron grinned mildly at Pepe.

There was a click and then Pepe lowered the camera. "That's no good," said Pepe. "Don't be so shy, Cameron. You are with a professional."

Christine turned her head and nuzzled the side of Cameron's face. They both began to laugh.

"Perfect," said Pepe. The camera clicked again. "Now one with the hound."

Christine smugly pushed her lips up and swatted her brother's knee. "Moby is not a hound," she said.

"Excusez-moi, s'il vous plaît pardonnez," said Pepe.

"How about we get a picture together," said Cameron. "Let's ask that man by the tree."

CHAPTER 52
ILE DE LA CITÉ, PARIS

Cameron squeezed his hands into his hips. His blood still pumped hard. He darted his eyes across place du Parvis-Notre-Dame, scanning for anyone that could have recognized him. The square's name had changed to Place John Paul II, after the dead pontiff, yet regardless of title he finally felt he was someplace safe. The spot where he stood to the side of the square, between the great bronze equestrian statue of Charlemagne et ses leudes and the edge of the trees, was familiar to him, a constant in a world that was becoming increasingly tumultuous with amazing momentum.

Cameron had exited Place Dauphine as expediently as possible without breaking into a suspicious run. To elude authorities, he had crossed the square to the northern bank of Ile de la Cité and nearly run into oncoming traffic of emergency vehicles. Cameron did not want to be seen. Without hesitation, he veered away from the flashing lights and squawking sirens coming from mid-island. He continued his stride north along the sidewalk and away from the trail of first responders that were filing onto the avenue behind him. He made his way onto the Pont Neuf, the city's oldest bridge. He was about to cross the Seine when he heard the emergency squawks of additional vehicles rushing from the Paris Metro center. He doubled back to avoid being noticed. He followed the southern walk and at the first chance, slipped down the steps to continue along the Seine. Cameron kept moving toward the area of Ile de la Cité most infested with tourists.

Surrounded by tourists, Cameron was able to blend in almost seamlessly.

Cameron now stood safely in the shadow of the patina Olivier and Roland. The famed sword Durendal hovered above Cameron, eternally leading the Frank King Charlemagne and his warhorse Tencendor.

Cameron was reassured, yet this too reminded him of Pepe. Pepe Laroque, his friend of many years, more than a friend, a brother, now incinerated beneath the bursting plume of black smoke that poured skyward a short distance away.

Cameron had always been pleased by the mammoth sculpture, the representation of absolute power, of unification, of the good fight. Pepe referred to the magnificent work as a remnant of imperialism and, possibly worse, a recollection of a time when France and Germany were one. Pepe was, after all, a Frenchman.

Trained to fully be aware of his gear and surroundings, Cameron was unusually out of sorts. He had not taken the opportunity to regroup. The blade Pepe had given him was easily detected, heavy in his pocket, as were the Ruger and SIG tucked in his waist. Cameron reached inside the pocket of his sport coat. Another relieving autonomic breath pumped through his nose and into his chest. He had his mobile phone. His other belongings, and his friend, were lost in the explosion at the other end of Ile de la Cité.

The phone awoke with a full charge and reception. Cameron was thankful that he had powered the phone on the express train. That would mean–he patted the other breast of his coat and then searched inside that pocket–the charger was still with him, a small good thing. With his thumb, he zipped through the contacts to his restaurant Le Dragon Vert. Claude would assist him. Cameron tapped the screen and then held the phone to his ear. There was a series of clicks. Cameron imagined the signal being bounced against some satellite, and then the familiar ring. On the second ring, the other line picked up. Cameron spoke immediately, "Hello this is Cameron, I need to speak to—" the recorded voice of the restaurants hostess interrupted him. "Hello, thank you for calling Le Dragon Vert. Our hours are 10am to 11pm—" Cameron lowered the phone. The time difference from Paris to New York was six hours and the sun was high above the cathedral de Notre Dame. Stateside, Claude would be at the Union Square Greenmarket to greet the farmers and vendors as they set up.

  · Cameron slid his thumb down the screen to sort through the contacts again. He slipped too far into the letter R section. He went up the list to the first name, Claude Rambeaux and then double tapped the screen to make the connection.

"C'mon, Claude, pick up," said Cameron. He began to pace in a small circle.

On the third ring, Claude answered the phone, "Hello, this is Claude."

"Claude, this is Cameron."

Claude's voice elevated, "Cameron, I thought this was you. You are still away. The number was a bridge."

"I'm in Paris."

"Ah, Paris. I am at the Greenmarket, so beautiful. This morning I found some small aubergine to stuff."

Cameron lifted his chin. The words were a bit amiss. The events leading to this call were all too personal. "Listen," said Cameron. "Things are red right now."

Claude's tone became serious. The elation of a mere second before was lost. "What's wrong Cameron? How can I help you?"

"I am in danger," said Cameron. "I need to find somewhere safe."

"Where is Pepe?" asked Claude.

A punch of nausea landed in Cameron's inner gut as he mentally formed the words, yet to say them triggered a latent switch deep within him. "Pepe has fallen," said Cameron. He said the words in such a way that he was reporting matter of fact.

There was a pause.

"I see," said Claude. "You need the number for Absolon, correct?"

"The hotel in Asnières is the safest place I know right now," said Cameron.

"Do not worry," said Claude. "Make your way to the hotel, and I will make the call."

CHAPTER 53
ASNIÈRES, PARIS

So many years had passed for both Cameron and Asnières since his last visit, that he momentarily lost his bearing when he exited the metro station. Some of the buildings were the same. As with most old European cities, the eyesore flare-ups of modernization increase in relation to the distance from the city's metro center. Asnières was a suburb touched by such modernism. Convenience mart petrol stands, the bland architecture of new hotels, and anachronistic glass walled shopping centers peppered streets that held the generational homes he found familiar. He adjusted his mind to filter the transition of time, and then overlaid the Asnières before him, over the suburb of his younger days. The metro station, the pharmacy, and a few landmark buildings, now repurposed, led Cameron down a side street. He anticipated the old townhouse.

Cameron did not recognize the guesthouse until he was close, the facade disguised with newly coated stucco and partly hidden behind a lush floral garden. He may have continued past it, had the unique multi gabled frame not caught his eye.

The metal gate was the same, though there was no longer rust nor squeak. The fruit trees and slates of stone that composed the walkway were definitely a fresh part of the landscaped yard, as were the grape vines wrapped up and around the arbor trellis. The wooden door, no longer weatherworn, was a deep brilliant red, and partly open. Cameron gently pushed the door a bit further and then entered the foyer.

Cameron called out, "Bonjour, est quelqu'un à la maison? Is anyone home?"

"Un moment," came a younger man's voice from the back of the house.

The foyer also appeared foreign to Cameron, as did the adjoining library when he peeked further inside. The interior rooms had been renovated. Bright colors covered the once patina walls and some aged knick-knacks, none that Cameron recognized, peppered the few surfaces.

A thin mop haired man entered through the French doors from the opposite end of the library. The young man appeared boyish, though Cameron judged him to be near thirty. The man wore a Brown University sweatshirt and was wiping his hands with a cloth. He held out a hand, a slight hint of French in his English, "You must be Cameron."

Cameron was pleased Claude had eased his arrival. He smiled and took the man's hand. "Yes, that's right. I am looking for Absolon. Is he here?"

"That's me," said the young man.

"There is a mistake, I was looking—"

The young man finished Cameron's sentence, "For my grandfather, yes I know. I'm Abe—well, I am an Absolon too—I have always gone by Abe."

"Little Abe, yes of course, you have changed."
Cameron hovered his hand waist level. "You have grown."

Abe lifted his brow, "Yes, that's true."

Cameron placed his hands on his hips. "Where is your

245

grandfather?" he asked.

"He is no longer with us."

"I'm sorry," said Cameron.

"Oh, that sounded wrong. Don't be sorry, he moved back to Algiers," said Abe. "He is very happy there."

"Oh."

"Yeah, I run the hotel now," said Abe. He gestured past Cameron. "Excuse me, may I?" Abe slipped past Cameron to the still open door. He leaned his head outside, and darted his eyes through the neighborhood. "Monsieur Claude said you might be followed."

"I don't believe I was," said Cameron. "Though I am not so sure it's safe to walk the Avenue des Champs-Élysées."

Comfortable that nothing past his garden was out of the ordinary, Abe closed the door and then headed back through the library. "Follow me to the garden, we can talk out there."

The French doors of the garden opened to a stone patio, shaded by a vine-covered pergola. Soft jazz and the pungent sweet scent of lilies permeated into the house. Bordering the patio were a variety of lilies, roses, and surrounding a corner arbor, similar to the one in the front of the house, a few groomed outcroppings of wildflowers. The simple courtyard and algae stained birdbath of Cameron's younger years had transformed to the lushness of a miniature estate.

On a low metal café table, a blue tin-serving tray emblazoned with a vibrant Orangina logo held a sweating bottle of sparkling lemonade and three tall glasses a lighter hue of blue than the tray. On a matching bench behind the small table sat an attractive young Asian woman, her blouse fully open, nursing a baby, easily no more than three months old. She did not appear modest or to mind the stranger entering the patio. She continued to serenely caress the suckling child, her tired eyes pleasant. Abe's mop of dark hair and disheveled attire mirrored the young mother. Cameron understood neither had been getting much rest.

Abe inhaled deeply and then in a soft voice introduced the young woman, "Cameron, this is my wife Kim."

Kim subtly lifted her head, her smile still pleasant, her caresses a natural repetition as the baby fed. Cameron was surprised by her American accent when she spoke. "It's really you, Cameron Kincaid, the Dragon Chef."

Cameron's eyes went wide. The events of the last few days had taken him far from the world he had created in New York.

"That's me," said Cameron. "Pleased to meet you. What is the little one's name?"

"This little hungry fella is Jonah," said Kim, "after my father. I love your shows. We only get one here. In Boston I used to watch you all of the time. Abe has told me many times you were a friend of the family. I didn't believe him."

"It's true, I knew Abe's grandfather quite well, and the family. You're American?"

Abe answered Cameron, "Kim and I met at Brown my sophomore year."

"My mother is Vietnamese and my father is from Massachusetts," said Kim. She gazed back down at the closed eyes of the babe in her arms. "And now little Jonah is French like his Daddy."

Cameron smiled a bit uncomfortably. "I'm intruding."

Kim raised her head again. "Not at all, sit. Abe, honey, pour Cameron a drink and tell him what you know."

"Thank you," said Cameron. He sat in one of the two metal patio chairs. Abe began to pour lemon seltzer into the three glasses. "So as I mentioned, Monsieur Claude explained to me why you are here." Cameron shifted his eyes to Kim, once again soothing her son. "Don't worry," said Abe. He offered Cameron the beverage and then took a seat in the second patio chair. "She knows what I know."

Cameron compressed his lips and then nodded.

Abe lifted his brow in a matter of fact fashion, then continued, "Well, anyway, I still know all of Absolon's friends."

"And Abe has few of his own," added Kim in a soft voice, now rocking back and forth.

"And I have a few of my own," nodded Abe. "So tracking down this Dada character was not that hard."

"You've found him already?"

"Not exactly. I am still waiting for friends to get back to me," said Abe.

"Hmm," said Cameron. He sipped the sparkling lemonade.

Abe grinned, "I did find out where he is going to be."

CHAPTER 54
8TH ARRONDISSEMENT OF PARIS

The leather jacket Cameron had borrowed from young Abe hugged his shoulders and upper arms tightly. The sheen of the blackened lambskin reflected the amber streetlamps with the same glow of the scooters and autos parked beside him. He flipped the enduro's kill switch and straightened himself, his legs spread wide to balance the motorbike in between. Without movement, the matching black helmet was becoming warm. He plucked his head from the snug heater rather than flip up the mask. He adjusted each driving glove, pulling down hard on the short cuffs and spreading his fingers wide to dig in deeply, and then, satisfied by the fit, flexed each hand. Uniform silhouettes of horse chestnut trees lined the roadways, already damp from the subtle evening mist, and muted beds of perennials filled the medians. The moist air, dense with the sweet pungent perfume of night blooming blossoms, enveloped him.

Cameron began to wait, gazing stone-faced at the restaurant across the street.

A short way ahead of him, the driver of the white

Bentley was also in waiting. Behind the white car, two silhouettes sat sentry in a small indigo Renault. Abe's friend had been correct. Dada was dining tonight at the Egyptian Room. Cameron pondered whether the warlord was undeterred by the earlier events of the day, confident the explosion that had killed Cameron's old friend would not trace back to him, or did Dada simply not care, disregarding the matter entirely. Cameron decided on the latter.

A faint drizzle had come, gone, and returned, still Cameron stayed in wait on the side of Rue Marbeuf. The hours of heavy traffic flooded across Avenue des Champs-Élysées at the end of the block. Taxis and town cars slipped past Cameron down the one-way street to let finely dressed guests arrive and depart from the trendy velvet roped restaurant, which, by this late hour, had transformed into a nightclub. Some of the guests he recognized from New York, some from his own restaurant. To go into the ultra art deco lounge of Egyptian Room would jeopardize his search for Dada. The risk of being recognized himself, even to have his name mentioned in a greeting, was far too great. Better to remain incognito in the partial shadow of the street, his back to approaching vehicles, no one looking back at the man on the motorbike, a common sight in Paris.

A few times, he was wary of Dada's men, twitching and fidgety in their seats. Once, Cameron thought he would need to move on when one of the large bodyguards stepped out of the Renault to stretch his legs. The man had stared a moment too long in Cameron's direction, an animal suspicious of his surroundings, instinctually drawn toward the predator. Distracted by the scolding of his colleague, the bodyguard stopped searching the night, and returned to his assigned post inside of the car. The man was not mistaken in that Cameron was a predator. No matter that he'd redefined himself as a debonair restaurateur, a worldly television personality. No matter how he lived his modern life day to day, Cameron Kincaid was and always would be a specialized commando, a man still utilizing an alias, no less than in the last years he'd served as a deep cover agent. The part of his psyche overwritten by intense training and conditioning would forever leave him an alpha of alphas, an apex predator.

Half past midnight, the bodyguard again removed himself from the Renault. This time the driver of the white Bentley also exited his vehicle. Both of the standing men pressed a finger to their ears. The driver of the Bentley opened a passenger door slightly. Dada was leaving the restaurant. Cameron slipped on his helmet in preparation. He reached down and switched the fuel line back on. When Dada, accompanied by two more suited bodyguards, made his way from Egyptian Room to the Bentley, Cameron lifted the motorbike upright by the handlebars. With the tip of his foot, he flipped the folded kick-start away from the bike. Once Dada and his men were in the vehicles and had begun to pull away, Cameron pounced on the kick-start to ignite the bike's engine. He did not want to draw the attention of the men in the Renault. He left the headlamp off, and only when the small motorcade was near the corner of Avenue des Champs-Élysées, did Cameron pull away from the curb.

The white Bentley and indigo Renault continued forward across Avenue des Champs-Élysées, Rue Marbeuf becoming Rue du Colisée. Cameron held the motorbike at the corner. The Arch de Triumph towered over Place Charles de Gaulle to his left and an even distance to his right was the Obélisque of Place de la Concorde. When the light began to change for the oncoming traffic, he popped the clutch to gun the enduro. The engine whined loudly, jetting the bike through the intersection no differently than a scurrying rat. After he crossed the busy avenue, he eased off the throttle and tapped back a gear. The bike disappeared again into the shadows. The motorcade was already to the busy Rue de Courcelles. This time Cameron did not make the light. Confident he would not lose Dada, he watched the motorcade gaining distance and waited. When the light did change, the taillights of the Renault disappeared to the right.

Cameron flicked his thumb to illuminate the bike's headlamp. To remain dark on these streets could attract unnecessary attention. He motored steady to the corner and then rolled onto Rue du Faubourg Saint-Honoré.

Dada had not travelled far. The Bentley and the Renault were at the valet station of the Hôtel Le Bristol. Cameron's stakeout had been a success. He had discovered Dada's Paris lair. Cameron was familiar with the hotel. He attended a birthday celebration there every year for an aging friend, a Francophile fragrance mogul from the States, and had stayed there on many other occasions in his new persona. How predictable that Ibrahim Dada would make his Paris home in yet another a five star hotel.

There was an issue. The staff of the Hôtel Le Bristol was familiar with Cameron as well. There would be no way he could walk in incognito as he and Pepe had through the service entrance of the May Fair. He would have to use another skillset to get to Dada.

The enduro leaned a hard left short of the hotel. Cameron rode around the block, stopping safely in the shadow of the first intersection past the hotel. The north side of the intersection was a good place to hide. If the Renault or Bentley were to leave the Hotel, they would be forced to turn south, a lower risk they would see him.

Cameron rested his helmet on the handlebars. He pulled his mobile phone from inside the leather jacket and dialed.

"Hello," said Abe.

"It's Cameron."

"Yeah, I saw that. Did you find him?"

"Your friend was right," said Cameron. "Not only was he at the restaurant, I was able to follow him to the Hôtel Le Bristol."

"Well, that's good," said Abe.

"Not exactly," said Cameron. "The last time I was in the Hôtel Le Bristol I was in the bar all night with U2."

"The band?"

"Yeah, the band."

"So they know you, got it, I have someone I can call," said Abe. "Give me a few minutes."

"No problem," said Cameron. "I'll be waiting right here. This time I'm not letting him out of my sight."

CHAPTER 55
HÔTEL LE BRISTOL, PARIS

The information from Abe's friend came by late afternoon. The suite that Ibrahim Dada had made his own was on the top floor of the Hôtel Le Bristol, the eighth floor, facing the garden. Near Cameron, two French paparazzi, each with a 500mm camera lens dangling from their belt, were discussing another guest of the hotel, a young pop star. Cameron circled the block again. Paparazzi stalking the young pop star were staked out at every exit. Cameron had to wait for the photo parasites to leave before he could approach the hotel.

Cameron's opportunity came where he most desired it, the service entrance to the adjacent Epicure restaurant. The new restaurant and terrace separated the hotel from the 1,200 square meter French garden and was perfect cover to get him close. The street clear, he ducked into the serviceway that ran between the gate and restaurant toward the hotel.

Hidden in the shadow of the columned pergola, Cameron peered across the terrace to the back wall of the hotel. The white Botticino marbled terrace was empty except for two white jacketed workers removing and folding the last of the cotton-linen tablecloths from the cast iron tables. He waited for them to finish before making his way to the back wall. As they folded the last tablecloth, he sized up the best point of access. The bubbling 'Fontaine aux Amours' fountain at the center of the terrace appeared to be his best opportunity.

The two began to chat and then one lit a cigarette. Cameron was prepared to wait out the pair. From inside the restaurant came a loud pop, the opening of a champagne bottle, followed by a beckoning shout. The smoker stomped out his cigarette and, with smiles on their faces, the two headed into the glass walled dining room. Bending at his waist, Cameron skirted the hedge to the fountain. The fountain was a bit farther from the first ledge than he had calculated, so he deduced he would need to climb to the top and launch himself onto the wall. From behind the fountain, he peeked back toward the glass walls of the Epicure restaurant. The two white jacketed men had gathered with three of the kitchen staff and were raising glasses. None of the indoor crew faced the fountain or the back of the hotel. Cameron counted to three then stair stepped up the base of the fountain, placed his hands on either side of the top basin and, in a hop, lifted his feet up near his hands.

In the odd pose of an arched cat, Cameron froze.

Across the terrace, hidden to him from beneath the pergola, was the hotel's grand garden, a magnificent array of tulips, daffodils, azaleas, rhododendrons, and facing Cameron, the gardener. The gardener was spraying water from a hose onto a bed of tulips, meters from the terrace. Focused on his ground level task, the gardener had not yet noticed Cameron, directly to his front.

Cameron remained a statue, a new fixture to the fountain. He had not expected to see a gardener watering so late in the evening. Then from within the restaurant came another shout. Cameron's eyes darted to the indoor crew. One of the white jacketed men was walking to a garden door. "Bastian," the man called out toward the gardener. The gardener's head jolted toward the restaurant. Cameron could see now the man was wearing headphones and, caught off guard, had jerked his head to the side without looking forward, to where Cameron crouched, breathless. The gardener smiled, began to roll his hose, and headed toward the door and the others.

Cameron waited until the crew again were raising glasses and then flung himself up and back to the ledge.

Cameron propelled himself to exactly where he needed to be to clutch the ledge above his head. He briefly hung to assess those celebrating meters away within the glass walls and then, confident he was clear, he swung his right hand over to lead his body around to face the wall. As soon as his hand made contact, he hoisted himself up and then onto the ledge.

Cameron's deltoids burned.

With stealth and speed, he wasted no time getting to the third floor, scaling his way to the suite's terrace. The scent of magnolias shot up from the French garden below. Cautiously, he maneuvered himself between windows to avoid detection. He carefully placed fingers and toes onto the ends of the ledges, gradually lifting himself above the surrounding skyline. Though he had not scaled a building in years, the effort was second nature. Countless missions in the eastern bloc had required subtle infiltration. There had been a mission in Prague where he found himself scaling up and down the same building several nights in a row, primarily for visits to the wife of a former Russian General he was converting to an asset.

Each grip from Cameron's hand, each push of his toe maneuvered him farther up the wall until he found himself below the terrace of Dada's suite. The room above was quiet. He spun his weight so that his back was again flat on the wall. Climbing as much mentally as physically, he already had his next move planned. His plan was to swing himself up onto the edge of the terrace. His deltoids still burned, yet he had blocked out the sensation. From his perch, he could see the sterile light and contrasting shadows of the hotel garden below and in the distance, the Basilica of the Sacré Cœur, the church of Saint-Augustin, and the rooftops of Paris.

Cameron filled his lungs with air and then, with a pounce of a cat practiced a thousand times before, flung himself up, around, and onto the ledge of the darkened terrace. He peered under the railing. The French doors were open, framed by sheer curtain panels that glowed back at him. There was no motion, no shadows against the interior lamp lit wall. He held firm on the ledge.

Cameron made ready the Ruger and then eased himself up and over the railing. With the greatness of stealth, he slowly moved toward the open door. His adrenalin intoxicating him, overriding the exhaustion of the day. He was a good adrenalin drunk.

Through the sheer curtain, Cameron inspected the room. The only light in the room emanated from a tall standing lamp in the far corner. At rest in a cushioned chair beside the lamp was Dada, silent; he appeared to be sleeping. Also from the room came a familiar smell that Cameron identified immediately, the reek of a bowel movement, the particular stench of a man that has recently passed.

Cameron moved into the room to have a better look.

Dada was sitting in the chair. Dada was not sleeping. His face was beaten and cut, his left ear was separated from his head, the shirt of his fine suit oozed with punch colored blood, his throat was slit across the entire base of his neck. Cameron recognized the cut as well as any signature.

"Pepe," said Cameron.

A dark shadow filled the doorframe to the adjoining

room, and then a figure came into the light.

On the chair before Cameron was a corpse that had been alive moments ago. Standing beside that corpse was a man, now alive, that had been dead.

"I knew you would come," said Pepe. "I could not wait."

CHAPTER 56
HÔTEL LE BRISTOL, PARIS

Pepe rested himself into a cushioned chair opposite the doorway from the freshly dead Ibrahim Dada. Already pumped with adrenalin, a confused wave of emotion coursed into Cameron. His old friend, a fellow Green Dragon, the man he had counted on through countless missions, was alive. Cameron was elated to see his brother-in-arms, yet the carved up warlord across the room, the work of his friend, was jarring. He peered at the dead man, mentally recreating the slow death. Cameron had seen men killed in this fashion many times before, and certainly he had no remorse for the evil tyrant. But Pepe had been extreme. He had tortured Dada, beat him, and then slit his throat. He had not cut from behind by surprise, rather coldly from the front.

"You were looking him in the eyes," said Cameron, fixed on the glazed sightless orbs staring out to nothing.

Pepe had reclaimed a bit of the jolliness that had fallen from him the past few days. "I wanted him to see me as I took his future from him."

"I reject the glamour of evil," said Cameron.

"Do not quote verse to me, brother," said Pepe. "I have finally found Christine."

Cameron shifted his full attention to Pepe. "You have?" Cameron peered into the adjoining room. "She is here?"

"No."

"You know where she is?"

"I know much more than that. Sit. Sit."

Cameron dropped himself onto a wooden chair on the far side of the French doors, resting his hands, still holding the Ruger, on his lap. The exhaustion was beginning to take a toll on him. "The others, the bodyguards?"

"They are in the other room. I did not need them," said Pepe.

"So what happened? How are you—"

"Alive?" said Pepe. "I was going to the window to call down to you to ask the restaurant for some, um, what is the word for miel?"

"Honey."

"Oui, to get some honey. I saw Rudy from the restaurant offering you the box and wine. I looked to the table and thought very quickly. I ran to the door and was at the second floor when, boom."

"The explosion," said Cameron.

"Yes, the explosion came," said Pepe. "When I reached the gallery, I entered the cellar and then left through the sewer. I did not know if anyone was waiting in Place Dauphine so I thought better if I appeared to have died."

"Well, that worked," said Cameron. "How did you end up here?"

"Probably the same as you. On a hunch, I called my contact back in Montreal. He told me of a bar where Somali frequent. I went to the bar and waited. The barman told me the men that work with Dada came in every night when they are in town. I gave the man some euros and began to drink. I guess I drank a bit more than I planned. By late afternoon, some men came in and the barman gave me a signal. I watched the men until they left and then followed them. I peeled one away and hauled him below to the catacombs."

Cameron was unsure where Pepe's story was going. Pepe continued.

"I had a discussion with the man and could not convince him to tell me where Dada was staying. Then I realized the man's comrades had followed me into the catacombs and he was simply stalling me for time, so in the dark I killed them one by one until I got to the last man," said Pepe.

"And he told you Dada was here," said Cameron.

"He was easy to convince. Pepe reached into the pocket of his jacket and removed a fistful of something. He tossed what he held onto the floor for Cameron to see in the light. Cameron's eyes widened, his mind reeled. Pepe, without changing his tone, continued his story.

"I presented the last man with the ears of his colleagues. He was quick to tell me where to find his general."

"Hmm, I see," said Cameron, not wanting to believe what Pepe was saying.

"Then I came here and waited. Dada told me what I wanted to know and more."

"What did he say?"

"Listen for yourself," said Pepe. Pepe reached into an inside pocket and then tossed Cameron what he had found there. Cameron caught the small piece of electronics. He examined the digital recorder and then hit play.

Dada's pain immediately spouted from the tinny recording. Cameron sighed and continued to listen.

Dada screaming: "What are you doing? You are crazy."

Next came the sharp crack of a slap, followed by another, Dada screaming with each blow.

Dada beginning to whimper: "What do you want. I did nothing."

Pepe: "You know what you did. Now tell me!"

Another cracking sound cut through the recording, followed by another tinny and muted howl from Dada.

Pepe again, determined: "You hijacked the Kalinihta, now where is the girl?" another crack, "Where is my sister?"

Dada: "I did not do this. I let them stay at the compound and sent along some men."

Pepe: "That was your compound? Answer me," slap, slap. Cameron peered up at the bloody corpse in the chair, the bruising that had begun on the sides of the face, and the bruising that had ceased after death.

Dada: "Why should I tell you? You are a dead man."

Pepe: "Because I will cut this from your body."

Dada: "You will do no such, Aaaaaa! You are dead! You are dead!"

Pepe: "I may be dead, but I am a dead man with a knife."

Dada: "Yes, that was my compound. The plan was for him to hide until you came. Then his father would be happy to deal."

Pepe: "What are you saying? That Nikos was in on this?"

Dada: "Yes, Nikos, this was his plan to push his father Demetrius into a deal for a cut of the profit. This was his plan."

Pepe: "His plan?"

Dada: "Nikos said that if Christine were captured that you would ride in like the cavalry to rescue her. The kidnapping was a setup. All planned by Nikos."

Pepe: "And you took Christine in return?"

Dada: "No! I know nothing about her!"

Pepe screamed: "You lie! You lie!" along with repetitive slaps, screams, and moans.

Dada: "No, no. This was his plan from the beginning.

262

Go to Gstaad and ask him yourself. Nikos Stratos. No! No! Stop this! You are a dead man!!"

Cameron stopped the recording and peered into Pepe's satiated eyes.

EPISODE IV

CHAPTER 57
GSTAAD, SWITZERLAND

The Volvo was travelling much faster than the posted limit, and as they traversed the incline of the winding road, Pepe continued to accelerate. The engine loaded RPMs onto each gear in succession, amplifying the illusion of speed and momentum. Cameron felt the sensation of being thrust up, out, and around the curves. He would have preferred to drive, yet had to defer to Pepe. Before leaving Paris, Pepe had secured the car, so there was never a question or an option for Cameron to do more than ease back and take in the Alps.

Of things to see in the world, the scenery of the Alps was among the most beautiful. A Mozart sonata filled the car. Cameron tapped his knee to the exhilarating tempo. The thinner air of the higher elevation gave the shimmering surface of Lake Geneva a fairy tale glisten. The iconic Alps, the pastoral valleys, and glacier groomed slopes were all postcard perfect. From the French Alps through the Swiss, the villages became evermore ornate. Even the jumbled architecture of Montreux, spanning from medieval snapshots of eras past to modern symbols of culture and the utmost wealth, had an enticing appeal.

Cameron and Pepe would soon arrive at their destination in the Bernese Oberland, a fairy tale in the Alps, brought to life by the architectural wonders of the Gstaad super rich. Each chalet was a paradise, an oasis, a manifestation of the vanity of artisans, architects, and interior designers with no budget limitation. The breathtaking uniform chalets, ornately carved from local wood, each hid a literal underground fortress with which Cameron was familiar. The picture perfect facades, a modest three meters above the surface, hid high-tech fortresses five times as large in the depths of Oberbort, Gstaad's most fashionable area. Reinforced by nuclear bomb proof concrete, these mansions under the earth held in their bellies swimming pools, fitness centers, spas, movie theaters, vintage car stocked garages, and wine cellars large enough to store a small vineyard. Cameron had been here several times before as a chef, and to play, and years ago as an agent. Quieter than St. Moritz and far more exclusive, the unscrupulous found comfort amongst celebrity and wealth.

Five minutes from the Gstaad Palace hotel, the valley's monument to prestige, Pepe found the driveway to the home of Demetrius Stratos. Demetrius' home, arguably the most expensive estate in Gstaad, audaciously boasted two massive chalets on the inclined field, two heads attached to a far larger beast below.

Pepe and Cameron were fresh, clean, and in surprisingly good spirits. The death of the Somali warlord Ibrahim Dada at Pepe's hand was an apparent catharsis. Though he had not yet found his sister Christine, taken from the hijacked yacht Kalinihta, Pepe was jubilant, almost his old jolly self. Pepe's mood in turn lightened Cameron's. The violence of the previous evening and the day before, of every day of the past week in Somalia, Dubai, London, and Paris, had become a perverse normal. The reinforced conditioning and training of his younger super commando self had overridden any morality play his mature psyche had applied to the events of the preceding days. Cameron was, after all, stoic by nature; that had been a key factor in his promotion to the Green Dragons. He accepted, believed, that the actions of the past could not be prevented or changed, only avenged, and that was what they were here in Gstaad to do. Avenge Pepe's sister, Cameron's former lover, Christine, for the wrongdoing at the hands of Nikos Stratos.

Neither Pepe nor Cameron had spoken of Alastair Main. Three days prior, their friend Alastair had been by their side. He had split off to piece together information that could help them in their search. That the two had not mentioned him did not mean their friend was absent from their thoughts. Alastair had a history with Nikos. To openly speak of their friend could lead down a path that neither wanted to walk.

Without words, Cameron and Pepe had made the mutual decision that they alone would deal with Nikos.

CHAPTER 58
GSTAAD, SWITZERLAND

Despite the prominent portion of Demetrius Stratos' estate being hidden below them, deep beneath the earth, what was above ground still gave the impression of grandeur. The first of the two mammoth wood faced chalets towered above them. The Greek shipping tycoon was obviously immune to the visible height limit imposed on the mere millionaires that peppered the mountainside around him. To their front was a garage door that Cameron calculated, by the dimensions, was the entrance not to the garage proper, rather to an auto elevator designed to transport the Stratos fleet of unique Ferraris and Lamborghinis to and from the depths below. Attached to the garage overlooking the valley was a building aligned in style with the two brethren above, yet miniature in size and status.

Cameron gazed out over the town of Gstaad in the valley below and then, momentarily unsure, asked Pepe, "Demetrius is expecting us?"

"He is expecting us," said Pepe.

"And he knew who you were?"

"I believe he knows who we are, he has been funding

our expedition. Anyway, I did not speak to him, I spoke to an assistant."

The heavy wooden door of the miniature chalet opened and from within stepped an exquisitely beautiful young woman. She wore tight fitting slacks and a wool sweater, predictable Alpen garb.

"This must be her," said Cameron.

The young woman said nothing. As the door pulled shut behind her, she looked fixedly at Pepe and Cameron. Her eyes appeared to pair with each of them. That her sultry gaze was at the same time obviously innocent yet seductive was provoking. She reminded Cameron of paintings he had seen, the Mona Lisa, or the Girl with a Pearl Earring, the way the women in the portraits poured out in a gaze, fixed on the observer, in silent communication. She offered them a pleasant smile, the knowing kind of smile that said, *Feel at home, you are welcome here.* Her light hair was full, blown out, and her relaxed nature implied a woman on holiday rather than an assistant to an industry mogul. Cameron pondered that she could easily have been a model, or an actress, and that perhaps at one time she had been.

The young woman's voice was full and confident, "Hello, you must be Mister Laroque and Mister Kincaid."

"Yes," said Pepe, he stepped toward the front of the Volvo to meet their greeter. "I am Pepe Laroque, and this is my colleague, Cameron Kincaid. Please call me Pepe, mademoiselle."

"And please, call me Cameron."

"Okay, Pepe, Cameron, I am Mister Stratos' assistant, Annalisa Droukos. Please call me Annalisa. Mister Stratos is expecting you, if you could follow me."

Annalisa offered another pert smile and then led them to an entrance set in the stacked boulders that composed the lower wall of the chalet. From a treetop to the left of the mammoth chalet came a sharp flash of light. Cameron met Pepe's eyes to see if he had noticed the sniper in the trees, obviously a member of the Stratos' security team. Pepe winked back and subtly nodded, shifting his brow in the direction to the eave above Cameron's shoulder. Cameron casually looked back over the valley and then forward again, catching the subtle red LED adjacent to the buttonhole camera that undoubtedly filled the screen of some internal security room deep in the belly of the estate. Though Annalisa did not wait for any signal or clearance, Cameron was sure he heard a faint click the second before she touched the handle of the door. If she had heard a lock releasing, she appeared not to notice, pulling the door open as casually as one goes from one room to the next.

The interior of the chalet was radically different from the fairy tale facade. The walls were rosewood paneled midway up to a small ledged molding, and then papered deeply red the remainder of the way up to an intricately carved wood ceiling. The indirect light cast the illuminating effect of oil lamps or candles, reminiscent of a train car or old Victorian manor. Along the crimson wall were photographs spaced every half meter. In an automated rehearsed fashion, Annalisa began to list off the people pictured by rote.

"On the wall you will find photos of some of the illustrious guests of the chalet as well as friends of the Stratos family. Pictured with Mister Stratos' father you will see Mister Churchill and in the next, you will see Mister Stratos himself, with the Queen, and in the next with Prince Charles and Princess Diana." Cameron recognized the Greek shipping mogul from the photo back at Alastair's cottage on the Laikipia plateau. Demetrius' well-groomed midnight hair was slicked back and below his chin; he wore a cravat, and on his finger, a wide gold ring with a red ruby setting. His hair, the cravat, and ring were consistent, no matter the age of the photo. Cameron had a brief imaginative flash of Demetrius as a small schoolboy with the same slick hair, silk cravat, and large gold ring.

As they continued through a maze of corridors and

stairwells, Annalisa continued describing the endless pictures and shelved artifacts. Along the way, they passed several dark lacquered doors that appeared, after a few hallways, confusingly the same; the same crystal knobs, the same order of sconces, and the portraits only subtly different than the last. Occasionally there would be an open room or a few open rooms together. Always the tour pressed on, focusing on the portrait collection of the world's elite. Initially, Cameron thought the tour a mere embellishment on the part of Demetrius, showing off the aristocrats, new and old, which were friends of the Stratos family. Then Cameron deduced the true purpose of the tour. The trivial information was meant to distract guests as they were led through the complex interior of the mansion.

After fifteen minutes of photos and trinkets, they came to a set of wooden double doors, black lacquered as the many before. Again Cameron heard a faint click before Annalisa reached for the lead crystal knob.

"This is Mister Stratos' library," she said. "Please wait here and he will join you shortly."

The Stratos library, in the same manner as every other part of the chalet they had been shown, resembled a museum. The walls of the large library were entirely covered, with the exception the wall bordering the door. The wall was rosewood paneled midway and topped with the same crimson that papered the hallway. On either side of the door were recently stocked sidebars, one with assorted cheeses and meats, and the other with decanters and a crystal bowl of ice.

The ceiling was a continuation of exaggerated ornate woodcarvings, including two wooden cherubs at the base of a high backlit stained glass dome in the center. The sidewalls were shelved, floor to ceiling, with dark hued leather bindings, bright with accents of pressed gold and silver letters. On one shelf was a solitary device to detect moisture, and in another section, backlit behind glass, were ancient and rare tomes. The entirety of the back wall was also an exhibit behind glass. Covering the back wall from one side to another was an array of modern and ancient weapons. On the right side, a glass door shielded a recessed anteroom, the size of a large closet, lined with handguns of every age and make. The rest of the wall was adorned with antique edge weapons. Neatly displayed were row after row of swords, scimitars, spears, knives, and daggers. In the center of the room was a low table display case housing aboriginal blowguns, each surrounded by various feathered darts. Around the low table were four heavily cushioned dark leather chairs, and another four sat on the outer edge of the room, one in each corner.

The room was magnificent.

"You can help yourself with a drink from the sidebar," said Annalisa. "Is there anything special I can have brought in for you?"

Cameron raised his brow. "I believe we're fine, Annalisa."

"Excellent," said Annalisa. She gestured to an intercom near the door. "Just tap that button if you need anything. Mister Stratos will be with you shortly." She put a finger to her ear revealing a small emerald that mirrored the glint in her eyes. An earpiece. She smiled and then tilted her head toward the wall, fixed intently on a conversation that Cameron and Pepe were not privy to. Then Annalisa nodded her head, removed her finger, and returned her attention to the two men. "He is still on a call, so please make yourself comfortable."

"Thank you," the two said in near unison.

"And Mister Kincaid, um, Cameron," said Annalisa.

"Yes?"

"I enjoy your shows."

Cameron near winced. Though he had received many unexpected compliments that had caught him off guard, Annalisa's was different. He had begun to forget about his celebrity chef persona.

"Thank you for watching, I am glad you enjoy the

shows."

Annalisa's gaze appeared more intense, more eager to please, "As I said, if you need anything." Her last word hung in the air as she left them alone in the library.

Cameron shifted his eyes to Pepe. "Don't start."

"Dragon Chef," said Pepe haughtily. He winked at Cameron.

Neither took the offered drink, rather they both went to inspect the weapons display at the back of the library. Though Cameron and Pepe were not exactly weapons enthusiasts, they certainly had a predilection. Cameron's curiosity drew him toward the gun closet. Pepe, by no surprise to Cameron, was instinctively drawn to the edge weapons. The handguns in the recessed display case were no doubt some of the rarest, and those that were more common, Cameron surmised, had a special property or past. Cameron imaged a man of Demetrius' wealth would have the gun that killed Hitler if that device was obtainable.

"Cameron," said Pepe, his voice low. "Come here for a moment. I want you to see this."

Cameron joined Pepe, scanning the iron and steel as he passed the wall. "What did you find?"

"You are not going to believe this," said Pepe.

In the case in front of Pepe, a series of fifty daggers were pinned to the red velvet wall, in two rows of twenty-five. The daggers appeared to be arranged by age. Some of the daggers were very ornate, others mere missiles, all of them with the same Latin inscription, 'Caedite eos! Novit enim Dominus qui sunt eius.'

Cameron translated the familiar phrase, "Kill them all. Surely the Lord discerns which ones are his."

"Can you believe he has these?" asked Pepe.

"Well, he is a collector, and we have a few of our own."

"You think they belonged to the agents of the same clandestine group we met up with?" asked Pepe. "Some of these are very old."

"If you would have asked me before Quebec, I might have said something different. Marie said the Rex Mundi has many agents, knowing and not knowing. Who knows how far back in history the cells go. Marie said they went back to the beginning."

"The beginning of what?" asked Pepe.

From the door of the library came a deep voice, "To the beginning of the world."

The two spun to see Demetrius Stratos enter the room. Stratos lifted a finger in the direction of the case. "You find the daggers interesting?"

CHAPTER 59
GSTAAD, SWITZERLAND

Well-tanned and debonair, Demetrius Stratos could have been posing for a portrait. Framed between the library doors, the crimson at his back exaggerated the brilliance of his pressed white shirt, and, as in every photo, his dark hair was slicked back, around his neck he wore a silk cravat, and the gold ruby ring, as crimson as the backdrop, was on his hand. Stratos' blue eyes penetrated the room. The kind look on his face did not disguise the fact that he was intensely and steadily assessing his two visitors.

Having previously met a number of people associated with wealth or celebrity, Cameron was not put off by the man's scrutiny. The pause was becoming slightly uncomfortable when Cameron realized Stratos was exercising a familiar technique. The confident gaze was to give the impression that Stratos could judiciously size up a man. Cameron and Pepe were to understand him to be serious and reliable, or that Stratos had tallied their flaws. Cameron deduced that the magnate probably thought the two men had come to Gstaad for an additional fee for saving his son Nikos from the coastal pirates. The correct soldier's response was to mirror Stratos with a stern gaze to set him at ease. A stare that would instill in the rich man the impression that Cameron and Pepe were not mere fortune hunters. So Cameron and Pepe returned the stare.

"Those daggers are a very rare find," said Stratos, before either Cameron or Pepe spoke. He crossed the room to join Cameron and Pepe near the glass-covered wall.

Pepe began to speak, "Mister—"

Raising a quick hand, Stratos cut Pepe off, "Yes, yes, we can forego the formality of introductions. You know who I am, I know who you are. Now let me tell you about these daggers you are admiring." From his pocket, Stratos pulled a small fob, similar to one used as a car key. He subtly tapped a button with his thumb and the glass began to slide to the side, disappearing into the end of the shelved wall. When the glass cleared the fifty daggers, Stratos removed one from the section that appeared among the oldest. Stratos chose one of the few with a hilt, a white hilt. "These daggers are very rare finds," said Stratos. He held the dagger to demonstrate the peculiarities. "Take this specimen for example. Fine metallurgy, a perfect balance, and the hilt—"

"Made of bone, correct?" asked Pepe.

"Yes," said Stratos, pleased by Pepe's assessment. He held the dagger by the blade between his knuckles and thumb so that the hilt was fully revealed. "In fact this hilt is made of bone, as are a few others. Some collectors have asserted the bone is from a large mammal, a cow or a horse, others say a predator. They are wrong, of course. I had a DNA test performed, not on this blade alone but the other bone handled daggers in this collection as well. You know what I found?"

"They are all human," said Pepe.

"That is correct." Stratos handed the blade to Pepe. "Each one, including the one you are holding, proved to be human bone. European, as a matter of detail."

Pepe inspected the dagger, twisting the blade from one side to the other. "For an older knife, this has fine craftsmanship."

"I agree. The articulate manner of the metal craft around the top and bottom of the hilt and the delicate inscription along the blade, all of the daggers share this. That is what ties the collection together, yet the style of lettering on this dagger... Well, the intricacy is unique."

"'Caedite eos! Novit enim Dominus qui sunt eius,'" said Cameron. "Kill them all. Surely the Lord discerns which ones are his."

"That is right, Mister Kincaid. Your Latin and vision are both spectacular. I find the inscriptions difficult to read in this light."

"We've actually come across these before," said Cameron.

Stratos peered into Cameron's eyes, his expression knowing, "So I've been told."

Cameron's throat slightly tensed. With his best face, he pretended not to have been surprised by the statement. Besides, Stratos must have heard him wrong. Stratos could not possibly guess that Cameron and Pepe once had such daggers in their possession. Stratos could not possibly be aware of how the daggers, worn by the Rex Mundi operatives, came into their possession—by the death of Rex Mundi agents. Perhaps Stratos was aware of the terrorist cult. Maybe Stratos was quite comfortable knowing that these instruments of death were all tokens of a cult. A cult, Cameron and Pepe realized, that went back hundreds of years, as dear Marie had told them before she died.

Stratos did not let the conversation pause. Cunningly, he changed the subject so as not to linger on his statement. "Well," he took the dagger back from Pepe to place back into the special reserved space in the collection. "I do want to welcome you. I want to thank you for saving my son, and insist you share a drink with me in thanks." Stratos turned toward the sidebar across the room. "I of course want to offer my condolences for your sister, Pepe. Dreadful, these animals." He spun around to face them, approaching the bar blindly. "And I do mean animals. I could not begin to tell you the trouble I have had with them in the past." At the bar, he again turned his back to them and began preparing three rock glasses of scotch. "Hijacking, hostages, the disregard for life and property. I understand the two of you have been pursuing her whereabouts." He spun back around, a scotch glass in each hand for the two men. "Here, have a seat."

"You should sit with us," said Cameron.

"Certainly, I intend to."

"Um, that is not what I meant. You see, we have found Christine, or at least finally know where to find her."

"That's fabulous," said Stratos. "We should be toasting." Cameron and Pepe each took a seat on the cushioned leather chairs in the center of the room. Stratos joined them.

"You might not think so in a moment," said Pepe.

"I don't understand."

"You will," said Pepe. He placed the small digital recorder on the display case table between them.

"You see," said Cameron. "We spoke with Abbo and Dada about your relationship with them."

Stratos' brow dropped.

"And we don't really care about that. But there is something else Dada shared with us. Well, you should hear this yourself. Pepe, if you please."

Pepe placed his index finger on the top of the recording device and pressed play.

CHAPTER 60
GSTAAD, SWITZERLAND

After listening to the torture of Ibrahim Dada and the coerced warlord's account of the hijacking of the Kalinihta, subsequent kidnapping, and the claim that responsibility fell on Nikos Stratos, Demetrius Stratos straightened in his chair. He ran his finger around the rim of his scotch glass, sipped, and then relished the alcohol for a moment.

Cameron sensed the cognitive dissonance plainly on Stratos. The inconsistent beliefs in the deceitful spoiled playboy Stratos knew his son to be conflicted with his implicit faith the boy would never be disloyal to his father. Cameron could not fault Stratos for believing the best of his only son. Every parent should be on the side of their child.

"That man would have said anything," said Stratos, affirming the reaction Cameron had predicted.

"You know who the man was on the recording," said Cameron. "You know Ibrahim Dada."

"Of course. I know that man is a scoundrel and despite his title as admiral or general or his diplomatic status. He is not much more than a common thug."

"We know of your dealings with Abbo, and we know Dada was trying to work with you."

281

Stratos raised his hands. "So you know. Business on the high seas is very complex. Since you have obviously come into some information I will tell you that many men do business with these and other unsavory people, small things, unavoidable, necessary evils." His face shrugged. "You have to imagine I run, not one, but rather several fleets of tankers and commodities." Stratos leaned in to the display case between them, resting his elbows on his knees. He set his rock glass on the table and then clasped his hands together. "That is why I find this impossible to believe. The idea my son would stage his own kidnapping in a plot to undermine me, a ridiculous notion. My son is many things, conniving and clever, yes. Disloyal he is not."

"Believe what you will," said Pepe. "We conducted more than one, shall we say, intense interviews. I do not believe these men were wanting to lie."

Stratos smirked at Pepe, "Interviews? A more precise description would be interrogations. Everyone knows tortured men will say anything. Dada was in fear of his life, and rightfully so if I understand correctly, and Abbo, what you did to him, really." Demetrius shook his head. "The local papers reported a high altitude gas accident. Don't forget I financed your endeavor. I know you two were behind the whole thing. Blowing him out the window of the Burj Khalifa." Stratos shook his head again. "That was unnecessary. Abbo was a lecherous, greedy man, yet he did business wisely. He kept his people reigned in and he was good for his word."

"I am sure Abbo was a great man," said Cameron.

Stratos appeared disgusted. He spoke coolly, "I am only saying that Abbo was not merely a thief," he flashed his eyes between them, "or a pirate. He knew how to do business in a way that was mutually beneficial to all persons."

"You call what you do there business?" asked Pepe.

Stratos rolled his eyes. "Business of a sort. I thought you were here to discuss something else."

"We are," said Cameron sensing the blood rising between Pepe and Stratos. "We do not wish to offend. We believe Nikos can help us to find Christine."

In contemplation Stratos wrapped his knuckles against the top of the display case glass in slow repetition, pausing between each tap. Then after a long pause, he congenially spoke again. "I will indulge you because you saved my son, and I understand your concern for the missing girl. Annalisa tells me that when Nikos left Lamu he went directly to Monaco, then sailed our yacht down to Ibiza. Apparently, he plans to stay at our Ibiza estate to do some sailing and clear his head. I will fly the two of you down there to confront Nikos. Then we can settle this once and for all."

"Ibiza, you say?" asked Pepe.

"Annalisa will have my jet prepped. I have a few things to tend to. Someone will be along to sort you so you can freshen up and we will leave in—" Stratos put his finger to his ear as Annalisa had earlier. "Yes, we can leave within the hour. I will meet you at the chopper."

CHAPTER 61
PARIS, FIFTEEN YEARS BEFORE

The bathroom floor was covered with layers of newspaper. Cameron had cleared one of little Moby's messes earlier and already there was another pool in the corner. Christine sat on the edge of the bed gazing down at the small brown ball frolicking at her feet. "He is so cute," she said, "this petit doggy."

Ten million years of evolution coursed through Cameron. He had made Christine happy and countless sparking endorphins issued his biological reward with a sense of elation, a euphoric well-being. The wine and chocolate did not hurt either. In his hand, he held the last of the wine, a half bottle of vin rouge pulled from the top of their short refrigerator. In his other hand, two small fruit glasses were pinched between his fingers. Cameron winked at Christine, put the bottle to his mouth, pulled the cork with his teeth, and then with a huff sent the plug flying across the room.

Christine giggled. She spoke softly, seduction in her eyes, "So gallant."

Cameron filled the two small glasses with a single pour and then offered one to Christine. "I aim to please, mademoiselle."

"Merci, monsieur," said Christine. She sipped, then stopped, overtaken by another giggle.

Cameron leaned forward to give Christine a quick peck. When he placed his mouth upon hers, she hooked an arm around his neck and squeezed, lifting herself from the bed to pull him down. Caught in the embrace, Cameron's balance wavered and he began to sink forward. The further he leaned the more passionately she kissed, melting into him, drawing him to the mattress. Awkwardly contorted, he continued to kiss her until he could lean no further without spilling wine. He shifted his foot to correct himself and lowered her gently back onto the bed, extending his arm up and away to balance the glass in his hand.

Free of her weight, Cameron unlocked the kiss and rubbed his nose against Christine's. "Careful, unless you want a wine shower."

"Would that be so bad?"

Cameron scrunched up one side of his face. "Maybe white wine would be better."

Christine set her glass of wine down on the bedside table, raised her arms up to embrace an invisible shower, and exclaimed, "Bathe me in a shower of champagne?"

"You would like that, would you?"

"Oui," said Christine, her voice cute. "Then you can clean me." She lifted her arms open to him. Cameron had another sip of his wine, set the glass near Christine's, and then settled into her embrace, this time falling with her onto the mattress. She touched her lips softly to his, her mouth open, not a full kiss, a precursor, a tease of what was to come next. She pulled slightly away and then kissed him again, this time with more intensity, more passion, and then the two rolled on their backs. They gazed up at what could have been a field of stars yet was merely plaster, dinged in spots, and yellowed in others. Cameron raised his forearm and Christine coiled hers so that the palms of their hands met and their fingers could clasp. This happened so naturally, in unison, their bodies and minds synchronizing.

Christine's voice was musically dreamy, "Today was perfect. I want you to be with me always."

"That would be nice," said Cameron. He wanted to be calm, truthful, and not let the reality of the short time they had together slip from him. Moments such as these, he thought Christine had tossed reality away, and that concerned him. Not in the sense he thought her irrational, rather he did not want to see her hurt.

Christine continued, "You could stop with the Legion, and then you could come to Paris, to always be here to look after me."

"One day I will," he said. "You know I am under contract."

Christine sighed. "Oui," she said. She rolled onto her side and brought her free arm around to run her fingers across his chest. She continued to softly rake him for a long moment and then, with a tint of intrigue asked him a question.

"Cameron?"

"Yes, Christine?"

"What if something were to happen to me?"

Cameron tilted his head toward hers. "What do you mean, something happen to you?"

Christine raised her brow. She had not actually thought of any one particular thing. "I don't know. What if somebody tried to hurt me, take me away in a grand kidnapping?"

"No one is going to kidnap you."

"What if somebody did? What if they try to steal me and you are not here to protect me? What if you are across the sea with my brother on some mission, doing who knows what?"

Cameron rolled to face Christine. "I promise. If anyone ever tries to take you, I will come to your rescue."

"You promise? You will be mon chevalier?"

"I promise, on my honor," said Cameron, and then he

kissed Christine again, harder than before, embracing her until their passions were satisfied.

CHAPTER 62
IBIZA

The group enjoyed a four-course dinner aboard Stratos' private jet. The meal consisted of salad, fresh Maine lobster, Wagyu steak, and black currant custard, and lasted the flight from Gstaad to Ibiza. No sooner had the dessert plates been collected than the jet prepared to touch down at the Ibiza airport, where two four-door Aston Martin Rapides were waiting. Stratos and his assistant Annalisa drove one, Cameron and Pepe the second. Because of his familiarity with the island, Cameron drove.

Cameron's past visits to Ibiza had not been as a chef. His time on the island had been spent as an agent of the Legion, posing as a civilian. His missions were of the same nature as those in Gstaad. Though not as exclusive as the Swiss enclave, Ibiza was simply another playground for celebrity, wealth, and the unscrupulous.

Tiers of holiday villas appeared to pop out of the ocean side hills surrounding the town of Ibiza, in the same fashion as the chalets that filled the mountainsides of the Bernese Oberland. On Ibiza, the facades peering down to the sea were all glass rather than carved wood, yet they created the same illusion of multi-dwellings peppering the island heights. The glass facades, the same as the wooden, were actually multi-levels of single homes, stealthily attached within the sparse forest and hillside. Hidden as well from the beautiful bay below were the sun decks, infinity pools, and the rear garages that housed high-end sports cars of all makes.

The wealthy occupants residing in the hills far above the crystal blue ocean, predominantly young foreigners, collectively slept until noon, napped late in the day, and then clubbed all night, making the sunrise their second sunset, what those of their ilk tagged as a 'disco sunrise'. The authorities' highly tolerant, blasé attitude toward the illicit behavior of the hill dwellers and Ibiza hippie kids that slept on the beach had earned the small Spanish island the well-deserved moniker, the 'Gomorrah of the Med.'

With the huge help of Annalisa's congenial demeanor and feminine wilds, Stratos had worked to calm the intentions of Cameron and Pepe. Requisitioning them a car from his fleet was part of the effort to build trust. Stratos had Annalisa call the staff ahead of the group's arrival to determine if Nikos was at the compound. Apparently, he was not. So when Cameron drove the Aston Martin into the parking bay, their expectation was that Nikos was already out for the evening. The playboy was surely at a café, preparing to watch the sunset, and would soon be partaking one of the islands famed mega-clubs. Nikos' absence suited Cameron fine. Without games or confrontation, the search for Christine would be easier.

The Stratos Ibiza compound was architecturally similar to the chalet in Gstaad, but at a smaller scale. When Annalisa led Cameron and Pepe into the principal dwelling, the main difference from the Gstaad decor was that the walls were ivory as opposed to the crimson paper they had seen during their small tour of the chalet. The walls were lined with photographs, as the chalet had been, however there were no signs of the antiqued Victorian motif. The décor of the Ibiza villa was youthful, modern, and tropical.

The central room opened to a high ceiling and the rooms of the next level shared the glass walled cerulean blue ocean view from the interior balcony. A tall bright tapestry hung on one side of the room and a large Britto multicolored pop canvas spanned the height of the other. Large fronds shot out of planters near the edge of the room and large puffy brilliant colored pillows covered the three white sofas and floor.

"Feel free to check every part of the house," said Stratos. "Annalisa has shut down security and will open any door that remains locked. I want this to be settled once and for all."

Cameron detected the temper of the Greek man was sneaking in. He deduced that Stratos was sure the villa was empty. Stratos certainly would have had Annalisa ask the staff. "We'll be quick," said Cameron, and to keep Stratos' temper from flaring added, "We appreciate the indulgence."

Already walking toward the white bar on the side of the room, his lip curled, his head nodding, Stratos turned his head back toward the two men. Precisely at that moment, Annalisa entered the room from behind them. She had excused herself to 'freshen up' on their arrival, and had changed into a revealing full bikini top with a flowing white wrap around her waist. When Cameron had first met her at the chalet he had been taken by her stunning beauty, yet her well-endowed proportions had been hidden beneath the slacks and wool sweater.

Annalisa raised her hand toward the staircase as if she were a hostess greeting the two men at a spa resort. "Gentlemen, if you can please follow me, we can begin the tour."

Annalisa had called it a tour, and her description could not have been more precise. The two followed her through every luxurious upstairs room, each with fine furnishings and an oceanic view. They followed through the glass walled suites to the sides of the central room, each with hot tubs and other amenities. Along her tour, Annalisa described the photos on the walls of the hallway and the special aspects of each room, as she had done at the chalet. They returned to the lower level and then toured every room there, and then went through a subterranean passage to the other villas. They toured the fully industrial kitchen equipped to cater hundreds, the large courtyard containing two infinity pools and three spa bathhouses, and then the staff villa, with a private pool and bathhouse that alone could compete with any resort.

For Cameron and Pepe's satisfaction, Annalisa took the time to openly speak with each staff member they came across. For each maid and gardener, she made an introduction and asked if they had seen Mister Nikos and when they each replied yes with an overly warm, pleasing smile that barely masked their individual disgust for the young master, she would ask if he had brought any guest to the villa, to which each of them replied no, or they did not know, or referred another staff member better fitted for ratting out the boss.

When they reached the wine cellar, Annalisa excused herself to get a key from the chef, explaining, "Some of the staff cannot resist temptation."

Alone, Pepe muttered to Cameron, "She knows we are not going to find a sign of Christine here."

Cameron whispered back, careful not to move his lips, due to the camera he was sure had them in focus. "I came to that conclusion the moment we arrived."

"They are nervous, though," said Pepe.

"Yeah, something is up. She may not be here at the villa, yet they certainly don't trust Nikos."

"I picked up on that as well."

Christine, of course, was not in the wine cellar, nor was she in the tree hidden security barracks, the movie theater, on the tennis court, or lastly, in the private rooms of Nikos and his father. These rooms were true examples of the extreme wealth of the Stratos clan. Annalisa was insistent that to visit the inner sanctum of Demetrius Stratos was a privilege granted to very few. Cameron imagined that to be true. There were plenty of other rooms to entertain any trysts the older bachelor may decide to partake, where the voluptuous Annalisa could assist him in other entertaining matters besides business. The study alone, the only darkened room in the compound, showed signs of wealth in every deep detail, from the soft leather paneled walls to the rare Brazilian hardwood desk.

Yet in all of these rooms there was no sign of Pepe's sister. Not even in Nikos' private wing. Cameron and Pepe were a bit perturbed for being granted access to the rooms of highest suspicion last. Granted, as Annalisa led them through each immaculate room, they saw no signs of foul play. Neither of the two suspected any evidence had been hidden or washed away as they were being distracted with a tour of the rest of the compound. These were the last rooms to visit because they were not on the tour map, not part of Annalisa's rote breakdown of each room and element.

Nikos' study is where they found their single clue. Much much simpler than his father's, the study's walls had the same ivory white as every other room, the desk a small wooden table, the shelves vacant of any collection of books. Of interest, though, was the picture-covered wall. Like his father and grandfather's thousand photos covering every bit of hall space in the chalet and villa, and most likely every other estate and home the family owned, these photos were of Nikos with an assortment of people. Yet the people pictured in these photos were no dignitaries or titans of business, all of these pictures were of Nikos and his friends. There was a picture that they had seen before, the one with Alastair by his side; a small brass tab on the frame said 'Kenya.' What drew Cameron and Pepe's interest was another photo. A picture of Nikos and another man, arm in arm, a half naked woman held by the waist on either side, surrounded by the colorful party array of a rave. Etched in the small brass plaque tacked to that frame were the words

'Ibiza, Stratosphere.'

Cameron and Pepe looked at each other knowingly. The Stratosphere was a club of repute where famous deejays flew in to host regular parties. The name had not clicked before.

Pepe tapped the bottom of the picture. "This is a great picture. Where was this taken?"

"Oh, that is Stratosphere, a fabulous club that Nikos co-owns. Very fun, you should try to visit—" she caught herself and stopped.

Pepe appeared jovial, "Stratosphere, a great name for a club. A nice play on words." He lifted his hands, molding some invisible clay. "A nice play on names." Then his tone shifted, "Is that where Nikos will be tonight?"

Annalisa's jaw tightened and her head shifted to the side to help fortify her resolve. She obviously realized she had said too much and that there was no backing away.

This was the time for Cameron to turn on his charm. He smiled subtly, and then with a low confident tone he asked Annalisa, "This club, Stratosphere, we are going to find him there, aren't we?"

Annalisa's eye darted from one side to another, searching for anyone that may be watching, or perhaps come to save her from betraying her employers. Then with obvious reluctance, she matched her eyes to Pepe and then to Cameron, and nodded her head, an affirmative yes.

CHAPTER 63
IBIZA

The taillights of the Aston Martin Rapide in front of them glowed unevenly against the late tangerine sky.

"Your boss doesn't know one of the LEDs is out on the right side," said Cameron. "I bet he won't be pleased."

Annalisa sighed, "I'll have the garage fix the light in the morning."

Pepe shuffled uncomfortably in the backseat. "How much farther do we have?"

"The club is off the main road between Ibiza Town and San Antonio," said Annalisa, "in walking distance to San Rafael."

"Near Amnesia?" asked Cameron. Cameron had one hand on the wheel and the other arm resting on the open window. The warm air of the island breezed into the car and washed over them.

"Stratosphere is between Amnesia and Privilege, Ibiza's other two famous nightclubs," said Annalisa. A subtle undertone to her voice told Cameron that Annalisa was still tense. Cameron had sized up Annalisa. She had not meant to lead them to Nikos, that was obvious, and the slip had her deeply concerned. Cameron also understood that describing the world around her comforted the beautiful Annalisa. He had met many people before that relished in dissociative context. Stratos had given Pepe and Cameron access to Annalisa and if Cameron wanted to turn her to his advantage he first needed to calm her. To get her talking before they reached the club. The club excited Annalisa and she'd lowered her guard. She had mentioned Stratosphere and then had she slipped. Stratosphere was a perfect topic for discussion. "Stratosphere is pretty famous," said Cameron. "I never put the two together, Stratos, Stratosphere. I can't say I'm surprised, yet I'm curious. How did Nikos end up with his own club?"

Cameron had been correct. He glanced into the rearview and caught a wink from Pepe. Annalisa's eyes lit up. "Stratosphere is one of the top three nightclubs on the island. My favorite, then again maybe I'm partial, and the story is a testament to Nikos."

"How's that?" asked Cameron.

"Like his father, if Nikos wants something he finds a way."

"And he wanted a club? That does not sound like such a challenge for the son of a billionaire."

"That's not what Nikos wanted. Since the sixties, the large discothèques of Ibiza flourished as the destination clubs of the Mediterranean. When disco died, techno music took the Mediterranean and the rest of Europe in a wave that would not catch on in the United States for almost another twenty years. The eclectic blend of deejay-led dance music, Balearic house, emerged as the new sound of Ibiza. The mega nightclubs evolved with new names and images for a new clientele, and Nikos Stratos was ripe for the birth of the ecstasy filled rave scene."

"Right," said Cameron. Annalisa had gone into rote brochure mode. "He was a rich playboy even then. I bet he wanted to be a deejay."

"That's right," said Annalisa. He was fascinated with techno. He owned a Roland TR-909 drum machine, and an array of top of the line electronics and turntables to create his own music. He even hosted a couple of nights."

"I get it. Daddy would not let him be a musician. Let me guess, did he threaten to cut off the piggy bank?"

"Not quite, we are Greek, we indulge our children. His father did, of course, frown on the idea of Nikos being a deejay, so they came to an agreement his father would condone. Nikos picked up a premiere nightclub. The venue had been a successful discothèque back to the early seventies, yet had not made the transformation. Then he renamed the place Stratosphere. Like Privilege, the world's largest nightclub, the dance floor is the size of an aircraft hangar with a twenty-five meter high roof. There is also a splendid open-air back patio with a fountain between two swimming pools."

Cameron saw Pepe roll his eyes at Annalisa's rote tour description.

"Sounds more like a testament to Demetrius," said Cameron. "He convinced his son to give up his dream in exchange for a nightclub."

"Just the opposite," said Annalisa. "Nikos convinced his father to let him continue to pursue his hobby and develop the club. The club is successful, and so is Nikos. He has a regular night there as well as nights in London and Vegas."

"I don't keep up with the scene. Still, I don't believe I have ever heard of Deejay Nikos."

"That's because he uses an alias to deejay and wears a costume," said Annalisa. "You must have heard of Deejay Roboto."

Pepe leaned forward, "No, really? He is famous."

"I told you. Like his father and his father before him, Nikos always has what he wants."

CHAPTER 64
STRATOSPHERE, IBIZA

When the Aston Martins reached the Stratosphere nightclub, the last remnants of fuchsia lined the western sky. A large crowd of excited clubgoers hovered outside the main doors. Cameron could hear and feel the deep base thump of the trance music playing inside. Stratos led Cameron to the VIP entrance around the side of the building. A team of valets in tight black t-shirts sprinted to the doors of both cars. When Stratos and Annalisa exited the Aston Martins, two muscular security guards at the door sporting the same tight black tees as the valets snapped to attention and unclipped the velvet rope that gated the entrance. Annalisa was stunning. She wore the wrap she had changed into at the villa with the addition of a sheer white blouse to cover the bikini. Stratos had provided Cameron and Pepe with lighter attire appropriate for the warmer Ibiza evening and the sure to be stifling club interior. Stratos himself wore white linen slacks and shirt and, of course, a thin cravat tied tightly around his neck.

Cameron was beginning to wonder what Stratos was hiding beneath the silk necktie.

Through the threshold, the electronic rhythm of the

dance music washed over the group. The soup of pulsing digital notes thickened, tactile as mist or fog. Flashing multicolor lights synched to the sound system added a physical quality to the electronic tones. The effect was compulsory autonomic acceleration of the heart and lungs. Cameron's nervous system heightened, high on contact with the interior rave dimension. He glanced at Pepe and the two shared a knowing glint.

The private entryway was a velvet-curtained foyer. The main dance floor split out to the right, and to the left, a set of stairs was ghostly shadowed by the bright blinking lights in the cavern above. Stratos led the group the route of the stairs. The first landing of the staircase opened up to a suspended catwalk that stretched along the length of the oversized tunnel to the next set of stairs. Across the stadium-sized dance floor, thousands of club-goers were already gathered, their arms waving together as a collective organism to the increasingly electric trance beat.

Spread throughout the writhing crowd were more than a dozen circular bars, the stainless steel bar tops lined with pyramids of bottled water. One of the bartenders poured a fluid onto a bar top and with a lighter created an instantaneous crescent of fire. This triggered other bartenders to do the same. As Stratos led the group across the catwalk, a cascade of small eruptions of flame burst from the stations across the dance floor. The fountains of flame burning off among the thousand blinking lights reminded Cameron of a chemical facility in full process. He was not far off. The group ascended a metal stairwell. Directly below, in a small sectioned off booth, a shirtless tattooist was inking a young lady's thigh, while next to him another partier reclined back in a barber chair rhythmically rolling her head side to side to the techno beat as a heavily inked bald girl slid an immensely long needle through the upper edge of her belly button.

Another story higher, the stairs opened to a raised platform. An intimate crowd of less than fifty lounged on the sofas, apparently oblivious to anyone not touching them, and a few were involved in some heavy touching. A few people, a bit more coherent, held company near the bar at the wall. A raised silk sheet, glowing peach from behind, lined the end of the platform farthest from the outer dance floor. Cameron imagined the extremes of the touching that was happening behind the privacy veil. The deejay was working some type of voodoo on a raised tier at the end of the platform. Surrounded by an array of small screens and electronic components, the Pied Piper of sorts enchanted, what appeared to Cameron as a mass of protoplasm, with musical mayhem.

Annalisa leaned into Cameron's ear. "He's great, isn't he?"

Cameron could barely hear Annalisa. "Who is he?"

"He calls himself MooreHouse, like more house, get it?"

"Clever," said Cameron.

"During the summer top producers and dance deejays come to the island in between touring and play at Stratosphere. Some of the most famous deejays run their own weekly nights right here. They use Ibiza for presenting new songs."

"Is that so?" asked Cameron, raising his brows.

"You can barely hear me?" asked Annalisa.

Cameron smiled and nodded his head.

Annalisa nodded and gestured for Cameron and Pepe to follow her, and then nodded to Stratos. Stratos returned the nod and headed toward the bar. At the wall past the deejay, Annalisa punched a keypad. The door opened to a small private lounge. The three stepped inside. The lounge was not that much different than a private box at any large stadium, the outer wall a pane of glass overlooking the entirety of Stratosphere. Once inside, Cameron noticed that there were several similar panes surrounding the upper level. The room was furnished with oversized stuffed sofas like those on the outer platform and the necks of champagne protruded from two buckets of ice.

Annalisa closed the door behind them, her voice clear and lowered to a normal level, "Would you be so kind as to pour, Mister Kincaid?"

The noise dissipation of the small lounge had an immediate sobering quality.

Cameron and Pepe each shifted their jaws opened and closed.

"Sorry," said Annalisa. "The room is soundproof," she shirked her shoulders, "also pressurized." Next to the door, Annalisa pressed a button on a small console and the remainder of the music dropped away. Even the incredibly deep thumps of the bass had disappeared.

"That's better," said Annalisa. "Now we can hear ourselves. Should I order something to eat?"

"No," said Pepe. "We should not be here so long."

Annalisa smiled, "Why, of course not. Will you indulge me with champagne, though? I admit I love the bubbles."

Pepe gave Annalisa a gracious smile. "Certainly, where are my manners? Kincaid, let me do the honors." Pepe removed one of the bottles from the ice and began to prepare three glasses.

Annalisa moved to the edge of the sofa. "May we sit, gentlemen?"

"Certainly," said Cameron. "After you."

The lounge was surreal in a way the world outside of the door was not. With the speaker to the sound system adjusted so low, the soundproofing and air system had the effect of sterilizing the environment. When they had first entered the room, Cameron had thought of the huge window as a voyeuristic display into the esoteric world beyond the glass. His perspective was shifting. Sitting with Annalisa on the sofa, he felt, with the long pause silences, that they could be on exhibit.

Cameron's mind raced. Perhaps they were on exhibit. "Will Demetrius be joining us?"

"Shortly, I believe," said Annalisa. She reached for the

champagne Pepe offered and then raised the glass. "I would like to make a toast."

"I will further indulge you," said Pepe. He and Cameron were not aloof to Annalisa stalling and, though they were sympathetic to the beautiful assistant, their mission was not to be subdued.

"To a wonderful evening," said Annalisa.

"Cheers," said Cameron and Pepe.

CHAPTER 65
STRATOSPHERE, IBIZA

Holding her champagne close, Annalisa peered deeply at Cameron. Her eyes burning coals, her hair blown and flowing, Annalisa began to slowly ease the sheer white blouse over her shoulders, in a very nonchalant, purposely seductive action.

Across the table, Pepe's lips tightened. Cameron could almost feel bad for this girl. So obviously put to task.

"Miss Droukos," said Pepe.

Annalisa kept her gaze locked on Cameron. "Annalisa, please," she said.

"Miss Droukos," Pepe repeated. "We have been waiting quite some time. Either Demetrius has found Nikos or he has not. Either way, I believe we are finished here."

"I told you. Mister Stratos will be along shortly. Please share some of this champagne with me. This second bottle is better than the first." Annalisa smiled softly. "You must tell me what it is like to be the famous Dragon Chef." She slid her hand across the cushion in Cameron's direction. "Women love a man that can cook. I bet you get a lot of attention."

Cameron sighed and straightened his back. "I am

sorry. We are here for one reason. I think it's time we speak to Nikos. His father has obviously found him."

Annalisa leaned forward, her breast revealed and almost falling away from the top that held them.

"Unless your next move is to strip off that bikini top and wrap and share your pleasures with us, I assure you, you have run out of game," said Pepe.

Annalisa sat upright. "Mister Laroque—"

"And I should further advise you that in this special instance, even the temptation of fruit such as yours will not restrain our pursuit of Nikos Stratos."

Annalisa went stone-faced for a moment. "Five more minutes, Cameron. Mister Stratos is on his way."

"Why five minutes?" Cameron's eyes flashed wide. "The earpiece. She hears them."

Cameron dashed to the windowpane. Demetrius and Nikos were fleeing to the exit off the edge of the catwalk below.

"We will be leaving now," said Cameron.

"Please, let Mister Stratos handle this and I am sure everything will be fine."

"Get her, the door is locked," said Cameron.

Pepe offered his hand to Annalisa. "May I help you up?"

"Why?" asked Annalisa.

"We need you to get us out of here," said Pepe.

"I suggest you do as he asks, Miss Droukos," said Cameron. "You will be very easy to carry, conscious or unconscious."

Annalisa stood and then finished her champagne in one drink. "They are not going to let you leave."

Cameron flashed his eyes up to Pepe. "I believe we can convince them."

Pepe reached for Annalisa's arm. She defiantly jerked away and went to the console. She tapped a short code. "Stay and there is no trouble."

"I find that is seldom the case," said Cameron. "Stand

back."

At the first crack of the door, the heavy trance beat bass flooded the room. The sense of urgency, the adrenalin, the force that was pushing Cameron, accelerated in intensity. He pulled the door in wide. The light of the lounge must have caught the peripheral of the deejay. Deejay MooreHouse shifted his gaze from his console to Cameron. The deejay held a sunglass stare that looked into and through Cameron, and then with a nod, slid a fader on one of his boards, leveling up a new rapid mix. Cameron returned the nod, unsure what prompted the deejay.

Instantly, Cameron had an answer.

A muscle bound Black Tee, locked onto Cameron, emerged from a dark shadow across the platform. Not to be too obvious to the approaching thug, Cameron relaxed and went into a subtle relaxed Taekwondo attention stance, the Charyeot stance. His body already in an upright standing position, his legs side by side, heels touching, toes slightly apart, Cameron dropped his hands parallel to his body and relaxed, proper to his training. To the arrogant Black Tee, Cameron would appear to be standing in the door waiting unprepared for a confrontation. Cameron was waiting, yet very prepared. Already ultra focused, the techno added a hypersensitivity. Cameron saw a slight acknowledgement in the approaching Black Tee's eyes, not toward Cameron, but to someone to the side of the door. When the second Black Tee spun into the doorframe, Cameron was expecting him. This Tee, a crew cut blonde, held up his flat hand in front of Cameron in a signal that the group should not move. Then in an action of brawn and inexperience the massive Tee smirked at Cameron and made the brutal mistake of shoving his meaty hand forward. The ape must have only seen a blur as Cameron slid to the side, clutched the man lightly by his wrist, and with little effort, used the man's own momentum to send him flying into the lounge. As he flew by Pepe, he received a solid elbow to the base of his skull that sent him crashing to the floor.

Upon seen his cohort disappear behind Cameron, the first Black Tee went rooster, his chest filling with rage and emotion, a critical flaw. The Black Tee raised his arms, his delts, pects, and lats pumped full. Cameron was sure steroids had dumbed down this giant. When the grizzly of a man was close, Cameron surprised the man with a quick Gunnun Sogi stance, a solid step forward followed through with a full on thrust to the Black Tee's breadbasket. The Black Tee's eyes screamed wide and his knees buckled. The tribal pulse of the music bore into Cameron's center. Another Black Tee thundered toward Cameron.

Cameron and Pepe exited the lounge. Pepe met the Black Tee first.

This third Black Tee was thinner, compact, and more agile than the first two. What he lacked in mass, he made up for in skill. Seeing Cameron's style of maneuver, the Tee approached in a Taekwondo fighting stance, rattled off two strikes that Pepe easily repelled and then fluidly went into a back-L stance, one foot on the ground, the other a flying kick toward Pepe's head. The blow may have been fatal had the man not failed at rule number one, know your audience. Pepe of course practiced Taekwondo. Pepe practiced Kung Fu. Pepe practiced Karate. Pepe was a master at Judo. Pepe effortlessly dodged the nimble assailant, his rotund upper body gyrating on his lowered knees, his head slipping back out of the way, his forearm sliding up to gently assist the younger man's leg away. Well trained, the Black Tee used Pepe's assist to thrust him into a spin and as his body curled around, raising his other leg to smash Pepe's ribs, forcing him to the wall. Pepe grimaced, the air crushed from his lungs. He dropped his arm over the young Black Tee's leg and rolled himself hard forward against the wall, splitting the limb out sideways away from the knee, the action and young man's anguish silent beneath the electronic beat, ever increasing to a mind blowing rate.

Everyone else on the platform seemed oblivious to what had happened. No one left for the other room or even sat up. No one appeared to notice, no one except for Annalisa. Outside the entrance to the lounge, Annalisa had lost expression.

"C'mon!" screamed Cameron.

Annalisa did not hear Cameron. He seized her arm, alerting her back from wherever she had checked out to. She turned her still vacant face toward him, and a glint of recognition filled her eyes. Cameron tilted his head toward Pepe and the stairwell and in a normal voice said, "Let's go." He was sure that beneath the volume of the pulsing unearthly music, she could not hear him.

Annalisa nodded and then began to move toward the exit.

CHAPTER 66
STRATOSPHERE, IBIZA

As more of a matter of training than formal protocol, Cameron remained by the door while Pepe led Annalisa down the metal stairs to the catwalk. He mentally divided the VIP level into quadrants and then scanned them one by one in search of anyone that was not subdued by a drug heavy trance or that appeared to be taking too much interest in him. Both he and Pepe had seen cameras hidden among the overhead lights. Regardless of whether the occupants of the VIP level had paid attention to their tussle with security, in a facility this size, someone was watching. Reinforcements were on the way. Confident the level was clear, Cameron twisted, clutched the rails of the stairwell, and slid down. They had almost crossed the catwalk when a Black Tee appeared from the exit, took two strides, and then nimbly sprung forward into a front facing stance. Pepe fluidly dropped into a shallow standing squat, an agile position giving him the flexibility to launch both attacks and defences against the formidable Tee.

The open catwalk was a maelstrom of electronic pulses, bass beats, and a sublime and ethereal swooning female chorus.

Panicked by the appearance of the Black Tee at the exit, Annalisa spun back toward Cameron. Her eyes flashed in horror, alerting him. He ducked and twisted short of an attack from a second Black Tee that had managed to elude him on the VIP platform and shadow them down.

Electric dance music was not something Cameron ever listened to, yet fighting was like dancing, and he was exhilarated.

The bass beat was pounding at a crushing speed. Bright flashes of brilliant color punctuated lightning fast punches. Cameron kept Annalisa in his peripheral. She appeared disoriented, stunned by the rapid strikes and blows, her head switching from one side to the other. Pepe moved uncomfortably close and she almost caught an elbow. She shuffled toward Cameron to a near miss as a foot flew past her face. She sidestepped up and down the catwalk, dodging feet, elbows, and open hands. There was never a need for her concern. Neither Pepe nor Cameron broke a sweat or an expression. The young Black Tees were fluid mechanized warriors. Every move made, whether by Cameron, Pepe, or the two agile security men, was cool and flowing, and occurring at a rate that, especially with the deep trance beat, was incredibly rapid, and remarkably predictable. The maneuvers were textbook, the only moves to make. As was the maneuver that made Annalisa gasp, when in unison, Cameron and Pepe positioned themselves on the far sides of the catwalk fight and their opponents close to her.

Between punches, Cameron caught Annalisa's eyes go wide and bright, and he shot her a devious smile. If she guessed the move was choreographed, she would have been right. Cameron and Pepe had practiced the move for staged bar brawls and the next part was Cameron's favorite. The two gave each other a nod when they were ready, and then each thrust a body blow to their opponent, penetrating to the true solar plexus, the dense cluster of nerve cells located behind the stomach, right below the diaphragm. The blow was intended to cause great pain, knock the wind out of the Black Tees, and most important, the simultaneous action was designed to shove the Tees into each other. The modification was that Annalisa was between them. The move worked. For a split second, the Black Tees' attention was drawn away from their opponents to the overwhelming pain in their gut, and to Annalisa between them. In that opportune slice of time, when the Tees turned toward her, Cameron and Pepe squeezed each by the back of the head, seized them by the crotch, and then flung the Tees airborne over the side of the catwalk.

In that sudden instant, as the two Black Tees arced high above the crowd, the thunderous backbeat that had shaken the building in a constant quake abruptly stopped. Silence, an unworldly hush, descended over the crowd, and then, echoing through the cavernous building in a soft repetitive whisper, "All for you, all for you, all for you—"

Cameron peered out into the hall, into the writhing mass gone calm, and then he looked up at Deejay MooreHouse. Deejay MooreHouse, way too cool in his sunglasses and heavy headphones, was smiling widely at Cameron. The deejay nodded his head, extended his arm, and then pointed his index finger straight to Cameron. "All for you, all for you, all for you—" Cameron smiled up to the deejay and shot his finger back, and then Deejay MooreHouse, in a dramatic motion, swung his arm up and around to jab down on the soundboard. The maelstrom of sound returned tenfold and the crowd of faithful thousands rallied. Deejay MooreHouse nodded at Cameron again, and Cameron returned the gesture.

CHAPTER 67
STRATOSPHERE, IBIZA

The two muscle bound Black Tees waiting at the valet stand were no surprise to Cameron. The calm of the fresh evening air, or maybe the reality shift of stepping out of the club, had subdued him. Cameron felt no need to launch into another confrontation.

Cameron smiled, sucked in a breath, and then said, "Gentlemen, the Aston Martin Rapide please."

The two men appeared uneasy. Their focus slipped past Cameron to Annalisa. "Miss Droukos," one of them said, "we have strict instructions from Mister Stratos that the gentlemen that came with you are to remain here until he returns."

Stepping forward Annalisa sighed, "I am sure you do. However, we are ready to go, so..." She shrugged her brows and reached for the velvet rope.

The second Black Tee found some confidence and moved to block Annalisa. "I'm sorry, Miss Droukos. Mister Stratos was very—" He paused searching for a word.

"Explicit?" offered Annalisa.

"Yes, explicit." He scowled, then said, "You need to go back in the club now."

Pepe put himself between the Black Tee and Annalisa to undo the velvet rope himself. His voice was stern, "I don't think that is going to happen."

The brave Black Tee threw his hand flat up against Pepe's chest and said, "I believe that's exactly what is going to happen."

Pepe slowly tilted his head up from the rope to meet the bouncer eye to eye with a look that let the Black Tee know he had made a mistake.

Annalisa scrunched her nose. Cameron winced an eye near closed, the image of a jet about to collide with a train and knowing that nothing could stop what was about to happen.

The velvet rope was no longer an issue as the bold Black Tee tore the hardware away when Pepe threw him into the driveway. The other bodyguard responded out of a sense of loyalty to his friend and duty to his job, yet only half heartedly, as he did not actually strike a punch at Cameron. He raised his fist into a boxing stance a safe distance away so he would still appear in play. The tossed down Black Tee began to stand. Pepe had taken two strides toward him when, from inside the nightclub, two more Black Tee security guards appeared. These two upped the game, as they each had Taser sticks in hand.

Pepe shook his head. "Really?" Then from the back of his waist he produced his Beretta M9, triggering Cameron to draw his Ruger.

The four Black Tees looked at each other and then the bold one said, "You cannot shoot all of us."

"I cannot believe you just said that," said Cameron.

The four Black Tees shared a glance, and then, bending forward, began to move toward Cameron and Pepe.

Annalisa screamed, "Stop! Stop!"

Everyone looked at Annalisa. They did stop. Right where they stood.

Annalisa spread her hands out, pressing them to the air, and spoke calmly at first, her voice rising as she went on,

"Okay, this is enough. These two men are obviously trained killers. Unless you all want to die, I suggest you prepare the car, and I will smooth things over with Mister Stratos."

The first bold Black Tee eyed Cameron and Pepe thoroughly, then asked, "Trained killers, Miss Droukos?"

Cameron flashed his brow.

"Get the car!" said Annalisa.

"Yes, right now," said the jolted Black Tee. "I'll get the car." He scurried toward the Aston Martin while the other three Black Tees began cleaning up the pieces of their broken velvet rope.

CHAPTER 68
IBIZA

The bi-xenon headlamps sprayed the road to Ibiza Town bright blue, far beyond the flying Aston Martin Rapide.

Pepe tapped his knuckles against the back window. "Can't you make this car go any faster?"

"It's an illusion," said Cameron. "We're moving fine."

"Huh?"

"We're almost to Ibiza Town."

Pepe curled his lip. He pushed his forehead against the glass and peered up through the darkness into the starry sky. In a low voice, he muttered, "Rich or not, who buys an Aston Martin with an automatic transmission."

Cameron flashed his eyes briefly from the road to the rearview, then dropped them back again. "A stick wouldn't move us any faster. Besides, they only make this model in automatic."

Annalisa reached for the stereo. "Mister Stratos is partial to Aston Martins. A close friend once owned the company."

Cameron placed his hand on Annalisa's. "Please, enough music for a little while."

Annalisa pulled her hand back to her lap. Cameron considered her situation. The situation Nikos and his father had put her in.

"Hey," said Cameron. "I thought you told us the garage in Gstaad was full of Lamborghinis and Ferraris. Are you telling me he has close friends in every one of those companies?"

Annalisa lowered her head, a bit embarrassed, and grinned. "You wouldn't believe it but, yes," she raised her head and looked at Cameron, "he does."

"In every one?" said Cameron.

"In every one," said Annalisa. Then they both began to laugh.

Annalisa sighed. "I guess it all sounds kind of ridiculous."

"He is who he is," said Cameron. He let the Aston Martin decelerate. On the road ahead of them, an unmoving line of red taillights trailed toward the glow of Ibiza Town on the near horizon.

"Is there always this much traffic on this little island?" asked Cameron.

Annalisa lifted her head in an attempt to see up and around the cars in queue ahead of them. "After sunset people are finding their way to dinner I guess."

Cameron rested his forearm on the steering wheel. They would have to wait for traffic to begin to move. With the tips of his fingers, he began to tap the top edge of the dashboard, a nervous habit that went with his mind wandering to where he may find Nikos, to where he may find Christine, because with one, would be the other.

Cameron tilted his head to the side and absently peered ahead to the roundabout. "There they are," he said.

"Where?" asked Annalisa. "Where do you see them? How do you know it's them?"

"Up there in the roundabout. The LED in the taillight is out. They didn't get far ahead of us."

Annalisa craned her head closer to Cameron for a clear

view of the roundabout. "I don't see them."

Cameron shifted his fingers on the dashboard to the left. "They took that turnoff. They're not going to the house or airport."

Pepe put his hands on either side of Annalisa's seat and pulled himself forward. "Where are they going, Miss Droukos?"

Annalisa's eyes, fresh a mere moment ago, were dark and tired. Cameron winked at Annalisa, triggering a frail smile in return. "I'd love to drive around all night, but we do need to help a friend."

This time Annalisa was quick to respond, "That turnoff leads to the port. They are going to Mister Stratos' sailing yacht."

"Of course," said Pepe, "that's why there were no signs of Christine. Nikos is hiding her on the yacht."

Cameron gripped the steering wheel and switched his head side to side. Driving forward to maneuver around the queue of cars was not an option. To the right was an iron fence and a boundary of boulders, and to the left was a meter high concrete median. Cameron and Pepe needed to uncomfortably bide their time until they made their way to the roundabout. After an eternal five minutes, they were clear of the median barrier on the left. Cameron gunned the accelerator and the Aston bounced up onto the curb. Dirt, dust, and stones flew up behind the car as Cameron tore through the loose dry sandy soil and shrubbery of the median and into the opposing lane. Circumventing the frozen traffic that had held them, he aimed the Aston toward the roundabout, ignoring any vehicles in his way. A small VW station wagon turned off the roundabout and into the lane, head on with the accelerating Aston. The horn of the oncoming Volkswagen blared as the vehicle swerved to miss the Aston Martin, then stopped abruptly as the car slammed up against an olive tree. Having barely missed crashing into the VW, the Aston entered the roundabout against traffic. The surprise chance of near collision sent the oncoming barrage of brilliant lights veering into rapidly deviating directions.

The Aston Martin had been still, a whirlwind, corrected, and then was again travelling smoothly. Cameron tweaked the rearview mirror to see if traffic in the roundabout was correcting as well. "You can relax now," he said.

"I'm not sure I can," said Annalisa. Her clawed hands were each clutching a part of the interior dearly, one hand the dash, the other the door.

"Which way now?"

"Um, turn right at the next roundabout then go all the way to the end. Mister Stratos keeps the yacht moored in Talamanca Bay."

The cadmium yellow lights that illuminated the white stucco buildings blanketing the hillside Ibiza Town, appeared an anachronism to the flowing headlights that weaved in and out of view. The harbor's forests of masts towering the mammoth powerboats produced the same sense of mixed century.

Cameron slowed as he approached the next roundabout that led down toward the port. The other Aston Martin was far ahead of them, yet in view, skirting the rows of the docked sailboats and cruisers populating the port. Cameron watched Stratos enter the far roundabout and then exit the spoke that led to the second harbor, Talamanca Bay. When Stratos had cleared his view, Cameron killed the lights of the Aston so he could shorten the distance to his quarry in stealth. The plan was good because when Cameron entered the far roundabout, he saw Demetrius and Nikos exiting their sports car at the shoreline parking area, mere meters away. Barely above an idle, the Aston loomed from the spoke onto the side street. The Aston came to rest curbside under the shadow of a tree. Hidden in the darkness, Cameron killed the engine and then decided to slip the key fob into his pocket.

The well-lit parking area, where Demetrius and Nikos

had left their Aston, was intended for those with boats moored out in the bay. From the shadows, Cameron watched the two men walk the length of a long concrete dock past a series of tethered dinghies. Nikos climbed into one of the dinghies near the end of the long dock, followed by his father. Demetrius untied the line and then pushed the boat away from the dock. Cameron watched Nikos tug a few times on the four stroke motor cable. With a purr, the dinghy veered out of the pool of light cast from the dock and into the bay.

A short way out, a number of masts sprouted from the surface of Talamanca Bay. Mooring lines, strung with lamps, appeared to rest on the reflecting amber sheets that shot across the still water from the shoreline hotels.

"Which one?" asked Pepe. His elbow supported him on the center console as he watched the two Greek men motor away.

"Excuse me?" asked Annalisa.

"Which sailboat? They are heading out to one of those boats," said Pepe. "I am guessing one of those three larger yachts."

"The smaller one on the side," said Annalisa.

"I would have guessed one of the larger ones," said Pepe.

"If you think thirty-eight meters is small. Anyway, the size is not what makes the yacht special. The Azulejo is over one hundred years old. Mister Stratos took great pride in restoring and racing the luxury yacht. His son shares the..." Annalisa hesitated, "affection."

Cameron smirked, "Another one of a kind."

"Hmm," said Annalisa.

"Well," said Pepe. "Demetrius and his family did not get to where they are without flaunting a little."

"I told you," said Annalisa. "The Stratos men have the means to obtain what they want, by purchase, or other... Well, they have the means."

"To take what they want," said Cameron

"I am sure they do," said Pepe. "Rather Machiavellian."

"To take what you want?" asked Annalisa.

"Not that," said Pepe. "I am referring to the power a one of a kind item brings to those like Stratos that wish to attain and maintain power."

"How so?"

"There is more to the acquisition of particular items. A key to creating and maintaining power is to create compelling spectacles, full of symbols that heighten presence. Machiavelli said people are always impressed by the superficial appearance of things."

"I may disagree that a century old luxury yacht is superficial."

"Does owning the boat make a difference in the man?"

"Fascinating, Mister Laroque," said Annalisa.

"Yes, fascinating," said Pepe. "There is another fascinating key to maintaining position and power that you appear to know so well."

"What is that?"

"Pose as a friend, work as spy."

"I'm sorry?"

Cameron smiled, "I do believe Stratos is genius for sending you in. You are top notch, short of weapons training. Where did you study?"

"Cambridge, then Harvard Law."

"Huh," Cameron glanced over at Annalisa, her naked flesh beneath the sheer blouse glistening bright in the dim interior of the car. "Brains and beauty," he said. "A slam dunk really."

"I'm not sure I follow," said Annalisa.

"Sure you do," said Cameron.

Annalisa hung her head down for a moment and then, in a soft tone said, "Foreknowledge cannot be elicited from ghosts and spirits, it cannot be inferred from comparison of previous events, or from the calculations of the heavens, but must be obtained from people who have knowledge of the enemy's situation."

"Sun-tzu," said Cameron. "He was right, tough to shoot ducks blindfolded."

Pepe held his hand out between them. "The earpiece please."

CHAPTER 69
TALAMANCA BAY, IBIZA

Even without the motor, the dinghy swiftly glided across the smooth surface of Talamanca Bay. From the dock, the bay had appeared mostly brilliant with the reflection from the lights of the beach hotels and mired with shadow where the light was absent. Out in the midst of the harbor, the above light of hillside Ibiza Town, and the myriad of stars that peppered the sky, made the interior of the small craft as well lit as the shore.

The Azulejo, like the other yachts near her, was lit by the strings of lamps along her moorings and up her masts. Cameron and Pepe saw two other dinghies tied to her stern. One of the dinghies had been brought out to the luxury sailing yacht by Demetrius and Nikos ahead of Cameron and Pepe, the other they surmised may belong to Azulejo. Perhaps Nikos had assigned someone with the task of caring for his captive. The task of feeding and securing Christine, ensuring she not leave the yacht, taking measures she remained below.

Men bickering, peaked with a few hollers, carried across the surface of the water.

Cameron's mind wandered to what he and Pepe would

find inside the cabin. His stomach tightened.

The end of the dinghy's towline was looped and ready. Pepe snagged a cleat at the stern. Cameron palmed some resistance to the warm hull as Pepe softly pulled the small craft tight to the yacht. No one was on deck. Light escaped from the open cabin.

The occupants of the yacht no longer quarreled loudly. The discussion ensued, muffled below within the hull.

Weapons drawn, Pepe and Cameron eased themselves onto the deck of the Azulejo.

Hunched over and incredibly nimble for the added girth of his age, Pepe scurried toward the foredeck hatch, the most likely place to find his sister. Cameron remained aft and waited until his partner was in position. From around the mast he could see Pepe lift the forward hatch.

His head focused below deck, Pepe threw Cameron a hand signal to signify he thought the forward cabin was clear. That was good and bad. The signal also meant Pepe did not see Christine. Then Pepe slipped into the yacht.

Huddling next to the main cabin door, Cameron began a slow count to five to allow Pepe to work his way aft. Though the forward cabin may be empty, Cameron was certain that at least Demetrius and Nikos were beyond the open hatch in front of him. There was also someone else with them. Cameron was close enough to make out the discussion. Someone was speaking with a British accent.

An accent Cameron immediately recognized. He knew the owner of the third dinghy well.

On the count of five, Ruger in hand, Cameron swung around and into the main cabin. Pepe pushed open the opposite door. Between Cameron and Pepe was Demetrius and Nikos. Signaled by the earpiece Demetrius took their entry in stride, while Nikos, having seen the two men kill firsthand, twitched his head uncomfortably side to side. On the side berth, in front of the Greeks, half awake, drugged, Pepe's sister Christine. Sitting on the berth next to Christine, one leg casually crossed over the other, his arm protectively wrapped around her, and his Walther PPK pointed at the father and son, was the yellow haired Alastair Main.

CHAPTER 70
TALAMANCA BAY, IBIZA

That Pepe had not shot every breathing being upon entering the cabin, besides Cameron and Christine, was a marvel. Cameron had his Ruger drawn in the general direction of father and son. Pepe had his Beretta raised to Nikos' head. Key to the two of them was that Alastair had his PPK pointed at the mogul and his scion, though neither Cameron or Pepe wanted to decipher Alastair's reason or intent. Unwanted doubt eased its way into their heads, memories of a past life flooding them with confusion. Not merely any other man, Alastair Main was brother-in-arms to Cameron and Pepe, more than that, a real brother, as tight as blood. The man was a Green Dragon of the highest honor. For an unfathomable number of missions Alastair, an unquestionable shot with camera or rifle, had been the unseen back up, hidden in a van or high on a perch. Alastair had saved Cameron's life on countless missions.

Neither Demetrius nor Nikos immediately spoke. Neither appeared dumbfounded, though Cameron calculated a safe bet would be that the two were not accustomed to having guns pointed at them, let alone three.

Cameron opted to size up what he and Pepe had

walked into. They were leaving with Christine in a matter of minutes regardless, and if Pepe lost patience and began to drop wealthy Greeks, well, that would have to happen. Cameron smirked in the most devious fashion. "Good evening, gentlemen," he said. "Sorry we were late. Did we miss anything?"

Pepe pressed his Beretta to Nikos temple. "We must be missing something."

"I had planned on having this wrapped up before you arrived," said Alastair. "Then again, I expected you a bit sooner, so I suppose the delay is mine."

A proper response from Alastair, a good sign.

Pepe grunted, "Cameron has spent too much time with Americans, always late."

Cameron whimsically raised a brow. "We were detained."

Apparently made confident by the banter, Demetrius spoke up, "And where is my lovely assistant?"

Pepe chuckled, "Miss Droukos is in the trunk of the Aston Martin."

"She's safe," said Cameron. "Pillow, blanket. We didn't want any interruptions, you understand."

Demetrius nodded his head, and then said, "I understand."

"I heard part of a..." Cameron paused flashing his eyes between Nikos and Alastair, "*discussion* when we arrived. Do continue."

Alastair raised his chin. "Mister Stratos was just asking Nikos to explain himself."

"Yes, gentleman," said Demetrius. He pressed his hands down into the air to express his case. "I assure you that I do not condone whatever has led to Miss Laroque residing on this yacht in—" he hesitated, "whatever condition she is in." He shifted his attention to Nikos. "Can you please explain to everyone what is going on."

Pepe pulled the Berretta a small bit away from Nikos' temple and then jabbed the barrel back against him with enough force to cause the playboy to shuffle. "Yes, please Nikos," said Pepe. "Explain to everyone what is going on."

Demetrius' eyes flared contemptuously at Pepe.

A spoiled man-child always told yes, and never maliciously assaulted, Nikos cheeks flushed at Pepe's blunt strike to his temple. His contempt, however, appeared to be directed at his father. Nikos acknowledged Pepe, his mouth tight across his face, leered at his father, and then he began to lash out. Tossing away the feint persona of the playful jetsetter, his tone became defiant and full of disgust, "You never believed I could set up my own deals. I wanted to show you I could."

Demetrius shook his head. "What are you talking about?" he asked. "That thug Dada had several contracts with me. He has done work for me and everyone else. You merely tried to broker a contract that was already set with Abbo."

"I wanted something more than that." Nikos' lip curled to a snarl. "Everything is you, you, you. I wanted to set up a future for myself. My empire."

"That is ridiculous." Demetrius held up a finger. "One day, everything that is mine will become yours."

Nikos raised his voice, "No. I wanted something that was mine. I found out from Feizel the deal you had with the National Volunteer Coast Guard. He bragged about the deal. For five euros a ton, his father allowed you to dump millions of tons of hazardous waste into Somali water. The fool thought his father was a genius. I know better. You charge one thousand euros a ton across Europe, pay the fool a fraction, and then pocket the difference. I made a better deal with Ibrahim Dada."

Demetrius frowned, "You found another fool."

Nikos scowled, "I figured if I could take Abbo out of the mix and get Dada the deal, he would cut me in, and I was right. We agreed he would charge ten euros a ton and give me three. He was happy to make the deal. He already had almost all of the arranged hijacking contracts. He was already going after control of Abbo's gun trade in Dubai, and with control of the waste and fisheries, he would have everything."

"You're heir to a billionaire," said Cameron. "Why bother for a few million euros?"

Alastair frowned, "All of this trouble because of daddy issues."

Pepe shook his head, "He wanted to prove he could undermine the old man."

Demetrius gazed at Nikos in disbelief. "You are my son," he said. "Why would you do this?"

"To show you I could," said Nikos. "Hijacking the Kalinihta was easy to pin on Abbo. Feizel was on board from the start. I convinced him we were the new generation, the next regime. He ate that up."

"You are the next generation," said Demetrius.

"Yes, but like me, Feizel did not want to wait for his father to die to take his turn. He wanted to show his father that he was capable of doing more in their clan. Dada provided the men to take the Kalinihta, and the Somali Marines had taken the compound north of Kismayu from the Merca Group, close enough to call the place Abbo's. Feizel loved the plan. My old buddy Feizel was partying with me all the way from the Seychelles to the compound. Dada even supplied the additional explosives to level the place when we left. Bit overkill, I admit. I thought the over the top explosions would be the give away."

Cameron was puzzled. "Feizel had a gun pointed at you."

"Yes, he thought that was part of the plan, and well, it was. I put an unloaded gun in his hands and told him we would be safe if he pointed it at me," said Nikos. "He was so high he would have done whatever I told him."

Pepe stared stone-faced at Nikos, and then said, "He kept waving the gun back and forth."

"My .50 caliber Desert Eagle is gold-plated, very heavy, and I don't think he'd ever held a gun before," said Nikos.

"He did not even know the thing was Israeli or he probably would not have touched it. The only part of my plan that was missing was how to safely get myself out of there without anyone finding too much out." Nikos leered at his father. "Your people may have been too thorough."

Alastair shook his head. "And that's where I came in."

Nikos nodded at Alastair. "Alastair had been my safari guide in Kenya, and I had gotten to know him. I knew he had once been a commando. I invited him to ski in Gstaad where he blended right in. Did you fellows know your friend here is descended from the peerage? His real name is not even Main, that's his middle name. His real name is Alastair Main Bulteel-Boyd." Nikos winked at Alastair. "You didn't think I knew. Bulteel-Boyd in the SAS before the GCP and then off the radar for a while. I did a background check, of course. That's how I found out we both knew Christine and then, more importantly." Nikos tilted his head back toward Pepe. "I accidently make the connection of how he knew Christine; he saw a photo of me with my arm around her, and recognized her right away. I remember he told me that if anything ever happened to Christine, there would be a string of commandos at the door." Nikos held his hands up in the air. "And then like magic, everything came together. And he was right, you two flew into the rescue with no questions asked."

Pepe swung his Berretta over toward Alastair's face. His already red eyes glazing, "You did this for money."

Alastair held his hand up in defense toward Pepe. "Whoa! Whoa! He played me the same as you. I thought we would find her in Dubai. When Abbo mentioned Dada I suspected a double-cross and tracked Nikos here."

Demetrius grabbed his son's shoulder. "Why do you have the girl?" he asked.

"At the compound, everything was falling into place. Dada's man Tijon, the bald giant, had shown me the exhilaration of pain when I let him beat me. The adrenalin mixed with the cocaine Feizel and I did back at the

327

compound helped me see my—" Nikos pursed his lips, "—invincibility. I knew I could finally begin to make things really happen, to shape things the way I wanted them to be. I had manipulated you, Abbo, Dada, Feizel, Alastair, everybody. I never felt so in control with so much power, a puppet master. I told Christine that soon I was going to be making changes when we were free–she of course believed we were prisoners. Anyway, I told her I was going to change my life and I wanted her with me, by my side." Nikos tossed his hands in the air. "She laughed at me, can you believe that? At me? She told me I had been doing too many drugs with Feizel. So I took her."

"So you took her?" asked Pepe.

"To teach her a lesson. To show her I could own her like anything else. I don't know. I did not think everything through. I flew her to the boat in Monaco and have kept her out of it until I could figure everything out."

"What is she on?" asked Pepe.

"Only tranquilizers, nothing more. I figured once she woke up and realized she had to stay with me, everything would work out."

CHAPTER 71
TALAMANCA BAY, IBIZA

Talamanca Bay was far cooler by comparison to the inland climes of Ibiza. With six adults occupying the Azulejo's main cabin, the small space was becoming quite warm. The fury of Demetrius Stratos and Pepe Laroque was increasing the temperature of the cabin several degrees. Both men were angry with Nikos, each for their own reason, yet the nature was the same. Nikos was disloyal and had betrayed the trust of those around him. Demetrius was angered by his son's disloyalty to him and Pepe was angered by Nikos' betrayal to Christine. Nikos was separated from reality, delusional. An heir to thousands of millions, he had created a deception within deceptions to suit unnecessary petty needs, manipulating some and sacrificing others indiscriminately.

Demetrius took in a deep nasal breath. "Take her out of here," he said to the three gunmen. "This needs to end now." He shifted his conversation between the three former Legionnaires. Each of them still held a weapon, all aimed in his general direction. "I did not want to believe you." He pressed his lips tightly together. "I have already set aside an account for you…" he paused, "for your

329

trouble." Demetrius flashed his eyes toward Christine, half conscious on Alastair's shoulder. "There is an exceptional amount set aside for Miss Laroque."

Cameron did not take Demetrius' statements as an offer to lower his weapon, nor did Alastair or Pepe. The tone in which the Greek spoke was not at all convincing. The three knew better.

To confirm Cameron's foreshadowing, Demetrius turned to him, and then slipped his hand under the bottom of his linen shirt. Cameron extended his neck and slightly raised his Ruger.

"Relax," said Demetrius. From the waist of his linen pants Demetrius retrieved an item familiar to Cameron. He held the piece of metal harmlessly across his open palm. Cameron's eyes went wide as did Pepe's. "Back in Gstaad you were admiring my collection," said Demetrius. "I know you know what this is."

Alastair craned his neck. "What do you have?" he asked. "A knife?"

"A dagger," said Pepe.

Cameron frowned, "A Rex Mundi dagger to be more specific."

"What is a Rex Mundi dagger?" asked Alastair. "May I have a look?"

Cameron glanced at Alastair, then back into the eyes of Demetrius. "Rex Mundi, King of the World," said Cameron.

"King of the what?" asked Alastair.

Cameron's brow furrowed. "A terrorist group Pepe and I stumbled upon up in Canada."

Pepe added, "More like a secret cult. They carry these daggers. Cameron and I have quite a collection."

Cameron stepped back from the Greek. "The Rex Mundi operatives we encountered were soldiers. The person that told us about the Rex Mundi implied the people running the show were quite well off."

Demetrius smiled and nodded. "Your friend was quite

correct," he said. "Then again, she is well versed in our ways."

Cameron noted the word 'is' and that meant that the Rex Mundi had never tracked down Nicole, and that they were unaware of what had happened to Marie. They were unaware that Marie had died in the cabin on Lake Ontario, a victim of the Rex Mundi's pursuit. To realize that Demetrius Stratos was part of the twisted clandestine organization that had relentlessly pursued him and the two innocent women of faith he had escorted from New York to Canada, wretched his stomach.

As if looking into Cameron's mind, Demetrius said, "The cell put into action was very sloppy." Demetrius shifted his body back toward the center of the cabin and at the same time, he twirled the dagger from his palm, toward his other hand, so that an index finger was on each end, and then he began to playfully roll the knife in concentric circles, appearing to amuse himself while he spoke. "Ironic that I now owe you a total of three counts of gratitude, Mister Kincaid."

"Yes, ironic," said Cameron.

"You saved my son." Demetrius flashed his eyes at Nikos, then back to his dagger. "Well, you and I both *thought* you saved him. Just the same. And you alerted me to this, shall we say, situation. The greatest thanks I bear is for the extermination of that cockroach Dada." He locked his eyes onto Pepe. "More accordingly, I should thank you."

In a challenge to himself, Demetrius began to spin the dagger more rapidly.

"Dada, you see, was not long for power anyway, a mere pawn. Worse, Dada resisted the true powers that be, colluding with my own son." Demetrius shook his head, "tsk, tsk, tsk."

Demetrius simultaneously straightened his neck and stopped the rotation of the dagger. "Things are in place for a reason." Reduced to a toy, he clutched the dagger by the hilt, yet held the knife away from himself, inspecting the ornament and design. The object appeared foreign to him. "You know my family, during and before World War II, were Nazi collaborators." He met eyes with Cameron and nodded his head. "Really, we were." He then turned to Alastair. "Immediately after the war, we allied with the British. Before all of that, we collaborated with the Turks, and the Brits again before that, always a grander plan spinning the wheel." He moved the hand holding the dagger in a broad circle to illustrate.

Demetrius stopped for an elaborate pause, the attention of the four other men in the room drawn to the hovering metal blade, drawn to him.

"Look, we need these people, people like Dada and Abbo, to serve a purpose. We create them by employing them to service a need. To transfer commodities under the guise of a hijacking, to fulfill insurance contracts that finance new fleets, mercenaries to eliminate non-players. Hell, the Chinese need a place to send the floating fish factory ships that feed their masses. Food, after all, means power. All these and other tasks need to be performed."

"Like dumping toxic waste in the open sea," said Pepe.

Demetrius absently nodded at Pepe. "Those men like Dada and Abbo are minions of a market, men that people like myself created. One might say—" Demetrius paused again. He glared into the shine of the metal blade he held out before him. "One might say, as the Texans are the Arabs, we are the real Somali pirates."

CHAPTER 72
TALAMANCA BAY, IBIZA

Demetrius was certainly convinced of everything he told those aboard the Azulejo. Demetrius held a Rex Mundi dagger, yet nothing that he said sounded anything like the fervor Cameron had heard from the Rex Mundi operative in Quebec. The way Cameron heard Demetrius, maintaining power and rank was justified by any means. Then again, Cameron was well aware that leaders are motivated by a different agenda than the many parts of an organization. Cameron himself had been a cog in a wheel when he was a super commando, never questioning, never daring to question. That same sense of honor had been used against him these last days, once again making him a cog in a wheel.

Cameron found himself angry. An anger he decided was justified. Nikos was the twisted arrogant son of a billionaire. But Cameron figured Nikos had done too much ecstasy and cocaine, or plainly was never rooted in reality. The audacity of this pretty boy to say outright that he took Christine to teach her a lesson, that he could own her.

Cameron's disdain for Nikos was great, yet it was no measure to Pepe's. Cameron could read Pepe easily from where he stood across the cabin. Pepe's own sanity had

333

been drawn and tested by this ordeal, and there was not much left keeping Pepe's finger from squeezing the trigger of the Berretta angled less than a muzzle flash from Nikos' skull.

Cameron shot his eyes to Alastair. Alastair was a fun loving man, easygoing by nature, a natural calm. To befriend Alastair was to gain a lifelong unquestioned loyalty. The back of Cameron's throat went acidic. The man that had saved his life more times than he knew—literally more times than he knew—had eyes fixed on Nikos no differently than a predator. That is what the betrayal meant.

Yet the playboy's father appeared far more furious with Nikos than the three former Legionnaires. His grandstanding finished, Demetrius gave the hilt of the raised dagger a tighter squeeze. Whether he was punctuating his the end of his speech, or beginning another, Cameron was unsure. Demetrius dropped the hand holding the dagger by his side and then turned to Nikos. He shook his head in short scolding turns. "Tsk, tsk, tsk. You are a naughty one, Nikos."

Cameron tilted his head to the side in disbelief. The father spoke to his grown son as to a three year old. No wonder Nikos was a mess.

Demetrius raised the dagger and began shaking the pointy end to Nikos face. "What would your mother say? You would break her heart. You break my heart. You try to negotiate around me, you deceive your friend Alastair, you double-cross Abbo, Feizel, and then you killed Feizel." Demetrius slipped the dagger into the pocket of his linen pants and then shoved Nikos back. Nikos cowered from his father. "You should know better, Nikos."

Demetrius stepped back from Nikos. He raised his hands in the air. Then Demetrius violently shoved his free hand under Nikos' shirt, into his waist. Nikos pushed at his father's hands. Demetrius slapped him across the face.

Demetrius held his index finger up to Nikos, glared at him sternly, and then he defiantly reached back to Nikos' waist and retrieved a small Ruger. He tossed the gun back and forth in his hands. "What is this?" he asked. "You carry a gun now, too."

Demetrius turned away from Nikos to address all the three Legionnaires. His head floated back and forth across all three as he spoke, "I am sure you are wondering why I so openly shared with you my involvement, my family's involvement, with the Rex Mundi, our relationship clandestine all of these years. They want me to apologize for my son." Demetrius shrugged. "What is a father to do? I have to apologize for my son, and there is only one way to make amends for the damage he has done. There is only one set of terms the Rex Mundi accepts for what he has done. They want me to kill him, of course, and if he were anyone else—" he twirled the barrel of the Ruger toward the ceiling. "Well, I have to spare my son."

Then Demetrius abruptly lowered the Ruger toward Alastair and fired.

Cameron released two rounds into Demetrius' side while Alastair simultaneously fired into his forehead, implanting fragments of the Greek's skull into the hull, killing him instantly.

What may have been a war cry began to escape from Nikos throat as he threw his body forward to charge Cameron. The cry became a gurgle as Pepe's blade clotheslined Nikos, slicing halfway through his neck. Cameron had seen Pepe do this before. The Berretta against Nikos skull had been a prop, the obvious weapon. Pepe had wanted to take Nikos' life with his hands.

Alastair sent a shot from the PPK into Nikos as well, though the partial decapitation was what killed him.

Alastair inspected his shoulders and then the hull around him. "Bloody hell, he missed me."

"He didn't miss," said Cameron. "He was in a corner. He said himself he had to spare his son. He knew we wouldn't. I think his heart was broken. He didn't want to see Nikos die."

"And what was with all of that rambling," said Alastair.

"Demetrius knew he wasn't leaving." Cameron knelt down and took the Rex Mundi dagger from Demetrius' pocket, far more ornamented than the others he had seen, this one had a crimson ruby set in the hilt. Cameron inspected the familiar ruby closely and then lifted Demetrius' hand. The ruby set into his ring was the same cut and size and was encircled with the exact design as the dagger.

"And what about that thing?" asked Alastair. He shifted to allow Pepe to exam Christine's pupils.

"Same thing," said Cameron. "He felt the need to let me know. They know who I am."

"They?" asked Alastair. "Who the bloody hell are they?"

"The Rex Mundi."

"Right."

"I'll fill you in after we get out of here." Cameron nodded toward Christine, her hair mussed, gaze dazed. "She's waited long enough for us." His face froze for a second, "And there is another woman waiting for us to rescue her from the trunk of the Aston Martin."

Alastair peered at Cameron, "We don't have to—,"

Cameron shook his head. "No, she won't talk." He glanced down at Nikos. "Besides, there has been enough unnecessary carnage." Cameron rested his hands, one with a Ruger, the other with the dagger, on his knees and sighed. "Listen, I'm gonna do a wipe down. Let's get her out of here."

Alastair eased Christine upright. "Christine, we need to go."

"Let me help you," said Pepe, slipping his arm beneath his sister. "The anesthetic effect of the drugs will wear off eventually, for now I don't believe she knows what has happened."

~*~

THE END

CAMERON KINCAID RETURNS IN
TEMPLAR FORCE

~*~

ABOUT THE AUTHOR

Daniel Arthur Smith is the author of the international bestsellers *THE CATHARI TREASURE, THE SOMALI DECEPTION,* and a few other novels and short stories.

He was raised in Michigan and graduated from Western Michigan University where he studied meta-physics, cognitive science, philosophy, and comparative religion. He began his career as a bartender, barista, poetry house proprietor, teacher and then became a technologist and futurist for the Fortune 100 across the Americas and Europe.

Daniel has traveled to over 300 cities in 22 countries, residing in Los Angeles, Kalamazoo, Prague, Crete, and now writes in Manhattan where he lives with his wife and young sons.

For more information, visit **danielarthursmith.com**

STAY IN THE LOOP

Following your favorite authors on Facebook, Twitter, or other social media has become a sketchy business. Facebook and other companies block authors from conversing regularly with readers unless they are willing to cough up BIG BUX to 'promote' every post. To make sure you are receiving the latest updates, freebies, and stories on everything in the Daniel Arthur Smith universe you have to join his email newsletter. As a subscriber, you'll receive early Advance Review Copies (ARCS) of all of Daniel's books and stories... for free! In addition to all of that, Daniel regularly gives away lots of other loot like signed books and posters, so make certain that you are subscribed.

Made in the USA
Columbia, SC
26 December 2023

29426208R00193